CHRISTOPHER BUSH
THE CASE OF THE
LEANING MAN

CHRISTOPHER BUSH was born Charlie Christmas Bush in Norfolk in 1885. His father was a farm labourer and his mother a milliner. In the early years of his childhood he lived with his aunt and uncle in London before returning to Norfolk aged seven, later winning a scholarship to Thetford Grammar School.

As an adult, Bush worked as a schoolmaster for 27 years, pausing only to fight in World War One, until retiring aged 46 in 1931 to be a full-time novelist. His first novel featuring the eccentric Ludovic Travers was published in 1926, and was followed by 62 additional Travers mysteries. These are all to be republished by Dean Street Press.

Christopher Bush fought again in World War Two, and was elected a member of the prestigious Detection Club. He died in 1973.

CHRISTOPHER BUSH

THE CASE OF THE LEANING MAN

With an introduction
by Curtis Evans

DEAN STREET PRESS

INTRODUCTION

THAT ONCE vast and mighty legion of bright young (and youngish) British crime writers who began publishing their ingenious tales of mystery and imagination during what is known as the Golden Age of detective fiction (traditionally dated from 1920 to 1939) had greatly diminished by the iconoclastic decade of the Sixties, many of these writers having become casualties of time. Of the 38 authors who during the Golden Age had belonged to the Detection Club, a London-based group which included within its ranks many of the finest writers of detective fiction then plying the craft in the United Kingdom, just over a third remained among the living by the second half of the 1960s, while merely seven—Agatha Christie, Anthony Gilbert, Gladys Mitchell, Margery Allingham, John Dickson Carr, Nicholas Blake and Christopher Bush—were still penning crime fiction.

In 1966--a year that saw the sad demise, at the too young age of 62, of Margery Allingham--an executive with the English book publishing firm Macdonald reflected on the continued popularity of the author who today is the least well known among this tiny but accomplished crime writing cohort: Christopher Bush (1885-1973), whose first of his three score and three series detective novels, *The Plumley Inheritance*, had appeared fully four decades earlier, in 1926. "He has a considerable public, a 'steady Bush public,' a public that has endured through many years," the executive boasted of Bush. "He never presents any problem to his publisher, who knows exactly how many copies of a title may be safely printed for the loyal Bush fans; the number is a healthy one too." Yet in 1968, just a couple of years after the Macdonald editor's affirmation of Bush's notable popular duration as a crime writer, the author, now in his 83rd year, bade farewell to mystery fiction with a final detective novel, *The Case of the Prodigal Daughter*, in which, like in Agatha Christie's *Third Girl* (1966), copious references are made, none too favorably, to youthful sex, drugs and rock and roll. Afterwards, outside of the reprinting in the UK in the early 1970s of a scattering of classic Bush titles from the Golden Age, Bush's books, in contrast with those of Christie, Carr, Allingham and Blake, disappeared from mass circulation in both the UK and the US, becoming fervently sought (and ever more unobtainable) treasures by collectors and connoisseurs of classic crime fiction. Now, in one of the signal developments in vintage mystery publishing, Dean Street Press is reprinting all 63 of the Christopher Bush detective novels. These will be published over a period of months, beginning with the release of books 1 to 10 in the series.

Few Golden Age British mystery writers had backgrounds as humble yet simultaneously mysterious, dotted with omissions and evasions, as Christopher Bush, who was born Charlie Christmas Bush on the day of the Nativity in 1885 in the Norfolk village of Great Hockham, to Charles Walter Bush and his second wife, Eva Margaret Long. While the father of Christopher Bush's Detection Club colleague and near exact contemporary Henry Wade (the pseudonym of Henry Lancelot Aubrey-Fletcher) was a baronet who lived in an elegant Georgian mansion and claimed extensive ownership of fertile English fields, Christopher's father resided in a cramped cottage and toiled in fields as a farm laborer, a term that in the late Victorian and Edwardian era, his son lamented many years afterward, "had in it something of contempt....There was something almost of serfdom about it."

Charles Walter Bush was a canny though mercurial individual, his only learning, his son recalled, having been "acquired at the Sunday school." A man of parts, Charles was a tenant farmer of three acres, a thatcher, bricklayer and carpenter (fittingly for the father of a detective novelist, coffins were his specialty), a village radical and a most adept poacher. After a flight from Great Hockham, possibly on account of his poaching activities, Charles, a widower with a baby son whom he had left in the care of his mother, resided in London, where he worked for a firm of spice importers. At a dance in the city, Charles met Christopher's mother, Eva Long, a lovely and sweet-natured young milliner and bonnet maker, sweeping her off her feet with a combination of "good looks and a certain plausibility." After their marriage the couple left London to live in a tiny rented cottage in Great Hockham, where Eva over the next eighteen years gave birth to three sons and five daughters and perforce learned the challenging ways of rural domestic economy.

Decades later an octogenarian Christopher Bush, in his memoir *Winter Harvest: A Norfolk Boyhood* (1967), characterized Great Hockham as a rustic rural redoubt where many of the words that fell from the tongues of the native inhabitants "were those of Shakespeare, Milton and the Authorised Version....Still in general use were words that were standard in Chaucer's time, but had since lost a certain respectability." Christopher amusingly recalled as a young boy telling his mother that a respectable neighbor woman had used profanity, explaining that in his hearing she had told her husband, "George, wipe you that shit off that pig's arse, do you'll datty your trousers," to which his mother had responded that although that particular usage of a four-letter word had not really been *swearing*, he was not to give vent to such language himself.

Great Hockham, which in Christopher Bush's youth had a population of about four hundred souls, was composed of a score or so of cottages, three public houses, a post-office, five shops, a couple of forges and a pair of churches, All Saint's and the Primitive Methodist Chapel, where the Bush family rather vocally worshipped. "The village lived by farming, and most of its men were labourers," Christopher recollected. "Most of the children left school as soon as the law permitted: boys to be absorbed somehow into the land and the girls to go into domestic service." There were three large farms and four smaller ones, and, in something of an anomaly, not one but two squires--the original squire, dubbed "Finch" by Christopher, having let the shooting rights at Little Hockham Hall to one "Green," a wealthy international banker, making the latter man a squire by courtesy. Finch owned most of the local houses and farms, in traditional form receiving rents for them personally on Michaelmas; and when Christopher's father fell out with Green, "a red-faced, pompous, blustering man," over a political election, he lost all of the banker's business, much to his mother's distress. Yet against all odds and adversities, Christopher's life greatly diverged from settled norms in Great Hockham, incidentally producing one of the most distinguished detective novelists from the Golden Age of detective fiction.

Although Christopher Bush was born in Great Hockham, he spent his earliest years in London living with his mother's much older sister, Elizabeth, and her husband, a fur dealer by the name of James Streeter, the couple having no children of their own. Almost certainly of illegitimate birth, Eva had been raised by the Long family from her infancy. She once told her youngest daughter how she recalled the Longs being visited, when she was a child, by a "fine lady in a carriage," whom she believed was her birth mother. Or is it possible that the "fine lady in a carriage" was simply an imaginary figment, like the aristocratic fantasies of Philippa Palfrey in P.D. James's *Innocent Blood* (1980), and that Eva's "sister" Elizabeth was in fact her mother?

The Streeters were a comfortably circumstanced couple at the time they took custody of Christopher. Their household included two maids and a governess for the young boy, whose doting but dutiful "Aunt Lizzie" devoted much of her time to the performance of "good works among the East End poor." When Christopher was seven years old, however, drastically straightened financial circumstances compelled the Streeters to leave London for Norfolk, by the way returning the boy to his birth parents in Great Hockham.

Fortunately the cause of the education of Christopher, who was not only a capable village cricketer but a precocious reader and scholar, was taken up both by his determined and devoted mother and an idealistic local elementary school headmaster. In his teens Christopher secured a scholarship to Norfolk's Thetford Grammar School, one of England's oldest educational institutions, where Thomas Paine had studied a century-and-a-half earlier. He left Thetford in 1904 to take a position as a junior schoolmaster, missing a chance to go to Cambridge University on yet another scholarship. (Later he proclaimed himself thankful for this turn of events, sardonically speculating that had he received a Cambridge degree he "might have become an exceedingly minor don or something as staid and static and respectable as a publisher.") Christopher would teach in English schools for the next twenty-seven years, retiring at the age of 46 in 1931, after he had established a successful career as a detective novelist.

Christopher's romantic relationships proved far rockier than his career path, not to mention every bit as murky as his mother's familial antecedents. In 1911, when Christopher was teaching in Wood Green School, a co-educational institution in Oxfordshire, he wed county council schoolteacher Ella Maria Pinner, a daughter of a baker neighbor of the Bushes in Great Hockham. The two appear never actually to have lived together, however, and in 1914, when Christopher at the age of 29 headed to war in the 16th (Public Schools) Battalion of the Middlesex Regiment, he falsely claimed in his attestation papers, under penalty of two years' imprisonment with hard labor, to be unmarried.

After four years of service in the Great War, including a year-long stint in Egypt, Christopher returned in 1919 to his position at Wood Green School, where he became involved in another romantic relationship, from which he soon desired to extricate himself. (A photo of the future author, taken at this time in Egypt, shows a rather dashing, thin-mustached man in uniform and is signed "Chris," suggesting that he had dispensed with "Charlie" and taken in its place a diminutive drawn from his middle name.) The next year Winifred Chart, a mathematics teacher at Wood Green, gave birth to a son, whom she named Geoffrey Bush. Christopher was the father of Geoffrey, who later in life became a noted English composer, though for reasons best known to himself Christopher never acknowledged his son. (A letter Geoffrey once sent him was returned unopened.) Winifred claimed that she and Christopher had married but separated, but she refused to speak of her purported spouse forever after and she destroyed all of his letters and other mementos, with the exception of a book of poetry that he had written for her during what she termed their engagement.

Christopher's true mate in life, though with her he had no children, was Florence Marjorie Barclay, the daughter of a draper from Ballymena, Northern Ireland, and, like Ella Pinner and Winifred Chart, a schoolteacher. Christopher and Marjorie likely had become romantically involved by 1929, when Christopher dedicated to her his second detective novel, *The Perfect Murder Case*; and they lived together as man and wife from the 1930s until her death in 1968 (after which, probably not coincidentally, Christopher stopped publishing novels). Christopher returned with Marjorie to the vicinity of Great Hockham when his writing career took flight, purchasing two adjoining cottages and commissioning his father and a stepbrother to build an extension consisting of a kitchen, two bedrooms and a new staircase. (The now sprawling structure, which Christopher called "Home Cottage," is now a bed and breakfast grandiloquently dubbed "Home Hall.") After a falling-out with his father, presumably over the conduct of Christopher's personal life, he and Marjorie in 1932 moved to Beckley, Sussex, where they purchased Horsepen, a lovely Tudor plaster and timber-framed house. In 1953 the couple settled at their final home, The Great House, a centuries-old structure (now a boutique hotel) in Lavenham, Suffolk.

From these three houses Christopher maintained a lucrative and critically esteemed career as a novelist, publishing both detective novels as Christopher Bush and, commencing in 1933 with the acclaimed book *Return* (in the UK, *God and the Rabbit*, 1934), regional novels purposefully drawing on his own life experience, under the pen name Michael Home. (During the 1940s he also published espionage novels under the Michael Home pseudonym.) Although his first detective novel, *The Plumley Inheritance*, made a limited impact, with his second, *The Perfect Murder Case*, Christopher struck gold. The latter novel, a big seller in both the UK and the US, was published in the former country by the prestigious Heinemann, soon to become the publisher of the detective novels of Margery Allingham and Carter Dickson (John Dickson Carr), and in the latter country by the Crime Club imprint of Doubleday, Doran, one of the most important publishers of mystery fiction in the United States.

Over the decade of the 1930s Christopher Bush published, in both the UK and the US as well as other countries around the world, some of the finest detective fiction of the Golden Age, prompting the brilliant Thirties crime fiction reviewer, author and Oxford University Press editor Charles Williams to avow: "Mr. Bush writes of as thoroughly enjoyable murders as any I know." (More recently, mystery genre authority B.A. Pike dubbed these novels by Bush, whom he praised as "one of the most reliable and resourceful of true detective writers"; "Golden Age baroque, rendered remarkable by some extraordinary flights of fancy.") In 1937 Christopher Bush became, along with Nicholas Blake, E.C.R. Lorac and Newton Gayle (the writing team of Muna Lee and Maurice West Guinness), one of the final authors initiated into the Detection Club before the outbreak of the Second World War and with it the demise of the Golden Age. Afterward he continued publishing a detective novel or more a year, with his final book in 1968 reaching a total of 63, all of them detailing the investigative adventures of lanky and bespectacled gentleman amateur detective Ludovic Travers. Concurring as I do with the encomia of Charles Williams and B.A. Pike, I will end this introduction by thanking Avril MacArthur for providing invaluable biographical information on her great uncle, and simply wishing fans of classic crime fiction good times as they discover (or rediscover), with this latest splendid series of Dean Street Press classic crime fiction reissues, Christopher Bush's Ludovic Travers detective novels. May a new "Bush public" yet arise!

Curtis Evans

The Case of the Leaning Man (1938)

"He's dead?"

"As mutton," said Wharton, laconically.

"An Indian, isn't he?"

"The Maharajah of Amli."

"The secretary pronounced it Oomli," Norris remarked tentatively.

"Oomli or Amli don't matter a damn," said Wharton contemptuously. "I call him a corpse." He gave a grunt. "Too important a corpse, that's the trouble."

The Case of the Leaning Man

LOVE FATEFULLY BLOSSOMED at the Victory Ball held at the Royal Albert Hall on November 11, 1919, one year after the signing of the Armistice that ended the First World War, when on a visit to England twenty-four-year-old Sir Hari Singh, nephew and heir of His Highness Pratap Singh, Maharaja of the princely state of Jammu and Kashmir, and his Indian secretary took their seats in a box adjacent to one occupied by Florence Maud Robinson, a vivacious thirty-one-year-old Englishwoman, and her friend, Mrs. Bevan. So swiftly, seemingly, did their ardor for each other grow that the Indian Price and his English *inamorata* were soon planning to travel together to his homeland, despite the fact that both of them were married. At a hotel in Paris, however, love's castle crashed into scores of jagged little pieces when a man purporting to be Mr. Robinson, Montague Noel Newton, stormed into the Price's suite at the St. James and Albany hotel and dramatically declaimed to Mrs. Robinson: "Now I've got you!"

Embarrassed and eager to extricate himself from a personal scandal that might imperil his royal succession, Sir Hari Singh on the advice of his Irish aide-de-camp, Captain Charles William Augustus Arthur, formerly of the Indian Army, wrote two checks, to the staggering sum of 300,000 pounds (over 15 million pounds today), in a bid to compensate Mr. Robinson for the grave harm the Prince had done to him by stealing his wife's affections. Although payment was stopped on the second check, 150,000 pounds in spoils was divided among the conspirators against the Prince—for Sir Hari was a victim of a particularly elaborate badger game, one involving not only, in all likelihood, Mr. and Mrs. Robinson themselves, but Mrs. Bevan, Captain Arthur, Montague Noel Newton ("an ingenious individual" with "a consistently villainous career of fifty-odd years," noted the distinguished lawyer and crime writer Bechhofer Roberts in his foreword to the *Mr. A. Case*, the trial record of the affair), and, last but certainly not least, William Cooper Hobbs. Hobbs was a managing clerk who acted as the conniving principal behind obscure yet conveniently pliable solicitors and was summed up by Bechhofer Roberts in 1948 as "one of the most considerable figures of the British underworld for very many years," being possessed of a seemingly unquenchable "passion for unrighteousness."

Unfortunately for the conspirators, rogues will fall out; and when Mr. Robinson, the supposed victim in the affair, discovered the extent of the Prince's bounty--the Robinsons had only received 21,000 of the 150,000 pound payout, despite the great load which Mrs. Robinson had taken entirely upon herself--he sued the Midland Bank. He argued that the bank should have only allowed him to draw the funds paid over by the Prince in his, Robinson's, name. The resulting 1925 trial—known as the Mr. A. Case, because in Britain the India Office persuaded the presiding judge not to allow Sir Hari Singh's name to be uttered in court—became one of the most notorious trials of the Jazz Age, a raucous era that certainly saw its share of notorious trials. Mr. Robinson lost the case, but as a result of the exposure of the conspirators' wicked plot, Hobbs and Captain Arthur were tried for fraud (Captain Arthur in France, where he has absconded) and duly convicted. "You are the last episode in a moving picture scenario," the media savvy French judge wryly informed the Captain as he sentenced him to a thirteen-month prison term.

Despite the notoriety of the case there were no film or stage treatments of it in Great Britain, the subject evidently having been deemed much too controversial. (A. A. Milne, creator of Winnie-the-Pooh and author of *The Red House Mystery*, sardonically pronounced at the time that "Mrs. Robinson has refused an offer to appear on the films, but will merely write her life for the papers instead.") However, the Mr. A. Case inspired a significant portion of Christopher Bush's nineteenth detective novel, *The Case of the Leaning Man* (*The Leaning Man* in the US), wherein the quasi-fictional Maharajah Bishan Singh is done to death in his suite in a London hotel. The Indian's death brings together our familiar old cast of regulars—Superintendent Wharton, Chief Inspector Norris, Police-Surgeon Menzies and, of course, that amateur sleuth extraordinaire, Ludovic "Ludo" Travers, who to help crack this case takes time off from his current book project, another criminological tome (following *Kensington Gore*, about murders of "bluebloods and intellectuals," and *Is this a Dagger?*, detailing "killings that had involved the stage and theatre"), which will include at least five of his and Wharton's previous cases. (Wharton is dubious about this latest effort.)

In Travers and Wharton's latest case—that of the murder of the maharajah--the police cast suspicious eyes at the Indian's English entourage, which includes a secretary, Bernard Thomas Osmund, racehorse trainer, Charles Willshed, and valet, William Bond. Then there are that unknown turbaned man who visited the maharajah on the night of his death and the mysterious "lady friend" his entourage keeps oddly mum about—what might they have had to do with the slaying? And what about the titular leaning man, whom Ludo had earlier by happenstance discovered expiring in the fog on Charing Cross Road? His death links up with the maharajah's murder in a most unexpected way.

Ludo is a bit abstracted at times in *The Case of the Leaning Man*, as he finds himself preoccupied with the lovely and accomplished stage performing sister act of Bernice and Joy Haire, old friends of his and "daughters of Sir Jerome Haire, that great survival of the old school of Irving and Tree." Recently the Haire girls have had a serious falling out, and Ludo tries, with no help whatsoever on the part of the amiably evasive siblings, to discover why this has happened. Increasingly Ludo finds his thoughts straying to the elder of the sisters, Bernice, who, having "spent some years in India with an aunt . . . had become . . . a classical oriental dancer," always giving performances of "an originality and a beauty that were curiously haunting. . . ."

A dozen years into the series, could the romance-averse Ludo finally be falling in love, just as other highly eligible British bachelor detectives—Dorothy L. Sayer's Lord Peter Wimsey, Margery Allingham's Albert Campion, Ngaio Marsh's Roderick Alleyn, Nicholas Blake's Nigel Strangeways, E.R. Punshon's Bobby Owen, John Rhode's Jimmy Waghorn—were similarly falling at this time, much to the chagrin of purist aestheticians of the detective novel like S.S. Van Dine, who groused that romance simply gummed up the workings of detection? The notice of *The Case of the Leaning Man* in the *New York Times Book Review* affords curious readers an important clue to this question: "Mr. Bush has produced another good detective story, this time with emotional complications such as the experts say should have no place in this type of fiction. But the experts are not always right."

POSTSCRIPT: In a seeming case of serendipity, William Cooper Hobbs of Mr. A infamy, who died at the age of eighty in 1945, was arrested and tried again in the UK in 1938, the same year that *The Case of the Leaning Man* was published, on the charge of forging the will of a late friend, William Clarkson, a West End theatrical costumier and fancy-dress provider who came out of the milieu about which Christopher Bush had written in his previous detective novel, *The Case of the Tudor Queen*. Hobbs, who had been left a large sum of money in the will, was sentenced to a term of five years penal servitude.

"There have been times when the methods of the police—and indeed, of myself—have reminded me of a certain aunt of mine who dabbled in water-colours. A tricky April landscape tempted her one day, but unhappily she got into difficulties with her clouds. Undaunted, however, she framed the gaudy result and christened it—*A Thunderstorm.*"

LUDOVIC TRAVERS
(Preface to a manuscript at
present untitled)

CHAPTER I

THE FIRST MYSTERY

THE MORNING OF Friday, the tenth of February, was a foggy one, but the fog was not a pea-souper but more of a whitish mist which gave promise of early dispersal. That was the opinion of Ludovic Travers, who inspected the weather from the window of his flat in St. Martin's Chambers before he settled down to work in the snugness of the study.

Life was running smoothly but uneventfully for Travers. For some months there had been no ravelled case of murder which might have meant days or even weeks of work with George—Superintendent—Wharton, but by way of compensation there was a third volume of literary criminology on the stocks.

Kensington Gore had been a causerie on crimes that, more or less happily, had eliminated bluebloods and intellectuals. *Is This a Dagger?* had dealt with those ironic killings that had involved the stage and theatre—ironic because they had been tragedies that had eliminated the tragedians. The volume on which Travers was at the moment engaged had no title, but was to criticize with a kind of playful admonition the murderers' handling of cases that had proved for them an exceedingly unfortunate speculation. Travers was trying to show, in other words, how the least bit more dexterity or forethought or even suavity might have saved various necks from the noose. The murders had all taken place within the last three years, and on at least five of them Superintendent Wharton and Travers himself had been engaged.

"What you're getting at is this," said George Wharton, when Travers confided to him the barest outlines. "You're going to show how damn clever you'd have been yourself." Then he grunted. "Any fool can be wise after the event."

"Precisely," said Travers amiably.

"And another thing," Wharton went on. "It ought to be made a criminal offence to show how murders ought to have been committed."

Travers's fingers went to his huge horn-rims. It was a trick of his to polish them when at a mental loss or on the edge of some discovery.

"A deplorable fallacy, surely?" he said. "You, objecting to respectably conducted murders? No murders, George, and where would you be? Handling petty larcenies and filling up forms."

Wharton gave another grunt and sidetracked the argument.

"What you want to write such damn rubbish for at all, beats me. If I had your money, and your brains if it comes to that, I'd find something better to do. Why don't you tackle something really worthwhile? A nice novel or something?"

"Nice is a relative term," smiled Travers, and left it at that.

But at about half-past eleven on that February morning Travers became aware that the sun had broken through, and at once he was pushing his work aside and ringing for Palmer. The venerable Palmer, who had once valeted Travers's father, was waiting with hat and overcoat when Travers emerged from the study.

"Rather alarming to have one's thoughts read like this," he said as he was helped into the overcoat. "What about this spell of weather? Is it going to last?"

Palmer gave that incipient bow of his.

"The glass is very high, sir. If I may say so, sir, I think we shall get sun during the day, which means fog at night—I mean, at this time of year, sir."

"Then we'll gather our roses," Travers smilingly told him.

He had no particular objective in mind, and after a few moments' walking, decided on Hyde Park. At the Marble Arch Barney Josephs, the theatrical agent, got off the same bus.

"How are you, Mr. Travers?" he said, and held out his hand.

Travers felt a warmth at the sight of Barney, whom he had known in the old days when the agency had been no more than a couple of rooms above a barber's shop in Walberry Street, Soho. Now, though Barney was a top-notcher and handled only class, he had not changed in the least. The same natural dignity was there; his manner was just as quiet and unassuming, and his burred voice as gentle.

"Keeping pretty busy, Barney?"

Barney spread his palms and gave a slight shrug of the shoulders.

"By the way," said Travers, "you're not looking any too fit. You're feeling well, are you?"

Travers, six foot three of lamp-post leanness, had adjusted his stride to Barney's as they made for the open park. Barney said that with a business like his, nobody could look well.

"Work and worry, Mr. Travers; that's what it all is. Work and worry, and, for a change, worry and work. You do not know."

"You're right," Travers told him consolingly. "Only this morning I was venturing to think of myself as a busy man, just because I was going to do a day's writing, and attend a committee meeting at the Hospital, and go to a cocktail party I can't wriggle out of."

"Cocktail parties?" He gave a prodigious shrug. "I never go. My digestion is none too good these days. I say I'm held up on business and hope to get along later."

"An excellent expedient," smiled Travers. "The trouble is I can't very well dodge this one. It's a kind of farewell party to young Chippenham, who's off to Brazil exploring or something. By the way, I might meet a couple of your clients there. I hear they're back in England."

Barney raised inquiring eyebrows.

"The Haires," explained Travers. "Bernice and Joy. I don't think Sir Jerome will be there. Something I wanted to ask you, by the way, though he isn't a client of yours. He's putting on a short act at the Paliceum and the Metropolis this week, and I was told he was getting eight hundred pounds. I know it means four shows a night, but isn't that rather a lot, even for an old master?"

Barney muttered something about the money coming in useful, and that surprised Travers, who had always assumed that the famous actor-manager must have clung firmly to much of the money he had once made. But Barney had apparently heard Travers's question from some immense distance, being busy with thoughts of his own. When he uttered those thoughts aloud, Travers was to be considerably surprised, if in a different way.

For Travers was always considerably puzzled why people should make him the grand depository of their secrets and worries, since he was unaware of those qualities of his own that invited the confidences. He was, for instance, the perfect listener, delightfully mannered and supremely well informed. Eccentric he might be at times, and unconventional, but even those who were for the first time in his company knew him for a man of taste and breeding, and of insight and sympathy; one with whom confidences would be safe and to whom sharp practice was an abomination.

"Mr. Travers," Barney said, and halted dramatically in his tracks, "I wonder if you'd do me a favour."

"Why not?" smiled Travers.

Barney took his arm and made for a side path.

Then his pace slackened and he began to relate his troubles with an earnestness that was singularly convincing and indeed affecting. Those troubles concerned Bernice and Joy Haire, whom Travers had just mentioned as likely to be at that evening's cocktail party.

The Haire girls, daughters of Sir Jerome Haire, that great survivor of the old school of Irving and Tree, had always been independent, and they owed little to the influence that might have been exerted on their behalf by their father. Bernice, the elder, had spent some years in India with an aunt, and had become what might be called a classical oriental dancer. Her performances had always had an originality and a beauty that were curiously haunting, and long before she became a client of Barney Josephs, she had had considerable success in London, though comparatively little financial gain. Joy had developed into a diseuse and mimic, and financially she had done much better than her sister, though it was Barney again who saw that there was really big money in her. Bernice, by the way, was thirty-five, and Joy twenty-six.

To Barney was due the credit for welding the twin acts into a show which, even before they left for their Australasian tour, the Haire sisters could rely on to fill any hall in town. Barney modestly disclaimed any credit for results so fortunate and spectacular. The sisters had it in their blood, he said, and their breeding and schooling and class gave them a quality and that essential something which was different.

The Australasian tour was a triumphant success and even before the voyage home was begun, Barney had drafted contracts—now awaiting only the sisters' signatures—for a tour of the States and Canada on terms that a year before would have seemed fantastically good for opera stars or virtuosi. From Perth the sisters had cabled their gratitude and delight. So to the trouble, and the mystery.

Joy and Bernice had quarrelled. Now the man in the street might find nothing unusual in that, for women are women, and differences in type and temperament might have accounted for it. The press, for instance, delighted to call Bernice exotic, mysterious and remote, which really meant that she had superb black eyes and hair, an ivory skin, a supple figure and a loathing for the vulgar sides of publicity. Joy, who took after her mother, was as multi-sided as her profession; neat and slim, red-haired and something of a gamine; adventurous, self-willed and obstinate—all of which Travers himself knew from even a haphazard acquaintance.

But the quarrel of the sisters was different from anything with which Barney had ever been acquainted. Maybe their breeding and the standards of their kind dictated aloofness rather than recrimination and bickering, but according to Barney it was something frightening. Each was wholly ignoring the existence of the other.

"How is Bernice?" someone might say.

"Bernice?" The answering question would sound like an allusion to a past incredibly remote. "I'm afraid I haven't seen Bernice for centuries."

Or the question might concern Joy, when it would be: "I haven't the least idea. We haven't seen each other for quite an age."

As for inquiries into future plans, they would be smilingly waved aside, and all that could be gathered was that the tour had been arduous and the sisters were spending an interlude wholly apart, much as husband and wife may find in separate holidays a kind of matrimonial spring-cleaning. But from Barney's angle, the whole proceeding had neither sense nor reason, and was far from being humorous. Each sister refused to sign the double contract, though willing to sign a new one which would provide her with some new but adequate partner. Each refused to meet the other, even in Barney's office. In their letters and talk to Barney, each avoided all mention of the other's very name.

"They're tied fast to you by contract?" Travers asked. "This is in the strictest confidence, by the way, but mightn't there be the chance of their holding out on you in order to get a still better contract? Mind you, I don't think Bernice would lend herself for a moment to double-crossing of that kind, but Joy is different. She's irresponsible and you never know when she's likely to fly off at a tangent. Besides, she wouldn't regard it as dishonesty."

Barney shook his head.

"I've handled all sorts, Mr. Travers, and I know the real quality when I meet it. They're ladies, if you know what I mean." Then his hands went despairingly to heaven. "I tell you I'm going crazy. What will my word be worth after this? I draw the contract and I promise. Thousands of pounds at stake, and they won't even listen to reason." The hands vibrated a last time and then fell helplessly. "If only I knew why, then I might do something, Mr. Travers. I ask you, why? Why?"

"Let's think it out," Travers said, and his hand went to Barney's shoulder. "You say that the sisters cabled enthusiastically from Perth, and therefore the break occurred during the voyage." His fingers were all at once at his glasses. "About you and me they'd say, 'Cherchez la femme.' Why not the other way about? Why shouldn't some man be the cause? A man they met on the boat on the way home?"

Barney remarked, most apologetically, that he didn't see how that explanation helped. If it were some love affair and jealousy, nothing he could do could smooth things out.

"Why not have a word with Sir Jerome?" Travers asked. "He must be aware of the situation. Besides, as a business and theatrical man, he'll be only too appreciative of the hole you've been landed in."

Barney said he had seen Sir Jerome, and from his sheepish looks Travers could imagine what had happened in the interview with the great man. He saw the hooked beak and the beetling eyebrows, he watched the ample gestures and heard the pompous, insistent, deliberate voice. Poor patient, pleading old Barney would have been led up the histrionic orchard while he tried in vain to put his questions and state his case.

"He said his daughters had grown past him," was Barney's version. "Then when I told him what I stood to lose—my money and my reputation—he told me to mind my own business, and he wouldn't understand that it *was* my business."

Travers shook his head and his hand once more went to Barney's shoulder.

"We'll get this thing straightened out, Barney. Don't you worry. I'll have a talk with both the sisters this afternoon—"

"They won't both be there," cut in Barney emphatically.

"Then I'll do my best with one," Travers said. "If neither is there, then I'll call on them at their private addresses. By some means or other I'll find out what stands in the way of their signing the contract. That's what you want, isn't it?"

Barney said it was, and the signing was urgent. The other parties were regarding things as settled, and so life for himself had become sheer bluff and lies. The tour ought actually to commence within three weeks.

"How long have they been back in England?" Travers asked.

"Six weeks."

Travers let out a whistle. "My hat, that lands me in a difficulty. I was abroad till a fortnight ago and I imagined they'd only just come back." He shook a dismal head. "I ought to have looked up Bernice. Still, I'll wriggle out of that. What worries me too is that they've kept up this silent quarrel business for six whole weeks." His hand went out. "Still, I'll bet you a new hat it's all straightened out inside another week." He smiled at

Barney's earnest, pleading look. "Something might even happen this evening. If it does, I'll ring you up."

There was a somewhat protracted meeting of the Finance Committee of the Central Hospital that afternoon, and Travers was late for the party. But he was lucky, for no sooner had he made a way through the crush and had a polite word with the Chippenhams, than he was actually hailed by Joy Haire, who led him aside to a comparatively lonely corner. Joy looked bewitching in a green costume that went ravishingly well with her red hair, and she seemed to be having a remarkably good time.

"Now you've got me, what are you going to do with me?" Travers said.

"Just talk," she said.

"The last time we talked," Travers reminded her, "you told me unashamedly that you were studying me for one of your five-minute impressions."

She laughed. "It was true. You must come and see me do it. A modern niece trying not to offend the susceptibilities of a favourite uncle."

Travers shook a reproving head. "You're a terrifying person, you know. Every woman who speaks to you must feel rather as if she's looking into a devastatingly candid mirror. Which reminds me. Whereabouts in this crush is Bernice?"

"Bernice?" She puckered her pretty brows. "Oh, Bernice. I don't imagine she's here. I mean, we see so little of each other these days."

"But, surely?"

She helped herself to cheese straws from a passing tray, and smiled back at him.

"Do try some of these. They're delicious."

He smiled a refusal, but halted another tray for his first cocktail. Joy took another too.

"About Bernice," Travers insinuated. "Why haven't you seen her recently?"

"Did I say that?"

The blandness took him aback for no more than a moment, but he decided to proceed more deviously.

"A great tour, was it?"

"Marvellous."

"And when do you set off again?"

"I don't know." She smiled dreamily at the cocktail. "One of these days, perhaps."

"Well, it's good to be young and with a bank balance," said Travers sententiously. "But isn't Bernice harrying you to be off again?"

Her eyes turned slowly towards him and the smile was provocative.

"You and Bernice used to be frightfully friendly once, didn't you?"

Travers flushed but managed to make an effective grimace.

"Why not? Bernice and Helen—my sister Helen—were at school together. But about that show of yours, I was thinking of—a show in town as a kind of follow on to that triumphant tour."

"I wonder," she said, and was all at once regarding him critically.

"Wonder what?"

She laughed. "Just another five-minute study. A feather-brained person like myself being interviewed by a really important Scotland Yard official."

"You're not referring to me?"

"But aren't you connected—is that the word?—with Scotland Yard? Everybody knows you are. And honestly, Ludo, wouldn't it make a perfectly lovely study?"

Travers smiled ruefully. "I imagine it would—as you would do it. By the way, what a perfectly charming ring!"

It was the finest square-cut emerald he had ever seen, and perfection itself for the red hair and the green of hat and costume. But she was smiling amusedly.

"Don't tell me it's paste?"

"Does it matter?" she said. "After all, even duchesses have ceased to be synonymous with diamonds."

"Yes," he said lamely. "I suppose they have."

"I must be running away," she was saying, but all the raillery had gone. Her brows puckered slightly.

"You're rather charming, you know, Ludo. What would you think of me if I asked you flagrantly to take me out some time to tea?"

Travers regarded her gravely.

"What would I think? Well, when I'd recovered from the delight of it—so to speak—I'd wonder just what it was you wished to talk over with me."

A quick alarm flashed across her face, and the words came instinctively.

"How did you know—I mean, what should I want to talk over with you?"

"Lord knows," said Travers. "But when shall it be? Tomorrow? Sunday?"

Her voice was little more than a whisper.

"Sunday. Somewhere out of town. You still have a car?"

"Yes," he said gravely, "I still have a car. And where shall I call?"

When he looked up from the quick glance at the card she gave him, she was making her way through the crowd again. Five minutes, and Travers made his own way out, and from a near-by phone booth he rang up Barney.

"Progress already, Barney. . . . No, not now. I hope to know all about everything by Sunday evening. I'm taking one of the principals—Joy, as a matter of fact—out to tea. At her invitation, Barney. See the point? Oh, and now I want to call on Bernice if she's in town. . . . She is?"

Barney gave the address and began mumbling his thanks. Travers cut him off with another optimism or two, and then had another look at the address he had written down. Barney was certainly right about the intensity of the rift. Bernice's address was a Bloomsbury private hotel, about as far as possible from Joy's flat at Lancaster Gate.

At once it must be said by way of explanation that a mystery was the breath of Travers's nostrils. Usually he was a lightning theorist, and George Wharton's latest quip about him was that he was the only living soul who could explain at a second's notice the amazingly elastic stowage properties of Noah's Ark.

Now the really curious thing about that mysterious quarrel of the Haire sisters was that Travers's nimble brain could suggest no immediate and satisfying solution. And, after all, why should it? But it nagged at him the more because he so desperately wanted to help Barney, and—less openly admitted—because he could not fit Bernice into the scheme of things.

The breach was a serious one, that much was obvious, or why should each sister throw away a contract that was worth thousands and end an association that looked as if it had acquired a permanent éclat? The association of Bernice and Joy was somewhat on a par with that of a Pavlova and a Ruth Draper, moreover it required little in the way of scenery or elaborate effects.

Again, as Travers saw things, two sisters might be at daggers drawn professionally and yet might agree to appear to the public as possessing a perfect professional harmony. And the more he thought things out, the less he was disposed to find any fault in Bernice, unless the fundamentals of her gracious personality had utterly changed. Serenely self-centred she might be, and rigid in her views, but Bernice Haire as he had known her could not conceivably be guilty of needlessly seeking or maintaining a quarrel.

Travers went deviously to work as became an unraveller of mysteries. Even if Joy was going to explain the mystery on the Sunday, that was no reason why he should not first see Bernice and try to arrive at her point of view. So as soon as he was back at the flat he rang up Helen. It was always his habit to spend his weekends at her place in Sussex.

"Can't get away this weekend," he said. "Just pressure of business. By the way, did you know Bernice was back in England?"

"I saw it in the paper weeks ago."

"Seen or heard anything of her?"

"My dear Ludo! You know I'm too busy for anything."

"Well, I might run across her somewhere. Give her your love, I suppose?"

That much of ground prepared, Travers set off for the Bloomsbury hotel. Bernice's maid said her mistress was just going out, but Travers was told to wait in the anteroom of the small suite. Then suddenly Bernice came in, face aglow.

Many things came back at that first new sight of her. There was no change; that he knew at once. The same quiet smile and the same graciousness, and a loveliness about her that was remote and austere.

"Ludo! But what a pleasure!"

"Unpardonable calling at this unearthly hour," he said, and bent over the white hand. "But I happened to have been talking to Helen, and I was this way . . ."

She smiled. "But I'm happy to see you." She hesitated for a moment. "You've been abroad?"

"I know," he said. "I ought to have come before. But I didn't know you were back. Believe me, Bernice."

"Of course I believe you." She smiled happily. "And how is Helen? We must really arrange a day in town."

"She'd love it," he said. "And now I won't keep you a moment longer. I hear you're due out."

She glanced at her watch, then sank into a chair.

"Plenty of time yet. And now tell me all about yourself and everything."

"Lord, no," said Travers gallantly. "I want to hear all about you. How the tour went, for instance."

"Magnificently."

"And Joy? How is she?"

"Joy?" She frowned slightly. "One doesn't hear much of Joy nowadays." A smile. "Children will grow up, you know."

"Yes," he said, and hunted vainly for some word of challenge. After all, Joy, even at twenty-six, was something of a child compared with Bernice.

"You're staying in town for some time?" he said, and then quickly: "But of course you are. Half London must be crazy to see you both in a show."

"Don't let's talk about us," she said. "Tell me about yourself. What are you doing? Writing?"

It took him three minutes to extricate himself from that by-path, and then she was rising to go.

"I'll tell Helen I saw you," he said, and then appeared to remember something. "By the way, didn't somebody tell me you and Joy were shortly going on another tour?"

She shook her head. "It's frightfully unlucky to talk about the future. And now I must fly." Her hand went out. "Guess where I'm going."

"Ultimately, I know," he said. "Immediately, to some friendly place because of the quiet way you're dressed."

She laughed. "How clever of you, Ludo! Actually I'm going to the Paliceum to see father. He rather expects it, poor darling."

Travers nodded. "Tell me, isn't he rather overdoing it at his age? Four shows a night is heavy going."

"I know," she said. "He suffers very much from insomnia and his doctor was furious—but there you are. It's some time now since he appeared in town and he's most anxious to keep in touch with his public or he'd never have signed the contract. But they're putting him on very well, I believe."

"So they ought," Travers said indignantly. "A man of his standing and ability and—if you'll pardon the phrase—of his showmanship, ought to be a colossal draw when he makes himself accessible to the music-hall public." He turned at the door. "When may I come and see you properly?"

She pretended to think.

"I'm frightfully busy, of course. Would you think me too unconventional if I rang you up?"

"My dear Bernice! I'd love you to ring up. Early next week? Or might I call before if the weather holds, and take you out?"

"But I might be out," she said.

But he held her to the promise, and departed head in air.

As he walked along to the Tube station he was feeling more satisfied about Barney's problem. Joy would be solving it on the Sunday—he was sure of that—and there would be no need to hear Bernice's side of the affair. How could a living soul ever quarrel with Bernice? The most her worst enemy could ever say about her was that she was over-reserved; puritanic maybe, which was a sound fault in the present times. And that quality merely helped to make her the unique thing she was; unique in her superb assurance, her perfection of poise, and that something that gave the steadfast impression of loyalty and safety. Remote she might be, but only to those who had no insight, or who failed to call forth a womanly sympathy and understanding.

It was when he happened to catch sight of a clock that he had a sudden resolve. It would be too late to go to that first house at the Paliceum as Bernice was doing. But why not go to a later show? The second house at either the Paliceum or the Metropolis, for instance? Each act of Sir Jerome's would take up about a quarter of an hour. Better ring up both houses and find the times of Sir Jerome's appearances at each.

Those time-tables proved remarkably convenient. Sir Jerome was on at the Paliceum from 7:00 to 7:20, and at the Metropolis from 7:35 to 7:55. Then came a long interval between the two houses, probably in order that the great actor should have ample time for his dinner, for the acts at the second houses were 9:15 to 9:35 at the Paliceum and 9:50 to 10:10 at the Metropolis.

Travers resolved therefore to eat his own dinner in comfort and he chose the second house at the Metropolis, where he booked a circle seat by phone.

CHAPTER II

THE LEANING MAN

PALMER HAD CERTAINLY been right about the weather. There had been a mist in the early evening when Travers set out for Bernice's hotel and it had thickened as night came on-Then it settled into a peculiarly swirling kind of lightish fog, as if there were breeze enough to harry it but not to disperse it. Travers, for instance, could scarcely see a yard before him when he left the flat again, and yet when he crossed Leicester Square he could read the signs above the Metropolis at the width of two wide streets.

The house was full, and as Travers waited for the show to begin he could not help remembering how earlier in the evening Bernice had also sat waiting through the varied performance till her father should appear. The thought was a kind of delightful intimacy, and he actually found himself looking round him in case she might by some amazing chance have decided on a second visit. Then he could smile at himself for so ridiculous a hope.

Curious, he thought, how the meeting with Bernice had brought back so many things. It was as if something of himself and his memories had been dormant, and then at the new sight of her had come suddenly to life. Yet, as he assured himself, he was not in love, for if he were, there would be a far greater unsettling in his mind than the wish to be in her company. Besides, with one so rare as Bernice, there was almost a shock in associating things so gross as sex and marriage. Or were they gross? He shook his head at that. The mere fact that he had thought of them as such was a proof that he had seen them through no veil of romance.

The overture began, and then when he looked at his program he had the quick sense of disappointment that comes when one looks back and remembers a thing already seen. It was *The Decoration* that Sir Jerome was to do, and he had seen the great actor in that melodramatic tour de force as long back as just after the war. But maybe, he assured himself, this latest performance would be a mellowed one; and then again, when it came to owning up to the truth, he was forced to admit that he had not come to the Metropolis to see Sir Jerome at all, but merely to prolong in some tenuous way that renewed contact with Sir Jerome's daughter.

Sir Jerome would be well over seventy, he thought. A fine actor—even a great one, judged by the standards that had satisfied pre-war generations. Now he was scarcely a legend in an age which was prone to giggle at fine sentiment and stir restlessly at ornate periods and florid gesture. And, of course, it was useless to deny that Sir Jerome had much of Tree in him, who had always been Tree. What was it that had been said about the eighteenth century actor Quin?

Horatio, Falstaff, Dorax—still 'twas Quin.

That was it, or very near it, and Sir Jerome had always been a Quin. Through whatever masterpieces of make-up one could tell him by his mannerisms, and that throaty, deliberate voice was the voice of Jerome Haire, whether it roared as true lion or like any nightingale.

But Travers was in too comfortable a mood to let introspection or reminiscence spoil his evening. He enjoyed the various turns that preceded Sir Jerome's appearance and found even a crooner temporarily bearable. Then the last plaudits died and the orchestra broke into the stirringly melancholic strains of Tchaikovsky's Fifth Symphony, and as the curtain slowly rose the music modulated cunningly and all at once was blaring out the old imperial Russian national anthem.

A roar of applause that seemed to shake the very building broke out as the scene was disclosed. Travers was surprised and in some curious way gratified at the overwhelming warmth of the reception. Then his thoughts were busy with what was to come, for the sight of the attic room and the portrait of the Emperor above the rickety mantelpiece had brought back each detail of speech and action.

Melodrama and even claptrap the story might be but it was the perfect playlet for that kind of audience. As for himself, he might discern Sir Jerome through the masterly make-up, and but for a more natural quavering the voice might be the accustomed voice, yet he found himself immediately interested, and even absorbed. With the natural aging of the actor the drama carried a new conviction.

It was the story of an ex-chamberlain to the Emperor, scarcely managing to live on the barest pittance in a Paris garret, but each night donning his old uniform and his decorations that he had somehow managed to save in his escape from the Bolsheviks. His crazy brain knew that the Emperor was not dead after all, and he knew it because he was still waiting for that decoration that the Emperor had promised him—the Grand Cross of the Order of the Romanoffs—a few days before the great debacle.

That night of the story, the Emperor did come to reward his faithful old servant. In his hallucinations the old man knelt before his invisible master, and talked with him, and stood proudly while the decoration was at last pinned on his breast. That he then knew it for hallucination, and died as he knew it, was no matter, for the audience had seen the inevitable ending, and there was a long, almost reverent hush as the curtain slowly fell.

But then there came what was for Travers a definite anti-climax. The curtain slowly rose again, and a new tremendous roar burst from the audience. It grew deafening, was held for a long minute, then slowly died away as the actor held up his hand. He made two steps forward. The Jerome voice spoke with all its throaty and almost pedantic deliberation, and there was the deprecatory stoop of the Jerome shoulders.

"Ladies and gentlemen, I have always been, and am, and hope always to remain . . . your very . . . humble . . . servant."

The deepest of bows and he was making his exit to yet another tremendous roar. Two more curtains were taken and then the orchestra burst into the incongruous rhythm of the latest song-craze. Travers lasted through two minutes of the final turn—a lady described as Radio's Hot Pertoot—then made his way out. It was then exactly a quarter past ten.

The mist struck chill as he left the theatre, and as he stood for an indecisive moment, a voice hailed him. It was Percy Weiss, of Weiss and Glinn, with whom Travers was very well acquainted through various committees of the Central Hospital.

"Been at the show?" Weiss was saying.

"Yes," said Travers. "And you?"

"As a matter of fact," Weiss explained, "I went to see Jerome Haire. You in a hurry? Why not drop in at my club?"

They made their way carefully through the patchy fog, talking of Haire and the giants of their youth. Weiss too had been most gratified at the reception given to Sir Jerome by the Metropolis audience.

"The critics don't know what they're talking about," he said. "There's always sound sense in a typical audience like tonight's. They know the real thing when they see it."

Travers affably agreed, though there were reservations he might have made. In the hall that night he had never wholly recaptured much of his own youth, and now, at even a slight distance and in the chill of the night air, he knew a forcing and an insincerity about his own brief enthusiasms of a few minutes before. All the same, it was somehow pleasant to talk about Sir Jerome. And then he remembered that remark Barney had mumbled about the actor being in need of the money. Weiss was the very fellow to have inside knowledge about that.

"Sir Jerome must have made the very devil of a lot of money in his time?" he began cautiously.

"Oh, yes," Weiss said. "But between ourselves, there's not a lot left. Just think back. How long is it since he had a theatre of his own in town?"

"Since he played?" He shook his head. "Three years, perhaps, or even more."

"That's right, and the season wasn't much more than a flop. Isn't that just what I was saying? The modern theatre thinks him démodé, and it's only the non-theatre-going public that sees the truth, as you and I saw tonight."

They found the club almost empty, and in a corner of the smoking-room resumed the talk over a couple of drinks. Travers hoped Weiss wasn't implying that Sir Jerome was in any want.

"Heavens, no!" Weiss said. "He has enough to live on in his comparatively simple way, and no more. You know his daughters?"

"Well, yes," said Travers, startled.

"Extraordinarily clever girls!" Weiss said. "But in the strictest confidence I may tell you that for the last two years they've been helping out his means with an allowance. That's why I'm very glad about his success this week. The cash may put him on his feet for a time, and I hear he's shortly doing another week up North."

"Strange, isn't it?" Travers said. "A great national figure and a kind of unsuspected skeleton in the cupboard. But what's happened to the money he's made?"

"Well, he backed himself of late years and he backed an unlucky loser. Bad investments too, I believe. And—I think this is more than a rumour—he still likes a little bit on a horse."

"You said he lived simply?" said Travers, lingering out the talk.

"He's a Londoner to the core, and an old-timer," Weiss said. "No sherry parties or weekend cottages for him. He still keeps his flat in Shaftesbury Avenue and he takes his constitutionals like an old trouper. You know, wanders round the old haunts and drops in at the Spread Eagle for a drink, just as he and all the bloods did in his younger days."

Travers smiled. "A little foible of his now to be the Doctor Johnson of the theatrical world. By the way, I thought his performance tonight had much improved since I last saw it. . . ."

It was after eleven o'clock when Travers came out once more to the fog. A spell of wool-gathering made him miss his turn and he found himself in Piccadilly Circus. So he crossed to Shaftesbury Avenue, cut through Soho Square, and came out at Charing

Cross Road. Then, through a clearing in the fog, he caught sight of the man.

He was drunk. The first glimpse told that, and also that no man could be much more drunk and still capable of control over his movements. At the moment Travers first caught sight of him he was just inside that narrow way that leads through to the Garrick—Waterman's Court, they call it—leaning in an angle made by the wall and the protruding window of a small shop, and he was motionless.

Then it was seen that his face was a fiery red and that he was breathing thickly, with mouth agape, and as Travers moved to the far pavement to avoid the very unpleasant sight of him, he all at once began making queer choking noises and weaving the air with his hands as if he were clutching at something invisible to everyone but himself. Travers turned back at that strange performance, and at that very moment a constable appeared out of the fog. He looked hard at the man.

"Hallo? What's the matter with you?"

But the man began to slither to the pavement, then as he fell, his head struck the pavement with a sound that reached as far as Travers.

"What's the matter with him, officer? Drunk?"

The constable sniffed. "Looks like d.t.'s to me."

The man now lay in a stupefied sleep, mouth agape and with that same strange thickness in his breathing. The constable put him in a sitting position against the wall, then had a good sniff at his mouth.

"Drunk as a pig, sir. Anyone can smell him a mile off." He shook his head. "He's a case for the ambulance."

"Just a minute," said Travers, who had suddenly begun to wonder. "If he's all that drunk, how did he get as far as here? The nearest pub's the Spread Eagle, and that was closed over half an hour ago."

"Red Biddy, I shouldn't wonder. Methylated spirits and cheap wine and rubbish. It's not so bad when you're indoors, so I'm told, but soon as you get out in the air, down you go like a pole-axed bullock. Look after him, sir, will you? I'll get the station ambulance here."

He disappeared again into the fog. Travers, fingers at his glasses, was thinking that if the tipple had been Red Biddy, then it must have been drunk quite close at hand, for the constable had distinctly said that a man went down with it the very minute he got in the cold air. As for the stupefied man, Travers could see that he was neatly dressed, if with an air of what is known as genteel poverty. His boots, for instance, were clean but none too good a fit; the cuffs and trouser bottoms of the navy-blue suit were slightly frayed, while the old-fashioned velvet collar of the overcoat was greenish and much worn. Elderly, he looked; clean-shaven and keen-faced. What might he have been? A butler, fallen on hard times, thought Travers, or a doctor who had been struck off the register.

Then as Travers shook his head, the man's hand began clutching at his collar as if he wanted air, but it changed to a more feeble groping, and then the hand fell again. It was a thin hand, that had some strange touch of quality, like the hand of a scholar or musician, and Travers, all at once stooping, saw how white it was, and that the nails were clean.

Steps were heard in the fog and two men appeared. One gave a titter, the other spoke.

"What is he? Drunk?"

Travers said nothing, being in no mood for discussion, then all at once the man who had spoken was coming close and kneeling by the man.

"Don't do that," Travers told him quickly. "The police are in charge."

But he paid no heed. He was even undoing the overcoat and leaning his head on the sleeping man's chest. Then the constable appeared.

"Ambulance just—Hi! What do you think you're doing?"

The kneeling man got to his feet.

"Better get him to St. Martin's Hospital," he said curtly. "He's in a pretty bad way."

"And who are you?" the constable fired.

"A doctor, and here's my card."

More steps were heard. They shuffled, then stopped.

"Anything the matter?"

Travers started at that latest voice, and one look at the new-comer told him he was right.

"Just a drunken man, sir."

Sir Jerome came forward and stared hard at the sleeping man.

"Here, you keep out of this, sir," the constable told him.

"I'm Sir Jerome Haire." The voice had an immense dignity. "And I think I know this man."

"Know him, sir!"

Then the ambulance drew up. The doctor cut impatiently in.

"Pardon me, Sir Jerome, but he ought to be got away at once."

"What's the ambulance for?" asked the constable with heavy irony.

"I don't mean to the station," insisted the doctor. "He should be rushed to the hospital."

"Get him inside, Tom," the constable said. Then he looked round at the watching group. The doctor's friend would not be needed but the others, Sir Jerome included, would have to come to the hospital and have their statements taken there.

The ambulance glided off into the fog and the four men followed it. By chance Travers and Sir Jerome walked together, and it was the actor who spoke first while he turned up the collar of his old-fashioned and somewhat flamboyant fur coat. His voice was fussy and pompous.

"A raw night, sir."

"It is," agreed Travers. "By the way, Sir Jerome, I saw your performance at the Metropolis tonight. If you'll allow me, I would like to congratulate you."

"No talking, please!" barked the constable. "You can do all the talking you like when you get inside where we're going."

Sir Jerome waved an indifferent hand, and the four moved on through the fog.

The doctor's quick statement was taken first, and then he went off to the ward where the drunk had been taken. Then Sir Jerome's turn came, and his story was interesting enough.

When taking his various constitutionals, he said, it was his habit to drop in occasionally at the Spread Eagle for a drink and particularly the chance sight of any old theatrical friend. He was often accosted there by those of the profession who had fallen on hard times. That worried him little, since it rarely meant more than a drink and a meal maybe, plus perhaps a half-crown, and more than once he had been able to find a man a job.

The previous Saturday morning he had been so spoken to in the Spread Eagle by a man who had been most persistent, and to get rid of him, Sir Jerome had told him to call at his Shaftesbury Avenue flat, which he had done on that same Saturday afternoon. The man had given the name of Furloe, and had given an account of his professional career. But that career had ended many years back, and on being pressed to account for that, and to give references, the man had begun to hedge and to contradict himself. Thereupon Sir Jerome decided to have nothing to do with him, and, what was more, told him so.

Thereupon the man spoke of some mystery which he couldn't reveal and asked if Sir Jerome would reconsider his decision provided the references could be obtained. Work was what he wanted, not charity.

"To get rid of him I told him to come and see me in three weeks' time," Sir Jerome said. "In the meanwhile I thought I might make some inquiries of my own."

"There was something fishy about him, sir," commented the constable.

"I thought he was a—er—ticket-of-leave man. An ex-convict," Sir Jerome said bluntly. "That was for me sufficient explanation of the gap in his career." He shrugged his shoulders. "I have nothing personally against ex-convicts but I didn't like the attitude of the fellow, or his manner."

"I see, sir. Furloe was the name. And his Christian names, sir?"

"I forget. He may have said something, but I forget." The shake of the head became a lugubrious one. "All the same it was a great shock seeing him as he was tonight. When I set out on my usual constitutional—I'm a bad sleeper nowadays—I had no idea—"

"Of course you didn't, sir."

Sir Jerome nodded in sympathy with himself. "A great shock, as I said. Still, it confirms what I was telling you. Someone must have been induced to give him money, and he must have spent it on drink."

The words had so reminiscently Victorian an echo that Travers had to wince. Then the officer broke in breezily.

"That's all from you then, sir. We have your address and so on."

"Goodnight to you then," the old actor said pompously. A quick look at Travers. "And goodnight to you, sir."

"Goodnight, Sir Jerome." He hesitated. "My name's Travers, if it recalls anything to you."

The old man glanced at the card and it was on the tip of Travers's tongue to recall Helen and Bernice. Then something made him change his mind.

"I may be able to see that you're not unduly troubled over this affair."

"Troubled?" He looked up with a glare, and the hooked beak seemed to thrust itself forward.

"I mean, if Scotland Yard should have to inquire—"

"What the devil are you talking about, sir!"

Travers smiled lamely. Perhaps the offer had been something of a cheap attempt to make himself agreeable to Bernice's father.

"I beg your pardon, Sir Jerome. We'll say no more about it."

The other seemed somewhat mollified at that.

"Connected with Scotland Yard, are you?" Another glare. "Scotland Yard don't bother themselves about drunken men, do they?"

Travers smiled sheepishly again, knowing he had landed himself in deeper waters than he had intended.

"No, Sir Jerome. And I repeat—I beg your pardon."

The old man nodded.

"Well, I shall be happy to-er-assist the police in any-er-capacity they may consider necessary. My services are entirely at their disposal." A quick glance down at the card. "Travers," he said, as if the name recalled nothing. "Well, once more good-night to you, Mr. Travers."

The officer ushered him out, then came back ready for Travers's statement.

"Now about you, sir." He hesitated as if he were in some difficulty from which he hoped Travers would extricate him. "You're connected with the Yard, sir."

"At intervals, yes," said Travers gravely.

"I see, sir." He rubbed his chin. "All the same, sir, I don't see where the Yard can come in"—his face brightened—"not unless he pops off as a result of tonight. You have a card on you, sir?"

So Travers was allowed to go, but he had one request to make.

"If it could be managed officially, officer, I'd very much like to know how the poor devil gets on. Could you give me a ring in the morning?"

"I'll see to that, sir."

A nod and a smile and Travers departed. But the smile went as he stepped out into the fog again. Somehow he had known all along, and the attitude of that chance doctor confirmed the fact, that the case was not one of mere drunkenness. That knowledge had been at the back of his mind when he had so foolishly mentioned Scotland Yard to Sir Jerome Haire. The redness of the face, the weaving gestures, the clutching at the collar: all those he had seen before on a certain poisoning case on which he had been engaged with George Wharton.

But safer perhaps to dismiss the whole thing now from his mind. If there were anything to discover, that doctor—in conjunction with the hospital authorities—would discover it quickly enough. He began thinking then of Sir Jerome, and that first sight he had had of him at such close quarters. A good-hearted old chap, in spite of that pretentiousness and the pompous mannerisms. A fine figure of a man too, in spite of his age. Once he must have had a magnificent physique, and there must still be a certain robustness on which to draw for the desperate strain of that music-hall week.

In the flat Travers was surprised to find Palmer still up, and there was a quick reprimand.

"I should have been in bed, sir," Palmer said, "but I didn't want you to miss this message. Superintendent Wharton said it was most important."

"When did it come?"

"An hour ago, sir."

But no sooner had Travers read it than he was making for the door again.

"You'd better get off to bed. When I shall be back, I can't say."

Palmer saw him out, and gave that little deprecatory cough.

"If you'll pardon me, sir, is it another murder?"

"Looks like it," Travers told him from the door.

And if he had added the honest truth it would have been that he almost hoped so.

CHAPTER III
DEATH AT THE LEVANTIC

THAT EXTREMELY expensive hotel, the Levantic, which stands near St. James's, is in various ways unique.

It caters, in the first place, to what one may call the eccentricities of the colour line. Black men, yellow men, brown men and even mud-coloured men—of rank and standing, certainly, and wealthy enough to pay its prices—are never embarrassed there by looks either askance or supercilious, for whites are as rare as bishops at beanos. Some of its regular clientele would be welcomed anywhere—make no bones about that—yet the fact remains that they prefer the Levantic.

And naturally also the hotel can provide and serve the queer varieties of food which taste or caste or creed may demand, and it can accommodate and handle those mixed entourages that often accompany potentates. But its other peculiarity is that it does not consist of a galaxy of rooms with private baths, but consists almost entirely of suites varying in extent and adaptability.

That fact is important when one examines the murder of the Maharajah of Amli, for when a hotel is rather like a block of private flats with one main entrance, there should be considerable difficulty in supervising those who enter it. Yet the management would smile if one ventured to suggest danger from, say, thieves. They know that the long and specialized experience of their staff has made the detection of a rogue a matter of instinct, and they would remind you that no thieves, or even the unsavoury, had ever been seen in its corridors. And if they had, you would gather that they had been so dealt with that no scandal or alarm had ever been allowed to pass the hotel doors.

When Travers came through the swing doors that night, the only men he saw were whites—two of Wharton's men, and at the discreetly placed bureau, what looked like a clerk and a definitely agitated man who might be the manager.

"Mr. Travers, sir?" one of the men said. "The Super's expecting you, sir. Suite seventeen."

When Travers stepped from the lift to the corridor there was no need to ask wherever suite seventeen was, for most of what was known as the circus—print and camera men—were standing in a group as if waiting for orders. A man who evidently recognized Travers opened a door for him.

"There's ways and means. They won't get me tied up with their blasted red-tape."

That was the old General—as the Yard not unaffectionately knew Wharton—blaring his views to Chief-Inspector Norris. Then Wharton caught sight of Travers, and at once his voice was that of the mild and henpecked paterfamilias of whom his vast weeping-willow moustache and antiquated spectacles made him the very spit.

"Here you are then, Mr. Travers."

Travers took the outstretched hand, and nodded genially at Norris.

"Sorry I'm late but I only just received your message."

"You're not late," Wharton said testily. "That's the damnable thing about it."

He gave no explanation of that queer statement but made at once for the open door to the left. The room they were in was a kind of lounge but this new room was evidently a workroom, and furnished handsomely enough. But Travers had no eyes for the fine furnishings: all he saw was a man, head sideways on the red and black carpet, as if he lay in some careless attitude of sleep.

"He's dead?"

"As mutton," said Wharton laconically.

"An Indian, isn't he."

"The Maharajah of Amli."

"That secretary pronounced it Oomli," Norris remarked tentatively.

"Oomli or Amli doesn't matter a damn," said Wharton contemptuously. "I call him a corpse." He gave a grunt. "Too important a corpse, that's the trouble."

"I seem to have read the name somewhere," Travers remarked reflectively. Then his fingers went to his glasses. "I believe it was something to do with racing. I suppose it couldn't have been."

At the moment his brain, as he knew, was far from working. The preliminaries to the inquiry were the strangest he had ever known when working with Wharton, for everything seemed unreal and incongruous. There was a dead man on the carpet, looking as if he weren't dead at all, and everywhere was an atmosphere of discreet quiet. No print or camera men were at work, and the chief interest Wharton was taking seemed to be in some grievance of his own.

"How was he killed, George?" In that hushed atmosphere Travers felt constrained to whisper.

"Knife in the ribs." From the way he said it, one gathered that his main regret was that he had not done it himself.

"Know the time?"

"Ten o'clock to the dot. Someone in the room below here heard voices and a scuffling, and then a thud as the body fell."

"Scuffle?"

Wharton began making a circuitous way round, and nodded for Travers to come round too. Then Travers could see that the dead man's wrists were bruised and there was a disorder about his neckwear.

"He's wearing morning clothes, George. Isn't that unusual?"

"How?"

"Well, wouldn't you have expected him to dress in the evening?"

"Oh, he was the unconventional sort," Wharton said. "The secretary told me he generally preferred to have informal meals served up here."

There was another awkward silence, then Travers smiled.

"We seem to be proceeding by jerks, George. Anything to do with what I happened to overhear you saying about red-tape?"

That set Wharton going.

"You've got it," he said. "You see, I was a damn sight too clever. As soon as I got here and they told me who he was, I reckoned it was up to me to be a regular diplomat. Thinks I, this is likely to be in the line of the Special Branch; also as he's a maharajah, there might be interested parties who might like to be here during the inquiry—"

Travers cut in amusedly. "And who might kick up a fuss if they hadn't been asked."

"Well, yes," granted Wharton. "Still, as I was saying, I just had a quick look round and no more. I asked no questions and I examined nothing; I simply grabbed the phone and rang up the powers that be. What do you think happened? Before I could get going on the job, word comes from some of the high-and-mighties through headquarters that nothing's to be touched till one of their—"

The phone bell sounded like a fire alarm. Wharton nipped across at once. Grunts and agreements were all that came from his end, but his look was a vastly different one when he hung up.

"Said they didn't mean it literally. They meant his *private* papers. Wouldn't it make an angel weep?" He gave another grunt or two. "Get hold of Menzies, Norris, and have the others in."

But he dropped a quick eyelid as Norris moved off.

"Mind you, Mr. Travers, I haven't been wasting my time altogether. I've picked up a thing or two. Have a look here."

He straddled the body and hoisted it partly to one side. Now Travers could see the knife that stuck askew in the ribs. Along one wrist was a cut, but, strangely enough, no blood on either wrist or fingers.

"What do you make of the knife?"

"Rather ornate, isn't it?" Travers said.

"It was used principally as a paper-weight," Wharton told him. "One or two other curios on the desk there, you may notice. And have you seen this?"

His toe was indicating a handy-sized automatic that lay near the desk. Chalk marks already outlined its position.

"Amli's own," Wharton said, "and kept in a drawer of that desk. The chair's overturned, as you see. Ah! here's Menzies."

Travers, still in very much of a fog about everything, answered the police-surgeon's friendly nod. Wharton got breezily to work.

"The body first. You get the men to work, Norris. They won't disturb us."

Travers watched from a comparative distance, for there was something in Menzies' careless and even jocular handling of corpses that always made him the least bit uneasy, illogical though his feelings might be. So his eyes were mostly on the camera men, with lights flashing on and off, and the chatter from Wharton and Menzies was as audible as if he stood nearby.

"Curious sort of thrust," Menzies said. "Have a look at the wound."

"What's that discoloration on the chin?"

"Wrists pretty bad too," Menzies said. "Look here. The skin actually torn."

"I'd like to have seen the scrap," Wharton chuckled. "They must have had the very devil of a set-to. Forceps? Here we are."

Out came the knife as easy as drawing a skewer.

"Handsome affair," Menzies remarked. "Brought from India, I'd say. Point's pretty sharp."

Collins, the print sergeant, took the knife over. It took him less than two minutes to declare there were no prints on it but Amli's!

"What the devil!" Wharton stared at Collins, at the knife, then down at Amli. "What do you make of that, Menzies? How could his be the only prints on the knife that killed him?"

"Easily enough," Menzies said dryly. "There're bruises on the wrists, aren't there? Why shouldn't the knife have been forced into his chest against his own resistance, so to speak?"

"Or why shouldn't Amli's prints have been faked on it after the stabbing?" asked Travers.

"Wait a minute." Wharton raised his hand. "Let's get this right. I say the knife couldn't have been forced down into Amli's ribs. It's physically impossible, at least while he held the knife above his head. You're the strongest man here, Norris. Pick out the weakest man—Menzies, say—and try it. I know. I've been over all this years ago."

"I expect you're right, sir," Norris said. "But what if both of them were struggling on the floor?"

"They weren't," Wharton told him. "In the room under here they heard the fall of a body. Amli was struck, and fell. My impressions are that there was no more struggling." He smiled grimly. "There didn't have to be."

"What about Mr. Travers's theory then, sir?"

Wharton shrugged his shoulders. "What about the prints, Collins? Clear, are they?"

"Have a look for yourself, sir. It's a whole blur of his prints."

Wharton had a look, then did some illustration.

"If the killer faked the prints after wiping off his own, then he'd have faked a clear set. As Collins says, all these shifting prints couldn't have been faked. Still, I think I can see everything pretty clearly now. Let's have the clothes off him, Menzies."

The running commentary continued to be illuminating.

"Lovely silk, this underwear. Must have cost a packet . . . A wily customer, I'll bet. . . . Bit gross, don't you think, or do these chaps run naturally to fat? . . . How old? I'd say somewhere about thirty. We can very easily find out."

The examination and comment went on, till at last a sheet covered the body. Travers looked down at the dead man's face. Somehow he looked much younger than thirty, though it might be the plumpness of the cheeks that gave that younger look. As for type, he was the kind of Indian that so fitted the imagination as to be far too close a fit—full lips, jet black hair and sloe-like eyes, and skin the colour of fumed oak.

"I don't like those chaps and I can't say why," Wharton said at Travers's elbow. "They make my skin ruffle."

"What's his height?" asked Norris.

"Five feet six or seven," Menzies said, and then the phone rang again.

Wharton slipped across. There were the same grunts and nods, and once more his lip was drooping ironically as he hooked up.

"You'll be pleased to hear he wasn't as important as

they first thought he was. All we have to do is seal up every private paper and item of correspondence and send it you know where. An official or two will be along in the morning. Pretty quick going, that. Only three hours since Amli was done in. However"—he heaved a sigh—"we'll do what we can. Go through all the rooms, Collins. Finish his pockets, Norris, and make an inventory. Like him in the bedroom, Menzies? By the way there're strict orders. No slicing him up to see how he worked. Time, and exact cause of death—that's all."

The body went through a door at the far corner, and Travers knew that things were likely to move along at top speed. Wharton looked limbered up, for one thing. Up to the moment he had displayed poor showmanship, for the various inhibitions had cramped his style. This was a pity, for a first-class actor had been lost when Wharton joined the Force, as Wharton himself was very well aware. Cross-examination was his particular delight, and now he was rubbing his hands at the prospect.

"We'll have that secretary in. No, we won't; we'll have the valet. I don't know, though. Better make it the secretary. Bring him in, Norris."

A man of about forty-five came in, and he was dressed in a neat grey suit. The bald area on his skull-top shone in the light, and there was a general shininess about him. Even his voice seemed hardly his own but one he had acquired somewhere and polished up for professional purposes, and though he was above medium height and well built, there was something definitely dapper about him. Travers felt a quick distrust but Wharton was greeting him with much affability and many apologies.

"Just a friendly talk. Nothing official," he said.

"You'd like to get to bed, the same as we do, so we'll take an official statement in the morning. The name is Osmund, isn't it?"

"That's correct," he said, and gave a little jerky bow. "Bernard Thomas Osmund."

"You were secretary to His Highness?"

"Yes, sir. I was engaged on His Highness's arrival six weeks ago, through a friend."

He mentioned a name, and Wharton, who had never heard it, decided to look impressed.

"Now about tonight. His Highness's movements, and your own. Anything that might help us." He smiled jocularly. "And don't tell me you told me anything already. Let's hear the whole lot again."

Osmund said he worked mornings and afternoons, and admitted that the job was the easiest he had ever had. That afternoon he had left at four for his flat in Wardour Street where he could always be reached by phone if urgently needed. He had not been rung up that evening and normally would not have returned to the hotel till nine the next morning, but while he was at a cinema—the Rembrandt in Gwynne Street, of which his brother was manager—he remembered something he should have brought away with him, so he at once came back to the Levantic.

"Then you left the cinema at about a quarter past ten?" Wharton said.

"That's correct, sir. I got here, as you know, at twenty-five past."

"Exactly," said Wharton, and pursed his lips. Then he gave a confidential nod. "Just between ourselves now, give us the inside information about His Highness."

Osmund shot a quick look that tapered off into a kind of archness: the sort of look a dark horse of a curate might feel constrained to give when invited to contribute a smoking-room story.

"In strict confidence," Wharton went coaxingly on. "Did he often come to England, for instance? What did he do when he got here and why did he come at all?"

Osmund relaxed, and there was an obvious relief that he had misread Wharton's first question. His Highness, he reminded his listeners, to whom everything was news, had been educated at a famous public school and at Oxford. His state might be a small one and politically he might be of comparatively no importance, but he was exceedingly wealthy. In spite of that he was most unostentatious and when in England preferred to live like an Englishman, which was why he had no native servants or entourage.

"I don't recall his name in connection with Oxford," Travers said. "He didn't play cricket at all, did he?"

"His Highness had no use for games of that sort," Osmund said.

"And why didn't he stay at the So-and-So or the So-and-So?" went on Travers, mentioning two most exclusive hotels. "I mean this: If it was his wish when in England to live like the English, then why didn't he live *with* the English?"

Osmund had no idea, unless it was because His Highness's predecessors had always chosen the Levantic. As for his interests when in England, he was going in for racing on a fairly large scale. The flat-racing season was due in a very few weeks and His Highness was naturally most interested in the work and trials of his horses.

"Trainer?"

"Charles Willshed, at Banthorne."

"Near Lewes, isn't it?" Wharton went on.

"That's correct," Osmund said. "His Highness was down there this morning and arrived back at three. That was when I saw him last."

"Any conversation?"

Osmund shot one of those queer looks that might mean anything. Then he shook his head.

"With His Highness, sir, you never spoke unless you were spoken to. He had no orders to give me. I saw him come in and that was all."

"Quite so, quite so." Wharton frowned in thought. "And now this automatic again. This was the drawer it was kept in?"

"Just here—"

"Keep back, if you please!" An arch look. "Many a man's been hanged, Mr. Osmund, because his finger prints were in the wrong places. And now will you look at his belongings and this inventory."

It seemed to Travers that the secretary's lip rather drooped at the gaudy ornamentation of the gold cigarette case and the fob watch. Then all at once he stared.

"His wallet's not here."

"Wallet?" said Wharton, interested enough to come peeringly forward. "What sort of wallet?"

"Just a small leather pocket wallet," Osmund said. "About this size. He had had it specially made for himself. It had A-M-L-I inlaid on it in platinum and diamonds."

"What'd he keep in it? Private papers and money?"

"That's all, sir, so I think. I used to see him take it out of his breast pocket occasionally."

"Hm!" went Wharton. "And the appointment book. Where's that kept?"

Osmund said there wasn't one. Sometimes he was asked to remind Amli about something but as a rule His Highness was secretive about his plans. As far as he could gather—without, of course, being curious—His Highness had no English friends. Willshed, the trainer, had come to the hotel once or twice.

"His Highness had his own interests then," Wharton said. He frowned again, then gave a beckoning glance. Osmund came nearer; Wharton craned forward.

"A pretty lady, was there?"

Osmund absolutely gaped, so startled was he. Then he moistened his lips.

"I can't say, sir. I mean, that would have been His Highness's private business, sir."

"And what did you think—privately?"

"I'm not paid to think, sir, if you'll excuse me."

Wharton heaved a sigh. "Well, we'll forget all about it. Know anybody who'd have killed him if he had the chance?"

"Why, no, sir."

Wharton's look became almost whimsical. "Know a friend of his called Smith?"

"Smith?" He must have thought Wharton was laughing, for he gave a little smirk. "I expect he knew quite a lot of Smiths, sir, same as we all do."

"He ever mentioned anyone of that name? Or did you ever know him correspond with anyone of the name?"

"Why, no, sir."

"Well, I think that's all," said Wharton with yet another pious sigh. Then all at once he was beckoning the secretary across to the far corner of the room. His tone was tremendously confidential.

"Now, Mr. Osmund, we're all men of the world. Absolutely between ourselves, what sort was he?"

Osmund hesitated, then nodded.

"He wasn't—well, one of our sort, sir."

Travers was startled at that amazing reply. Wharton merely chuckled.

"I guessed it. A bit of a flyer, was he?"

"I won't say more than I have, sir. He prided himself on being as English as the English, if you know what I mean, and he wasn't anything of the sort."

"What was he then?"

"He was boastful and showy." There was real venom in the reply. "And God help you if he didn't have all his own way."

"What did he do?"

"He'd get his own back somehow. And the way he'd look! Just as if you were dirt."

"Too bad, too bad," said Wharton, with a dismal shake of the head. Travers cut in.

"What was his race?"

"A Rajput, sir. Amli is in Rajputana."

Out went Wharton's hand. "Well, we're grateful and we won't keep you from your bed any longer. Tomorrow morning at eight suit you?"

At the door Osmund turned to make a request. Might he look on the desk for that urgent paper he needed? Or perhaps it might be in one of the drawers.

"Look on the desk by all means," Wharton told him. "About the drawers, I don't know. If you tell me just what it is, then I'll let you have it later if I run across it."

Osmund seemed a bit taken aback and Wharton could see his brain working.

"It's a private document of my own," he said. "I think His Highness must have mixed it up with his own papers. But I'll just look on the desk if you don't mind."

A quick whisper from Wharton reached Travers.

"Watch him while we pretend to talk!"

In two minutes Osmund was saying that now he came to think of it, the paper wasn't important after all. Wharton showed no surprise. So with a goodnight, out Osmund went, and a man went on his tail.

"Well," snapped Wharton at once, "what'd he do at the desk?"

"He had a good look at the blotter," Travers said, "and he surreptitiously tried the drawers. He was interested in one that appears to be locked."

Wharton examined the blotter at once. It seemed to have had plenty of use, but among the ink blottings one pencilled note stood clear, and it was in the top right-hand corner.

S 10

Wharton smiled grimly. "That would be a reminder of Smith at ten o'clock. And jotted down by His Nibs himself."

"Who *is* this Smith you keep mentioning?" asked Travers.

"Don't know yet," Wharton said. "Plenty of time, though. Plenty of time."

He frowned to himself as he stood there, pursing his lips in thought. There was nothing of the harassed paterfamilias about him then but, as it always seemed to Travers in those deliberate moments, something of the law itself—unhurrying, tenacious and remorselessly sure.

Then at last Wharton turned to Norris.

"No prints in the room?"

"Nothing but what we don't want," Norris told him.

"Right," said Wharton. "Ask that valet to step this way."

The man who entered was dressed in sober black. He looked about fifty and there was an air of impeccability and supreme competence about him. Wharton's geniality was met with exquisite reserve.

"Now, Mr. Bond, I'm sorry to have kept you waiting all this time. William Bond, isn't it?"

Bond bowed his reply.

"You were engaged by His Highness six weeks ago?"

"Yes, sir."

"And who was your previous employer?"

"Lord Francis Gaunt, sir."

"Really? Then why'd you leave?"

Before Travers could cut in, Bond's answer came with its delicate reproof.

"Lord Francis died two months ago, sir. He left me five hundred pounds, sir, as an appreciation of my services."

"Good luck to you!" said Wharton, not the least abashed. "And now tell us all that occurred between yourself and His Highness from three o'clock onwards."

That was easy. His Highness was out in the early evening and at seven o'clock ordered Bond to serve a light meal in one of the other rooms. Bond waited at table. Then at about a quarter to nine Bond was rung for and His Highness apparently took a pound note from his wallet—

"One minute," said Wharton. "A leather wallet with his monogram on it in diamonds?"

Bond said that was the one. Wharton then gathered that His Highness flicked the note contemptuously to Bond and told him to clear out and go to the devil till half-past ten.

"And did you?"

"I walked along the Embankment, sir, as far as Chelsea," said the unruffled Bond. "Then I misjudged the time, sir, which is why I was back at a quarter past ten."

Wharton nodded. "And then you found the body. Know anyone who'd have been likely to have done it?"

"I have no idea, sir."

"Ever hear him refer to anyone named Smith?"

"Smith, sir?" There had been the faintest flicker of horror. "Never, sir."

Wharton beckoned him to the far corner. There was the old blather about men of the world, then the question was put.

"Just what sort was he, personally?"

"Personally, sir?" He became human enough to gaze reflectively at the ceiling. "All employers are not alike, sir."

"Come down from that perch of yours," Wharton told him impatiently. "What was he, in himself?"

"He meant well, sir, according to his lights. He paid well, sir, but there were times when he was trying."

Wharton smiled. "Now we're hearing something." Another motion of secrecy. "Still, between ourselves, was there a—lady friend?"

Bond regarded him for a moment or two with unblinking eyes.

"I understand there might have been, sir."

"Know who she was and where she lived?"

"It was not my place to be interested, sir." He coughed. "I beg your pardon, sir. I should not have put it like that. May I suggest, sir, that you speak to the chauffeur."

"Thanks for the tip." He nodded. "Now I think that's all. In the morning we might have to take an official statement, but that needn't alarm you."

"Just one question," broke in Travers. "Since His late Highness was what you've told us, why did you continue in his service, Bond?"

Once more the reply was to contain the utmost delicacy of reproof.

"I had already given in my notice, sir. It expires tomorrow, sir. Perhaps in view of the hour, sir, I should have said today."

Wharton couldn't help a chuckle, and he took the hint. Bond was allowed to go.

"A great lad, that," Wharton said to Travers. "What'd you make of him?"

"A charming soul," Travers said. "He reminds me of that butler in the song—the butler comparing his old master with the parvenu.

> *It wouldn't have done for the Duke, sir;*
> *It wouldn't have done for His Grace.*"

"Yes," said Wharton, and rubbed his chin. "I rather think he could tell us a bit about Osmund. You summed him up, didn't you?"

"Osmund?" Travers smiled wryly. "I didn't like him a bit. He was too veneered."

"His time's coming," said Wharton darkly. "And what now, Norris?"

"I think the manager must be getting a bit anxious, sir."

"So am I, and so are all of us," said Wharton airily. "Still, apologize, and ask him to come up."

"A slow business, this," he said to Travers.

"Yes," Travers said. "That's why it's such a pity about those private papers we aren't allowed to examine. They might have told us a lot."

"They wouldn't."

Travers raised surprised eyebrows.

"That's right," Wharton told him. His voice lowered. "You didn't think I was going to be such a fool as to cool my heels here for an hour and more while the high-and-mighties made up their minds?" He snorted contemptuously. "There are only two things among those so-called private papers that interest me."

Travers's eyebrows lifted inquiringly again. Wharton chuckled.

"How do you think I came to suspect the existence of a pretty lady? And that Osmund was a twister?"

"I see. And what about Smith?"

"Smith?" said Wharton. "Smith's a bit different. Here come the ones who're going to tell us all about Smith."

Chapter iv
WHARTON IS STAGGERED

It was plain that Maroulis, the manager, was in an exceedingly nervous state, and there was little wonder. Only the most meticulously tactful handling could, according to his apprehensions, save the hotel from the worst possible kind of publicity. Wharton, who could adjust his manner to suit all occasions, was now the mere servant of the law and its sympathetic representative.

"No reason for alarm, I assure you," he said. "When you wake up in the morning you'll feel a different man."

Maroulis shrugged helpless shoulders. "Do you think I shall sleep, after all this?"

"Now, now," said Wharton soothingly. "We're in the hands of very high authorities who can be relied on in every way. They'll look after the political complications," and there he waved a vague hand.

But Maroulis didn't give a damn for political complications. What might happen in Amli, or even possible repercussions throughout the whole Indian Empire, were trifles to him. It was the terrible shattering of an established serenity, the break in the smooth running of the hotel and the effects on its clientele, that were his concern. Could Superintendent Wharton, he asked, do him at least the great favour of not questioning the Anonymous Personage whose Italian valet had been sent to complain of the scuffling and noise in the room above him?

"Give me your word the facts are correct, and I'm satisfied," Wharton told him handsomely. "If you're ready, Norris, we'll take down the evidence officially."

Maroulis motioned for the bureau clerk to come forward. He confirmed that at 10:05 the Italian valet had made the complaint. Thereupon he had rung through to the manager.

Maroulis took up the tale. He had personally apologized to the Personage and had given assurances. Since everything was then quiet up above, he had thought the complaint exaggerated, and, in any case, he had no intention whatever of antagonizing Amli.

"So far, excellent," said Wharton. "Now what about the description of Smith?"

Maroulis handed it over and said it was the combined work of the clerk and the elevator operator.

Age about fifty. Dark hair and eyes. Thinnish face and rather sallow. Height about five feet nine. Dressed in dark suit, check overcoat, bowler hat but no gloves. English, and looked like a sporting man.

"That's capital," Wharton said. "Now let's go over the events of the evening as near as you've been able to work them out."

The first facts were that two phone calls had been put through to the Maharajah's room, one at 8:15 and the other at 8:35. Immediately after the second one he rang down to say that if anyone wanted to see him, including a man named Smith, he was to come straight up.

"Just a moment. You're dead sure he used the word *including*?"

Maroulis was not sure. That was the impression, he was sure about that. Anyone inquiring for him was to be sent up, including a man named Smith. And Smith did come to the bureau just before ten o'clock, saying he had an appointment with the Maharajah. Thereupon he was taken up in the elevator.

Then came the curious thing. The elevator operator had shown Smith where the suite was, and the time then would be about a minute past ten. Yet, at five minutes past, while the valet was making his voluble and not too intelligible complaint, the clerk saw Smith leave the hotel, and he had come down by the stairs, not the elevator.

Maroulis then took up the tale again, and an important tale it was. Since he had last seen Wharton, and in the course of his own discreet inquiries, he had ascertained that a person who might be unauthorized had been in the hotel at the same time. An Indian, black-bearded, black-coated and wearing a white turban, had entered the hotel at about twenty minutes to ten. He had not used the elevator but had taken the stairs, for the elevator operator had seen him go that way. Then Maroulis insisted that Wharton must bear one thing in mind. The Indian was naturally taken for a guest of the hotel, and no report was made. But this Indian left the hotel again a minute or so before the departure of Smith.

"He left at, say, four minutes past ten and Smith at five minutes past," Wharton said. "And can I rely on you to find out if he were genuine or not?"

"I will find out," Maroulis said. "By nine o'clock tomorrow morning I will have seen everyone myself personally. But there is a difficulty. He may be what you call genuine, and a visitor, but the one he came to visit might not know of the visit."

Wharton smiled dryly. "Then you'd better try to find out what he was doing from twenty to ten—that was when he arrived, wasn't it?—to when he left. He couldn't have been lost and dumb in the wilds of your hotel for twenty-five minutes." He remembered something else. "Why should this Indian have been noticed at all? Is it unusual for people to come in and go out at ten o'clock at night?"

Maroulis explained. At that time of night people would be coming in, not going out. If Wharton preferred it to be put another way, there was just sufficient of the unusual in their leaving the hotel to bring them within the notice of the staff.

"By the way, there was no commissionaire on duty when I arrived," Wharton said. "What time does he go off duty?"

Again Maroulis explained. Uniformed commissionaires and the Levantic were hardly in keeping. The bureau was open till very late at night, and during the day a trusted employee was on duty near the door, but more to be at the service of guests than to scrutinize entrants.

The statements were read, but before they were signed Wharton remembered something else.

"What about the operator at your exchange?"

Maroulis saw the point in a flash.

"She is not the one who put through the calls. That one will be on duty again at eight o'clock in the morning."

Wharton turned to Norris. "Make a special note of that and don't let me forget. By the way, Mr. Maroulis, I don't want you to let that operator know I'm going to question her." He held out his hand, then drew it back. "If you're going down, I think I'll get you to show me the back entrances to this floor, and to this suite. I'll be back in five minutes, Norris."

Collins was standing by, but the rest of the circus had gone except for two men who were going carefully over the floors. Travers took an easy chair and lighted a cigarette.

"Not for me, sir," Norris said. "And what're your ideas about this affair, sir? It looks as if we'll be here a week, I mean if we have to go questioning the sort of coves I've caught a glimpse of since I've been here. A regular Tower of Babel job."

"I doubt if it will come to that," Travers reassured him. "As for ideas, I haven't a single one." He smiled. "It's rather like being in that fog outside there, with Wharton manipulating it. We keep hearing isolated facts-seeing clear spaces, if you like-then it's all dense again."

Norris lowered his voice. "What's that pretty lady business that was being harped on such a lot?"

"Don't know," smiled Travers. "When Wharton sees fit to move the fog on, we might have a look at her."

"And that mention of the Special Branch, sir. That was dropped like a hot potato, but why shouldn't there be some political jiggery-pokery behind this murder?"

"Why not?" said Travers. "But I hope to heaven there isn't. Suppose inquiries have to be made in India." He all at once looked up. "We've got to visualize it, as you say. If certain important authorities are coming in the morning—"

He broke off with a shake of the head. Norris clicked his tongue.

"Give me a straight job, sir, where you know—"

The far door opened and Wharton was beckoning to them. He had come up from that back way which led direct to the two rooms occupied by Bond. Then he had gone through to the annex to the palatial bedroom, and there Menzies, who had finished his examination, had something of importance to show him. Three black hairs had been entwined in the fingers of the dead man, and had escaped previous notice because of the colour of the skin.

"The left hand, just like this," Menzies said.

"Not human hairs?" asked Travers.

Wharton was running his glass over them once more.

"They're not human hairs. Menzies and I agreed on that when he just showed them to me."

Then there was a tap at the door and in looked one of the men who had been going over the floors.

"Just found something, sir."

"Well, what?" snapped Wharton.

"About a dozen black hairs, sir. Trodden in the carpet."

"The devil!" said Wharton. "Let's see where they were."

The spot turned out to be just beyond the chalk marks that indicated the shoulder of the corpse.

"Why didn't you leave them there?" snapped Wharton, and lay flat down with the glass. But he was in better humour when he got up again. None of his own people had trodden on those hairs, for whatever movements there had been about that room had been along routes already examined and cleared, like the passages made by mine-sweepers for following ships.

"Right," he said. "Get outside and work along the corridor to the stairs. Think of this. A man left this room hurriedly and he was wearing a false beard that'd had several hairs torn out of it. See if he moulted any more on the way down."

He gave a comical look over his spectacle tops at Norris and Travers.

"Well, that's beginning to clear the air. Now let's have a breather and talk things over."

It was about two in the morning when the brief reconstruction began. The hotel itself was deadly quiet and, for an Englishman, uncommonly stuffy.

"Amli was killed at ten o'clock," Wharton began. "The time of the fall confirms it. You confirmed it, Menzies, and there's something that confirms it that we shall come to later."

He consulted his notebook.

"Now we'll go back a bit. Two phone calls were put through to Amli. After the second one he did three things. First he noted down that Smith was coming at ten o'clock."

He paused, as if expecting a question. Norris duly obliged.

"How do you know it was Amli who made that note on the blotter, sir?"

Wharton fetched from the side-table the gold and inlaid pencil case from Amli's pocket.

"See this pencil tip? Extra black and worn square. Now compare with the S and the 10."

He peered amusedly again over his spectacle tops.

"Well, that was the first thing he did. He also got rid of Bond for a time, including the period from ten o'clock till half-past. Incidentally that shows that he didn't expect the interview with Smith to be a long one. He also advised the bureau that anyone was to be sent straight up."

"But there were two phone calls," Travers said

"Well?"

"Then he might have expected two callers. If so why didn't he make two notes?"

"I wish you wouldn't hustle me," Wharton told him testily. "Not that I don't see your point."

"And in that same context," went on Travers, "it seems strange that he got rid of Bond at about a quarter to nine when Smith wasn't expected till ten o'clock."

"You mean there were two callers?"

Travers smiled. "Well, weren't there? Your friend with the false beard, and then Smith?"

"But only one memo on the blotter," insisted Wharton.

"Well"—Travers shrugged his shoulders—"why write down what you can remember?"

Wharton pursed his lips.

"I don't quite get you. Still, to move on. Back to Smith, if you like. We agree that that was a fake name?"

Everybody apparently agreed.

"Right," said Wharton. "We know when he arrived and when he left. He was in this hotel about five minutes all told. Isn't it easy to see what happened?"

"Yes," Norris said. "He entered this room, saw the body, got the wind up and bolted down the stairs."

"Exactly! And he almost ran full tilt into the man who killed Amli. But we'll check all that later. All I'll call your attention to at the moment is that the Indian—we'll call him Turban—left here just ahead of Smith. Now to the actual killing."

He picked up the overturned chair and placed it in a natural position for a sitter at the desk. The desk itself was flat-topped, inlaid mahogany, with side wings and an inset for the chair.

"Did Amli know Turban, or didn't he?" went on Wharton. "I say he most certainly did."

"Sorry," said Travers, "but could you still bear in mind that there were *two* phone calls? If Smith rang up at eight thirty-five, then why shouldn't it have been Turban who rang at eight fifteen?"

"Why not? I'm saying that the meeting was expected to be a friendly one, or a purely business one. Think of something. Turban was in this room several minutes, and there was no complaint from downstairs about noise. The talk was therefore amicable or quiet and secret. Amli sat at this desk, and Turban stood. If Turban sat, where's the chair? If he moved the chair afterwards, why'd he move it? I can find no answer to that, so I say that Amli sat and Turban stood.

"What was Amli doing at the desk? Well, finding some paper or other, or showing Turban some document, or going into some problem that had to be illustrated. Then, close on ten o'clock, an argument began, and loud enough to be heard in the room below. There were threats, we'll say, and all at once Amli whipped open this drawer and covered Turban with the automatic. But Turban—a tallish man—came at him sideways, like this, and had him by the wrist—"

"Why did Amli let him, sir? Why didn't he shoot?"

Wharton sneered. "Because the gun was only bluff and Turban knew it. Amli daren't shoot. Turban came at him sideways—if he'd gone straight, then the desk must have been overturned. Also going sideways explains why the gun dropped just here when Turban twisted it out of his hand. But with his left hand Amli managed to reach back for the knife, and the struggle moved this way—"

"To where he was stabbed."

Wharton shot a curious look at Norris over the tops of those antiquated spectacles.

"Was he stabbed?"

The look shifted to Menzies, as if the two had some private understanding.

"Let me explain," he went on, "though as a matter of fact I think you've both seen and heard everything for yourselves. We agreed the knife couldn't have been forced into Audi's own ribs, unless his strength had given quite out, and that implies a very long struggle. Which there wasn't. Even if there were—and it wasn't heard in the room below here, then Turban the faker must have' had his beard badly torn and have been nicely mauled himself. But he came down practically at once and left the hotel under the eye of the clerk, with beard and all complete.

"Very well, then. The quick struggle moved over to here. Amli with one hand tried to grasp the beard, and Turban was afraid he'd rip it off. Turban therefore held the beard with one hand because it was vital to him as a disguise, if only for the purpose of leaving the hotel. So you see there was just enough resistance for Amli to have ripped some hairs out of the beard without tearing the whole beard off.

"Now then. I'm Turban. My left hand holds Amli's right which now holds the knife. Amli's left hand is at this beard and my right hand is holding down the beard. It all happens in a flash—remember that. Now I abandon the beard and swing back my right and catch Amli the devil of a wallop on the point of the chin. My beard has gone but down Amli goes with it. His wrist doubles up and he falls on the knife."

"The wound is torn where the knife sagged," added Menzies. "His chin shows the mark of the knock-out punch, and the fact that the cut on his wrist didn't bleed shows he was dead when his body relaxed and made it."

"Yes," said Travers. "I quite agree that we should have seen all that before. If the stabbing had been what we took it for, what need was there for the knockout?"

The whole working-out had certainly been conclusive, and Wharton could nod with pious humility.

"Well, there it is. And what did Turban do when he knew Amli was dead? He had to get that beard out of his fingers, and he also took Amli's wallet."

"I see it fitting in perfectly," broke in Travers.

"The cut was made on Amli's wrist when Turban either moved the body to make sure he was dead or moved it to take the wallet. By the way, is it possible to find out through Osmund whether Turban took anything else?"

"I don't like going as far as that with Osmund," Wharton said. "The interesting thing to me is that Turban didn't help himself to things like that cigarette case. To me that proves he wasn't after money. He was after the private papers in the wallet, and he took the whole wallet because he'd no time to sort out the notes. He must have worn gloves because otherwise he couldn't possibly have had the time to wipe off all the prints he'd have left. You've only got to check up times through Smith, the bureau clerk, the fall that was heard below here, and so on, and it's a dead cert that Turban wasn't in this room more than a minute after he knew Amli was dead."

"Smith couldn't have taken the wallet?"

Wharton's eyes popped open at that suggestion from Menzies.

"It's something we can't afford to disregard."

"Why shouldn't Smith and Turban have been confederates?" asked Travers.

"Why do you suggest that?"

"Well, how did Turban know that Amli would be alone, unless Smith told him? How was it Turban came so appositely?"

"Just a minute," Wharton told him dryly. "You can't have it both ways. First you base a theory on the fact that there were two phone calls, one by Smith and one by Turban, and now you say one told the other all about it. Mind you, I grant you there're wheels within wheels, but have you thought of anything that affects the main theory as I've just stated it?"

"One little thing," Travers said. "Just a point of confirmation. You can't imagine a real Indian giving that lovely knockout punch with the right."

Wharton fell into the trap. "Exactly! Turban was English, otherwise why the fake beard?"

"Then if Turban was English," said Travers, "so we know was Smith. All the more reason for the two being confederates."

Menzies chuckled at that, and Wharton had to follow suit.

"Your wits are too nimble for me," he said. "Anything else though?"

"Only one thing," Travers told him. "With regard to that getting rid of Bond. I rather believe that it was after all so that Smith shouldn't be seen. Smith must have been some kind of rogue, or why did he bolt when he saw the body?"

"There's a lot in that, sir," Norris said. "He never gave the alarm or anything."

"Yet when he entered the hotel he went up to the desk as bold as brass," said Wharton. "He didn't mind being seen. And no sneaking up the stairs for him."

"Quite so," said Travers. "But that doesn't conflict with the theory that he was a rogue and daren't let the police question him."

"No use arguing," Wharton said. "And you're all forgetting one thing. In the morning I'm having a talk with that phone girl here, to try and find out if she remembers the voices of the two callers. If she can swear one voice was English, then that will be Smith. If she says the other was like an Indian, then that would be Turban faking his voice to suit his beard. Once we get as far as that we'll have something to build on. And I've got another little trump card I haven't played yet. Not an ace, but a queen."

"The pretty lady?" asked Travers.

"Well, you're not far out. And now let's go outside and check up times."

The two men had worked their way past the lift but no more black hairs had been discovered. Wharton stood them by.

"I expect he was clutching that beard of his," he said, "and taking good care it stuck. This looks interesting, though."

He was pointing to a recess just past the lift. The curtains were drawn across its window beneath which stood two hand-some palms in large ornate pots.

"Here we are," he said all at once. "Now we know just what happened." There was dust behind the curtains and it had been disturbed. "Turban was making for the stairs when the lift was bringing Smith up, and he knew he would not have time to reach those stairs before the lift door opened. What he did therefore was to nip behind the curtains and wait." Then Wharton smiled hugely.

"Here he is, waiting. And quite close to the lift. But Smith and the lift attendant had some talk, therefore if Smith and Turban were confederates, Turban knew where Smith was going. When the lift went down again, all he'd do would be to slip along to warn Smith. But he didn't."

"I get you, sir," Norris said. "By the time the lift went down, Smith would at least be in this room, and he went straight out again. He was always just that much time behind Turban."

"That's it. He left the hotel a few seconds ahead of Smith because he went downstairs as soon as the lift started down. And he daren't hurry for fear of giving himself away. Smith did hurry. He was in a panic." He looked round inquiringly. "Everybody satisfied? If so we'll get back again. You two men go over this recess for hairs. You might also try it for prints."

Back in that room again, Wharton made for the blotter.

"Neither Smith nor Turban was interested in this sheet of blotting paper," he said. "They'd have ripped it off the pad if they had been."

He ran his glass over it and thought it at least two or three days old. Norris fetched a hand mirror from the bedroom and quite a lot of words could be made out. Two distinct hands were spotted at once—one neat, one sprawling.

"Osmund's and Amli's," Wharton said. "What's this? Here it is again."

"Bishan Singh," Travers said. "That would be Amli's name."

"I remember. That's how Osmund referred to him till I stopped him at it—His Highness Bishan Singh. Well, he's evidently written a letter or two. Lot of figures here. Osmund's accounts by the look of 'em. What's this cock-eyed bit?"

He was referring to a series of apparently connected words that ran slantingly across the general mass of blottings, both legible and illegible. Where the words met previous blottings, certain letters were obviously obscured.

"Mind if I try to take them down?" Travers said. "I'll leave the missing spaces if I can."

ine.. an ns. eakab ad

Wharton had a look at it, then shrugged his shoulders.

"Might be something in it, and there might not. Have the whole thing sent to the Yard, Norris. A nice little game for somebody to play picking out the words from that mix-up. Wouldn't like to tackle it—"

The phone bell rang.

"The Yard for a fiver! Why haven't we reported progress."

He took the receiver and his first words expressed considerable surprise.

"Divisional headquarters? . . . Yes, speaking. . . . My God! You don't say so! . . . Right. At once. Good-by."

"Well," he said, "if that wouldn't make you drop dead with a heart attack. That was the Division of the man who was called in here when Bond found the body. His inspector now says a man's just died in St. Martin's Hospital, and what do you think was in his pocket? *That wallet of Amli's.* No papers in it. Only small notes and fivers."

Chapter v
TRAVERS DROPS A HINT

Travers was as staggered as the rest at Wharton's amazing news. St. Martin's was a big hospital and there was no reason whatever why he should at once connect the man who had died there with that particular man—drunk or suffering from the effects of poison—whom he had seen leaning against a shop window in Waterman's Court.

As soon as Wharton stepped out to the misty street with Menzies and Travers, he began trying to fill in some gaps in his knowledge of India.

"You spent some years in India, didn't you, Mr. Travers?" he began.

"Only as a little fellow," Travers said, "when my father was soldiering there."

"That sounds good enough," Wharton said. "You might know enough to give me a sidelight or two on that chap Amli. Some of the evidence I've heard seems to contradict itself. Now in India, for example, would he be accepted as one of themselves by Europeans?"

"Most decidedly," Travers told him. "There's only one distinction, and it's always seemed to me to be very illogical and footling. Whatever his rank he wouldn't be admitted to the clubs. All other places and functions—yes."

"Then in spite of Osmund's explanation, I don't see why he didn't go to an English hotel."

"The Levantic's a very fine hotel," Travers reminded him. "Amli might have felt more really at home there. And, bearing in mind what Osmund and Bond admitted, we must assume that Amli was not the nicest of maharajahs. A hotel out of the lime-light is preferable when one's deeds are liable to be dirty."

Wharton clicked his tongue. "Now there's another thing I can't fit in. If he was at an English public school and Oxford—"

"Many an old Etonian's been in jail," Menzies cut in dryly. "You always did have a hankering after the old-school tie."

Wharton burst out explosively. Travers poured oil on the waters.

"I think it's a question of veneer. When that European polish goes only just below the surface, then it's dangerous to classify and formulate." His voice instinctively lowered. "Here we are then."

Wharton was first through the doors, and was hailed at once by the night porter.

"Mr. Wharton, sir? This way, sir."

In the room were waiting a doctor, a first-class inspector from the local division, and Travers's old friend the constable.

"Well, what's it all about?"

That was Wharton. The inspector replied tactfully, having sense enough to know that Wharton wanted no babbling to outsiders, even to the hospital surgeon.

"Well, sir, knowing you were dealing with a certain matter concerning a certain party, we thought you'd be interested when we found this."

Wharton's hand went out to the wallet, then drew back.

"Prints?"

"All over it, sir. No end of people handled it before we discovered it might be important."

Wharton picked it up. The leather was neat and the trimmings gaudy. The gold and diamond-studded monogram made Wharton grimace.

"Contents checked?"

"Taken over and signed for, sir."

"Found in the breast pocket of a man, you said. What else was in his pockets?"

"Here we are, sir. Two and seven-pence and one plain handkerchief."

"His prints on record?"

"They've been sent, sir, but no reply yet."

Wharton nodded approval.

"Now about the man. Accident case, was it, doctor?"

The doctor smiled wryly. "He was admitted soon after eleven o'clock supposed to be suffering from alcoholic collapse."

"You mean, he wasn't?"

"He certainly wasn't. He was suffering from atropine poisoning. Didn't emerge from the coma and died half an hour ago."

"The devil!" said Wharton. "I know atropine poisoning well enough. All the symptoms of the drunk. What form did he take it in?"

"That will be for your experts to determine," he was told. "It was taken in alcohol, if that's any interest. And my own opinion, for what it's worth, is that the general physique of the man and his age and so on indicated he could put up only a poor resistance."

"Or else he took a very big dose?"

"Not necessarily," broke in Menzies. "A big dose might act as an emetic or defeat its own ends."

"You people ought to know," Wharton said. "Did he talk at all?"

"He was in a state of coma," the doctor reminded him. "He never came out of it. By the way, he'd a nasty bruise on the temple, and some peculiar contusions which might have been due to his falling about. How far all that contributed to his death we don't at the moment know."

Wharton, frowning away in thought, noticed nothing of the uneasiness of Travers or the looks that passed between him and the constable.

"I'd better see the man," he said, and moved off at once. Travers stood fast, and he was the first to break the silence when the door closed on Wharton and the doctors.

"I didn't ask you earlier tonight," he said to the constable, "but I suppose you'd never seen the man before?"

"First time I saw him in my life, sir, was when he was leaning against that window."

"There's no possible means of finding out which way he came from?"

"I doubt it, sir," the inspector said. "That's a regular warren all round there. What I might be able to do, though, is find out where he'd been during the evening."

He began explaining ways and means, and then Wharton came bustling back, notebook in hand. He wanted to hear the constable's account of the finding of the supposedly drunken man. When Travers cut in, there was much peering from over Wharton's spectacle tops.

"Ah, well," Wharton said, after the explanations and apologies, "if you thought he was drunk, Mr. Travers, then no wonder the constable here was deceived."

The constable's own account was given, then Wharton decided on a bluff for the hospital's benefit and as an example of his own deductive powers.

"You thought it was Red Biddy," he said reflectively. "Well, it wasn't unreasonable. The first thing he did, apparently, when he found that wallet, was to break into a note and treat himself to a drink. The trouble is that certain information which I possess assures me he didn't find the wallet till well after ten. If he broke into a ten-bob note, then he spent seven-and-six. Quick work that, when the pubs closed at half-past ten." He shook his head. "He'd had some drink, that we know from the evidence of the authorities here, and from the smell of him. It certainly looks as if he did his drinking in some unauthorized place he knew of. He'd be charged pretty heavy there. What do you say, inspector?"

"And I shouldn't be surprised, sir, if I could find just where he got it."

"Good for you!" said Wharton. "That'll be killing two birds with one stone."

He was most interested in the evidence that had been given by Sir Jerome Haire.

"That ought to give us a line on him. Accosted Sir Jerome and called at his flat. Spun a yarn and tied himself up with lies."

He was moving across to the phone, and there was to be no secret as to what he was after.

"Wharton speaking. Put me through to C.R.O., will you?"

A short wait, then:

"Wharton speaking. You had some prints come from St. Martin's a short time ago. The name was given as Furloe. Any news? . . . I see. Thank you. Good-by."

"Well," he said, "we haven't got his prints, though that isn't conclusive proof that he's got a clean record. Not one of our ex-convicts, though, wherever else they might have jugged him, so Sir Jerome didn't make a good guess there." He looked round. "Nothing else, I think. I'll take those things of his with me, and you'd better let me have your official report, inspector. If I'm wanted, you know where I am."

"And we're to go on with the Red Biddy inquiries, sir?"

"Why not?" Wharton told him good-humouredly.

"Where now?" asked Travers when they came out to the street again.

"Back to the hotel," Wharton said, and then grunted contemptuously. "Red Biddy! Red Biddy, my foot! These fellows get things on the brain. Just because they've had a case or two, that's all you hear."

They were a hundred yards on before the last rumbling died, then his voice came dove-like.

"Well, what do you think about things? How's this man Furloe going to help?"

Travers shook his head. "It's a pity he couldn't conceivably have been Smith."

Wharton chuckled. "I'm very glad he isn't."

Then he thought perhaps he had admitted more than he was prepared to substantiate.

"By the way, I'm glad that affair at the hotel turned out to be an accident. Manslaughter, if you like, instead of murder."

"You think certain people will be pleased?"

"I'm sure of it. They're trying to avoid scandal and what they call complications. Well, now they've got their chance." He chuckled again. "From now on I don't give a damn about Amli—not directly. I've got a hunch that this chap Furloe is giving us our chance for a side attack. I shouldn't be surprised if he turns out to be our ace of trumps, and I'm taking good care that certain parties don't know we hold him."

"You mean, you don't think he picked up that wallet after all?"

"He *might* have picked it up," granted Wharton amusedly. "Then again he might not. By the way, does the wearing of a white turban denote anything?"

"You mean caste or creed or rank?" He shook his head. "Oh, no. A turban's according to the wearer's taste. A white one has no significance whatever."

"And what races wear black beards?"

"Mohammedans, Sikhs—"

He suddenly halted then and his fingers fumbled at his glasses. Wharton shot him a look.

"Got an idea?"

"I'm trying to work out an idea of your own," Travers told him. "Turban was a stage Indian, wasn't he? He was the average person's idea of what an Indian *ought to be*. Beard, turban, coat, colour and everything. Also a white turban would be the easiest to fabricate. What I'm getting at is that Furloe, you remember, claimed to Sir Jerome Haire to have been an actor."

"Yes," said Wharton, and coughed apologetically. "I admit I had that in mind when I said Furloe might be our ace of trumps. That's why I gave Menzies the private tip."

He halted outside the hotel entrance to explain.

"Just suppose—and it does no harm supposing—that Furloe was the Englishman who rigged himself up to be Turban. Then he had to use grease paint, and afterwards he'd have to use co-co-butter or something similar to get it off. However carefully he went to work he surely wouldn't get all the paint off, or all the butter. Menzies is looking out for traces of both when he does the post-mortem."

The hotel was like a mausoleum, with the dimmest of lights in the entrance lounge. Upstairs, the two men in the recess had found neither black hairs nor prints. Wharton stood them by again.

Norris was writing up his notes. Surprised he might be at what Wharton had to tell, but the surprise he had for Wharton was just as unexpected.

Just after Wharton left for the hospital, a phone message had come through from Prewitt, the man who hours before had been on the tail of Osmund when he left the hotel.

Osmund had been most careful, for he had acted as if he were being followed, and then had nipped into a passing taxi. But the amusing thing was that the fog was so thick towards Soho that Prewitt had no difficulty in keeping up with the taxi till it turned into Wardour Street. There he lost it, but a couple of hundred yards along, he found it waiting by the curb.

A quarter of an hour later, Osmund came out with a man who was wearing a heavy check overcoat. There was some bargaining about being driven to Enfield, but for overhearing which Prewitt would have lost the trail.

As it was he rang the Enfield police and warned them, then took a taxi himself. His driver took a circuitous way where the fog was less dense, and it was two minutes after their arrival at Enfield that Osmund's taxi came through. Eventually it drew up outside a detached villa in a quiet road.

Wharton held up a dramatic finger.

"Don't tell me where, Norris. Don't tell me where. But let me see. Was the house by any chance called Rose Bank, and the road Pendleford Road?"

Norris stared. "Good God, sir, how'd you know that?"

"Ah!" said Wharton, giving away no secrets. "You tell us what happened next."

Prewitt's own taxi was waiting nearby, and after an hour he sent it back to Enfield with a message. As a result an additional man, on a motor-bike, was sent along, and Prewitt was ready for anything if Osmund and his friend went different ways after leaving Rose Bank.

"A smart man, Prewitt," Wharton said. "I don't give a cuss about Osmund. We've always got him. It's Smith I want." He thought for a moment, then nodded to himself. "The other must be Smith, check overcoat or not."

He picked up the small ring of keys that had come from the dead man's pocket, and ran an eye over it as if he had never seen or handled it before.

"Well, about time we had a look in the drawers, don't you think?"

He admitted that he expected to find very little. Certain papers and valuables were kept in the hotel safe, and most of the dead man's transactions had been cash ones, the hotel acting as banking intermediary. And, of course, there had not been much time in three weeks for correspondence to accumulate.

But quite a lot of material came to light, and Wharton cast a quick eye over every sheet. Then at last they came to that locked drawer in which Travers had reported Osmund to be interested.

"A special lock on it!"-Wharton said, with much show of surprise. "Ah! this looks like the key. And now what have we?"

There was quite a collection of papers, and among them a legal-looking envelope. Wharton peered at it over his spectacle tops, then drew two papers out of it.

"Well, well, well!" he said. "If this isn't interesting. A twelve months' lease of a furnished house known as Rose Bank, situated at number sixteen Pendleford Road, Enfield, in the County of Middlesex."

He settled down to a detailed reading. Norris caught Travers's eye.

"And what's all this?" Wharton suddenly said. "Even more interesting! Would you believe it? A receipted account from Ropers of Bond Street. Ropers, mind you! Four hundred-odd pounds' worth of extra furniture." He whistled. "It ought to be quite a snug little place by now. I've half a mind to drop in."

He replaced the papers and got to his feet.

"Government departments can be pretty slow?"

"I think you can rely on that," Travers said.

"That's all right then." He nodded to himself. "I shall have to send those two papers, and as soon as they discover Rose Bank, you bet your life we'll be warned off it. The devil of it is, if I do go to Rose Bank, how did I come to know about it?"

Travers had to laugh.

"George, the way of deceivers is hard. But if you don't want them to know you saw the papers, you can always take Bond's tip and see the chauffeur."

Wharton chuckled delightedly.

"That's true enough. Norris, pack all that collection of rubbish and get it off. The more red tape and sealing-wax, the better they'll like it."

Norris got to work. Travers couldn't help pulling Wharton's leg.

"Quite an anti-climax, George, finding out how you arrived at the pretty lady. I thought it was some brilliant problem in deduction."

"They don't know everything at the Police College," Wharton said. "But it took a certain amount of deduction, didn't it, to know that Amli hadn't got some old family retainer pensioned off there? And I'd happened to be through that very road last week, seeing a man about something. Soon as I saw the name of that quiet little road again, I thought to myself how near town it was. Just the place for love birds."

"Love birds?" said the guileless Travers. "It isn't a serious affair, is it?"

"Serious?" Wharton glared. "What do you take me for? I knew as soon as you saw Osmund try the lock of that drawer. Osmund's a go-between. You daren't bet me a fiver I'm wrong. Whether Amli sounded him or not, he provided the lady. It's proved, isn't it? As soon as he couldn't scheme to get those two papers out of the drawer, off he went to Enfield, and Smith with him. I shouldn't be surprised if they've fixed up all sorts of alibis." A smile of grim anticipation. "The lady's probably expecting me in the morning."

The phone rang and he was scowling away as he went across. In two seconds a look of extreme gratification was spreading over his face.

"That's right," he said. "Sit tight. Won't be long now before it's daylight. I'll get another man sent to you. . . . That's right. Soon as you know just who he is, report here to me."

"We're getting on," he said, and then a tap came at the door. In came Prewitt.

"Come to report, sir. The taxi dropped Osmund at Oxford Circus and I tailed him back to Wardour Street. The other man went on in the same taxi and Finley's with it, sir."

"That's all right," Wharton said genially. "You haven't done too badly. Finley's just rung up to say he's now watching number twenty-three Hardacre Road, Islington. I'll write it down for you. You nip along to there in case there're two doors that want watching."

He patted Prewitt's shoulder and saw him out. Then he picked up his hat again.

"Well, I'll move along to the hospital again. About time Mr. Travers was tucked up in bed." A sudden idea came and seemed to amuse him. "What about letting Osmund still go on thinking he's leading us up the orchard?"

"He's a clever one, that, sir," Norris warned him.

"So are some others," chuckled Wharton. "One of them was christened George. I think we'll give Osmund plenty of rope. When he's where we want him, then I'll have just a few homely words. You ready, Mr. Travers?"

On the way he drew up a brief scheme for next morning.

"Soon as I get rid of the high-and-mighties, I'll see the phone girl and the chauffeur. You might interview Sir Jerome and check up at the Spread Eagle. Then if we know all about Smith, we might decide to go to Enfield for a word with the lady."

They said goodnight at the private door to the flat. Then, just as Wharton was moving off, Travers called him back.

"About Furloe, George, since you're going to the hospital. If he was Turban; then he did that struggling with Amli, so oughtn't his hands to be scratched and his wrists bruised?"

Wharton gaped. Then he gave a wry shake of the head.

"Yes," he said slowly. "There's no arguing against that." He stared again. "Wait a minute, though. His wrists were bruised, now I think of it. So was his shoulder."

Then he began clicking his tongue. .

"No telling what he was up to after he felt the effects of that dope. He might have stumbled about and bruised himself all over. Mind you, if he gave that knockout punch to the chin, his knuckles wouldn't be skinned, because he was wearing gloves."

"There's something else," said Travers. "If he was Turban, you might find some black hairs on him, which would prove things conclusively."

"But he changed his clothes afterwards."

"He wouldn't change his shirt and vest. He had a vest?"

"Oh, yes," Wharton said. "He had a vest."

But in spite of the pessimisms he set off again in the fog like a man making for something urgent and worth while. Travers made his own quiet way up the stairs and then was all at once aware of something that concerned himself.

What had seemed of such moment, and had taken all his thoughts, had been altogether forgotten. It was hours since he had thought of poor old Barney and his worries, or of that queer quarrel between Bernice and Joy—or even of Bernice herself.

CHAPTER VI
WHARTON MOVES SIDEWAYS

TRAVERS SLEPT for no more than two uneasy hours, with Furloe always at the background of his dreams. Not the Furloe who might have been Turban, and not even the Furloe of his own and Wharton's theories. It was the man who still kept coming to his mind; the man he had seen leaning helplessly in the angle of the shop window; the man with sensitive fingers and the neat, shabby clothes.

As Travers dressed himself that Saturday morning, he knew that whatever Furloe had done to bring him within the law, he himself was feeling some queer sympathy. Out of the sympathy perhaps, came the doubts, and by breakfast Travers knew somehow that Wharton's main theory must be wrong. Then something else was remembered and Furloe went for a time from Travers's mind.

"We shan't be away this weekend," he said to Palmer. "But I'd like the garage people to see the car's quite tidy. I hope to be going into the country tomorrow afternoon."

He was wondering just what hotel would suit Joy best when the phone rang. Norris was ringing up about the morning's arrangements.

"The Super's changed his mind, sir," he reported. "He'll tell you what's on when you get here."

"I'll be along in ten minutes," Travers said.

"No, sir," Norris cut in quickly. "The Super thought about ten o'clock. The Chief and the A.C. are here and a couple of bigwigs."

Which meant for Travers that the Chief Constable and the Assistant Commissioner were there, and two officials from, probably, the India Office.

"Ten o'clock, then. Anything new?"

"No, sir. Expecting to hear at any minute who Smith really is. Oh, and you ought to have heard the Super with Osmund this morning, sir. You'd have died of laughing."

"Osmund smell a rat?"

"Not him, sir. Butter wouldn't have melted in his mouth."

"What about the girl at the exchange?"

"That's rather tricky," Norris said. "She says she's so used to foreigners of all sorts talking English that she never pays any attention. But she thinks—thinks, mind you—that the first call was a foreigner's and the second one English."

Travers finished his breakfast and then found himself with almost an hour on his hands. Then Furloe came to his mind again and he went through to his desk and began to jot down the known facts about the man, and how they affected the theory that he had been Turban. Then he jotted down a few ideas and made a copy for Wharton.

At ten o'clock Wharton was in high good-humour.

"We've had a regular spring clean here," he told Travers. "Everything gone from Maroulis' safe. By the way, nobody in the hotel knows anything about our friend Turban. Valuable collection of jewels in the safe, so I believe. Amli's gone to some private mortuary, or religious one. Everything's closing down here except that we're to have free access. Anything to do with His Nibs is to be passed on, but we're to make discreet inquiries about Turban. Osmund's being paid off, and our dear old pal Bond. Dammit, if I could afford it I'd hire Bond myself. Anything else was there, Norris?"

"The chauffeur, sir, and he's still waiting."

"So he is," said Wharton. "You'd better show him in."

Arthur Rann, the chauffeur, was thirty and looked younger.

"You were taken on about six weeks ago, I suppose?" Wharton began cheerily.

"Yes, sir."

"And what sort of car do you drive?"

"His Highness had two cars, sir: a Rolls and a Bentley."

"Is that all?" said Wharton. "Well, I hope he never had to walk. Mr. Osmund a friend of yours, by the way?"

"Him, sir?" For a moment he looked either sheepish or uneasy. Then he shook his head. "I never have anything to do with him, sir, except on Saturdays."

"I see. Pay day. What about Mr. Bond?"

"He's a bit of all right, sir."

"Glad to hear it. Know who I am?"

"Yes, sir. Scotland Yard, sir."

Wharton chuckled. "That's news to me. Still, whatever we talk about is confidential. Understand that?"

"Yes, sir."

Wharton looked him clean in the eye. "Make sure you do. And now tell me. When were you at Enfield last?"

"Enfield, sir?" He moistened his lips. "You mean, with the guv'nor, sir?"

"What else should I mean? You don't pay private visits to the maid, do you?"

"No, sir." He grinned feebly. "Yesterday evening early we were there, sir."

"When did you first go there?"

"About a month ago, sir."

Wharton gave a quick description of Smith.

"No, sir," Rann said. "I've never seen a man of that kind there."

"Who did you see there?"

"No one, sir. All I had to do was sit in the car and wait."

Norris took his address and then Wharton had a final word.

"Do you think you'll remember what we've been talking about?"

"Oh, yes, sir!"

"Oh, no, sir!" His chin went forward. "You've forgotten it. You've never even been in this room at all. Isn't that so?"

"Yes, sir."

Wharton heaved a sigh.

"Now something else, and no lies. When I first mentioned Osmund's name, why did you look uncomfortable?"

Rann moistened his lips again.

"Come on! I haven't got all day."

Rann took a breath. "Well, sir, I didn't want to get no one into trouble."

"Really?"

"No, sir. It was like this, sir. Mr. Osmund came to me this morning, sir, and offered me ten pounds if I'd keep everything dark about Enfield."

"You took it?"

"No, sir. I told him I was telling lies not for him nor nobody."

Wharton peered at him over his spectacle tops.

"Very admirable of you." He looked round and his voice lowered. "I like you, Rann. If I had two Rolls's and half-a-dozen Bentleys I'd hire you myself. Now you take my advice. Get Osmund to make a fresh bid. Run him up to fifteen quid—*and then take it!*"

Rann stared, then grinned.

"That's right," Wharton told him. "You haven't told me a thing about Enfield. I've been telling you."

He motioned him curtly out, and with a flick to his forehead out Rann went.

"No vice in him," Wharton said. "And what was I talking about before he came in? Oh, yes; we're to make discreet inquiries about Turban. If you ask me, they were more anxious to know whether he was English or foreign than anything else. Inside an hour it'll be in the papers that His Nibs met with an accident when tackling an intruder."

The phone rang again and Wharton lifted the receiver.

"Yes, speaking. . . . Wait a minute while we get that down. . . . He went out and you asked someone who he was and they said William Feathers. . . . He's known as Corney. . . . Right. Make dead sure. . . . You are sure? Then report back. Yes, both of you."

Norris had been staring.

"You don't say Corney Feathers is Smith, sir!"

"You can take it he is," Wharton said, and explained to Travers. "Corney's the kind who ought to have the cat once a month regular. One of the worst procurers we've had to deal with. Norris had him over a tea-shop affair in Bishopsgate about a year ago. What'd he get, Norris?"

"Six months, sir. The time before cost him about seventy quid."

Wharton was frowning away in thought.

"I still don't think we ought to make a move. We know where Corney is when we want him." He rubbed his chin. "Let me think now. If we call Corney in, he might clear up whether or not he was connected with Turban. But knowing Corney, I say he wasn't. Corney's far more likely to have been seeing His Nibs about something to do with the pretty lady. Corney specializes in pretty ladies. But if we do bring Corney in, then we'll disturb Osmund."

"But there's nothing definite against Osmund," Travers pointed out. "There's no suspicion that he was connected with Turban, and he has an alibi."

"Alibi?" He snorted. "Alibis have been bust before; you ought to know that. You have a look at things this way. Corney and Osmund were both mixed up with the lady. Osmund considered the lady so important that he offered Rann a tenner to keep her dark. If we pounce unexpectedly on the lady, we can play her off against both Corney and Osmund and learn the devil of a lot about both."

"That's the best move, sir."

"Right," said Wharton. "We'll pay a little visit to Enfield. The fog's cleared, but there wasn't any out there, even last night." He picked up his hat. "On the way back, Mr. Travers can see Sir Jerome while I do the Spread Eagle. By that time, Norris, you might have something in answer to that appeal about Furloe."

He paused at the door.

"Anything we can pull Corney in for?"

"Not a thing," said Norris regretfully. "The last I heard of him when he came out was that he'd joined up with Ike Lubeson the bookie."

"Ike," said Wharton, and grunted. "There's another bright lad for you." He swivelled a quick look round. "Wait a minute. Ike a bookie, Corney his pal, and His Nibs a racing man. Some connection there, isn't there?"

The phone rang once more. Wharton and Travers listened while Norris answered.

"He's just going out. . . . I see. . . . Yes, I'll take it down. No traces of grease-paint or butter, but eyebrows may have been pencilled. Suggest advice. . . . Yes, the Super says he'll attend to it at once. . . . Good-by."

"Menzies, talking about Furloe?"

"That's right, sir. He thinks the eyebrows were pencilled, and he'd like you to call in an expert."

"Hm!" went Wharton, and looked at Travers.

"I think I'd try to get Barney Josephs, the theatrical agent," Travers said. "He's an old hand and he might also recognize Furloe, if Furloe really had been an actor."

"The very one to get," Wharton said, and waved Travers to the phone.

Within twenty minutes the four were in the mortuary, and Barney had run his eye over the dead man.

"You suggest his eyebrows were pencilled?" he asked in his mild way.

"They look as if they ought to be white," Menzies told him, "but there's a trace of something which can be washed off. That's all I know."

Barney adjusted his pince-nez, accepted Wharton's glass, and had a look.

"Yes," he said at last. "I should say not only his eyebrows but his eyelashes. Touched up, you know."

"Then we can test for mascara," Menzies said.

"That's capital." Wharton rubbed his hands. "We're most grateful to you, Mr. Josephs. By the way, you didn't recognize him?"

"Well"—Barney's eyes went that way again—"I seem to remember him—you know, a long while ago. I may be wrong. The name? That recalls nothing."

"Well, if you do happen to remember him, no matter in what way, we'd be most grateful if you'd let us know at once," Wharton said. "Now we won't trespass on your valuable time any longer."

Travers contrived to line up with Barney who was clearly anxious for a private word.

"About tomorrow, Barney," he said. "I'm positive I'm going to learn something. When a charming young lady hauls me off to tea, I have no illusions about myself. I know it isn't for the pleasure of my company."

"If something doesn't happen by Wednesday, Mr. Travers," Barney said, and seemed to shrivel up within himself, "then everything's off. My reputation, my money—I tell you it's driving me crazy."

"No need whatever for panic," Travers told him, and took his arm down the steps. "Before Wednesday, Barney, everything will be all right, and I'll be buying you the best hat in town."

Barney shook a plaintive head.

"Mr. Travers, if everything *is* all right by Wednesday, then I buy *myself* twenty hats. The best hats in town." Then he shook his head. "If not, then I don't need any hats."

"Well," Wharton said, and opened the door of his car, "all that merely seems to prove that Furloe told Sir Jerome no lies when he said he was an actor."

"We're going to Enfield?" Travers asked.

"Why not? We can't do a thing more about Furloe till there's a reply to that description the papers. Inside half an hour everybody'll be reading it."

He moved the car on.

"I like the look of Josephs. It might help a good deal if he should happen to remember Furloe. There's a bigger mystery about that chap than we've realized. Sort of a down-and-out, wasn't he? Touting for work and a regular cadger."

"Yes," Travers said. "There's a pretty big mystery. Anything in yet about the clothes?"

"Devil a black hair anywhere," Wharton said.

"The scratches and bruises?"

"No scratches. About the bruises, they're not nearly so pronounced as Amli's were."

Travers's fingers had been grasping that copy of the notes he had compiled about Furloe. Now he put it back in his pocket.

"Just what was in your mind, George, when you mentioned the big mystery about Furloe?"

"Well," said Wharton, "there's the mystery why a down-and-out should call and see an Indian potentate. And if a man's down, then where can he change into Indian clothes and back again without calling attention to himself? Mind you, I've thought of that and I'm hoping it was done in some public lavatory because if it were, then the Indian clothes were left there, as we shall discover when we make inquiries."

Travers smiled to himself.

"But, George, you're assuming Furloe was Turban. Yet you just said his wrists weren't scratched, or his hand, and his bruises weren't pronounced."

"Well, what's wrong? Everything shows that Turban was grasping Amli's wrists, not the other way about. Turban was protecting himself from Amli's attack."

"Yes," Travers said, "but there's still a most important thing that hasn't even been mentioned. When a down-and-out takes poison, he dies where he takes it."

Wharton looked round from the wheel.

"I mean this. He chooses his lonely corner and dies in it, just as certain sick animals crawl into a lonely corner to die. But Furloe had been wandering about, so we must assume. Therefore he didn't poison himself. He was given the poison. In short, he was murdered."

"I'm with you there," Wharton said heartily enough. "No container of the poison was found on him or near him. But as the poison was taken in whiskey, you'll admit that he might have been given it—or even have taken it—in a pub."

"We're going round in circles," Travers said. "As you say, we'd better wait till news comes in. All the same, he had to sleep somewhere, though we've alluded to him as a down-and-out."

"If nothing comes in by tonight, then every kip and lodging-house is going to be questioned."

Wharton drew the car away from the main stream of traffic, and Travers sat thinking. Furloe, according to the impressions he had himself formed, was a man who had still kept his respect.

His clothes and appearance showed that, and there had been nothing rascally about his looks. As for Sir Jerome's story, that might have been exaggerated, and the telling overacted, since it was Sir Jerome's natural tendency to act what needn't necessarily be acted. What therefore had been described as pestering, had probably been a protracted and humble inquiry about work; and if Furloe had nothing decent about him, why had Sir Jerome allowed that call at the flat? And Sir Jerome had certainly been wrong in thinking Furloe an ex-convict.

"What's on your mind?"

Travers shifted uneasily on the seat.

"I don't know that anything is—except perhaps Furloe. He's beginning to haunt me, George. That's why I'd like to talk about him and find out things." He shook his head. "You didn't see him before he died. The leaning man—that's how I think of him. At his last gasp, leaning in the angle of the window. He saw me, George, and I now think he was trying to speak to me. I was the Pharisee, and crossed to the other side."

"What do you mean by haunts?"

"Well, I can't get him out of my mind. Nothing else in this case does that. Amli doesn't interest me much. And it may sound rude but I'm not enormously interested in where we're going now. It's Furloe who grips me. Furloe, as I first saw him. Who killed him, and why."

Wharton slowed the car to a dawdle.

"Well, give us your ideas."

"Then let me contradict myself," Travers said. "That's one way of arriving at the truth. Say that Furloe did take the poison himself in a fit of despair, and then picked up the wallet later. Everything that happened is in a small area. 'The Levantic, St. Martin's, Wardour Street'—no side of that triangle is more than four hundred yards."

"Yes, but how explain away the make-up round Furloe's eyes?"

"Even that can be explained," Travers said. "Remember there was no sign of grease-paint on him. I say he might have given a show at a street corner or have been working the theatre queues. He had loose change in his pocket, and it was small change. Besides, burnt cork doesn't cost anything."

"Ingenious," Wharton said. "Very ingenious. But what about the fact that there were bruises on his wrists?"

"I can't deny facts," Travers said. "All the same I refuse to give way on one point. Furloe hadn't the stamina to struggle with Amli. He hadn't the physique to scratch and bruise the younger man and wrench a gun out of his hand. He couldn't have given that wallop with the right that knocked Amli out. Why, the hospital doctor said he hadn't enough resistance to stand up to the poison for anything like the normal time!"

"I've heard doctors before," Wharton told him airily. "But you wait till you're attacked by a much bigger man than yourself and see if you don't get strength from somewhere." He shrugged his shoulders. "But why all the worry about Furloe? There's plenty of time. There'll be something in about him by this time tomorrow, or my name's Higgins." His voice lowered. "This next turn is Pendleford Road."

The car was slowed once more to a crawl.

"This is it." He stared ahead. "Hallo! what's going on?"

A taxi stood before the house and as Wharton's car passed, Travers saw through the gate a woman in hat and coat carrying a bag down the path.

Wharton kept going and stopped fifty yards on near a pillar-box.

"You get out," he said to Travers, "and act natural. Go to a house and ask for somebody. I'll stay here."

Travers nipped out. A young, attractive woman in a handsome fur coat was coming from the direction of Rose Bank, a letter in her hand. Travers made for the nearest house, asked for a non-existent person, talked for a moment or two and then came back. The taxi had gone and Wharton was reversing.

"Hop in," the General said. "There's a place just down the road where we can phone."

The car made for town again and Wharton explained. Travers had remarked that the birds had left the nest.

"*Birds* is good," said Wharton, and chuckled. "Maid, luggage and everything. Osmund couldn't get the papers out of that drawer last night, so he knew I'd see 'em sooner or later, and so last night he and Corney nipped over here and had a council of war. They decided to evacuate, though there was a twelve months' lease of the house. And I know why. By the way, did you see the piece in the fur coat?"

"Attractive-looking girl," Travers said. "And the coat wasn't coney."

"One of the smartest pieces I know."

Travers looked surprised. Wharton modified the claim.

"Know about, that is to say. Remember Corney and the Bishopsgate tea-shop? That was one of the girls. The pick, I thought her, when I dropped into court one day. She and another girl got bound over."

"Too smart for a tea-shop, surely?"

Wharton glared, then heaved a sigh.

"I thought you were pulling my leg. Tea-shop, my eye! Smart pieces, that's what they were. Decoys for old fools in the sixties. And you'd have taken 'em for perfect ladies—unless you'd got one of 'em riled." He chuckled at that. "But I'm not worrying about her now. That taxi's being picked up, and you bet your life she's going either to Osmund or Corney."

Outside a newsagent's the splash bills caught his eye.

MYSTERIOUS DEATH OF MAHARAJAH read one.

ACTOR FOUND DYING IN STREET read another.

"Get the whole issue," said Wharton, "and we'll read all about it."

The versions of both affairs were guarded ones. Amli was supposed to have caught an intruder and to have been struck down by him when making for the phone or the door to give an alarm. The affair, it was insisted, had no political significance. The only new thing about it all, in fact, was a picture of Amli in native clothes, taken just before his investiture as ruler some two years previously.

Furloe had little more than a paragraph, but the column was completed by the description and the request for information.

"Ought to bring something in," Wharton said hopefully. "Now I think we'll have a quick look in at the Levantic."

"Something I've just remembered," Travers said. "Those officials whom you saw this morning. Did they let anything fall about Amli's private life?"

"I gathered a few things," Wharton said. "He's only been ruling for two years but there's been an eye kept on him. I don't mind owning he sounded to me like the hell of a bounder. Oh, yes, and there were hints about difficulties over the succession. Just eye-wash, I shouldn't wonder, to explain away the red-tape."

Travers's fingers were all at once at his glasses.

"George, that gives me an idea. In spite of the beard, Turban may have been an Indian."

"But the beard was false!"

"I know it. But if Turban was of a race, like Amli's, that didn't wear the beard—a Rajput, we'll say—then he might have worn a false beard in order to give Amli the impression that he was of some other race—a Sikh, for example."

Wharton clicked his tongue.

"Damn all this political business!" Then suddenly he was looking round. "But you can't deny that it was Furloe who had Amli's wallet?"

"Didn't we agree that Furloe might have picked it up?"

"Wait a minute," said Wharton, and narrowly missed another car. "Combine your ideas and mine. Furloe had been nobbled by political agitators in this country and was made a tool of. He was sent to get the letters and his share of the boodle was the wallet and the money. Then he was poisoned so that he shouldn't talk."

But the car was at the door of the Levantic, and in a couple of minutes they were in the same old room again.

"Anything been happening?" was Wharton's first question.

"Plenty, sir," Norris told him.

He closed the door behind Wharton and his voice lowered.

"Osmund. He was under notice to quit. He should have left yesterday."

Wharton smiled. The smile was the kind that Travers had described as that of a lion which has missed a particularly plump Christian with his first snap.

"Yes, sir," went on Norris. "See this firm? Amli rang them up early this week and asked them to find him a new secretary by noon today. They saw the news in the papers, and rang Maroulis, and he put them through to me."

"Beautiful!" said Wharton, and rubbed his hands with glee. "Wonder what our oily friend got up to. And never a word to us, mind you." He thought of something. "By the way, if he was paid off at four o'clock yesterday, what right had he to be in this room after ten o'clock? And making up that yarn about urgent papers."

"There's just another thing," Norris said. "Willshed, the trainer, just heard the news and rang up. I told him how he stood, and said we'd like a word with him here. He's coming now."

"You see him," Wharton said. "Mr. Travers, you slip along and see Sir Jerome and then get yourself some lunch, and be back here at two o'clock. I'll slip over to the Spread Eagle."

Travers was waiting but Wharton waved him on.

"Don't wait for me. I don't know that I shan't arrange a little firework display for two o'clock. We might see Osmund and Corney."

"And the lady."

"Yes," echoed Wharton. "And the lady."

CHAPTER VII
CLEAR AS DAYLIGHT

SIR JEROME'S FLAT turned out to be above a lingerie shop. On one side an alley led through to Soho Square. The door was on the south or Piccadilly side, and when Travers opened it he found himself in a narrow passage. On his left was another door that evidently communicated with the shop, and ahead lay the stairs which he mounted.

He rang the bell of the door that faced him, but there was no answer. Then he knocked, and listened, and then knocked again, but the flat appeared to be deserted and, somewhat puzzled, he made his way down again. As he was passing that side door, now on his right, it all at once opened, and later he knew it had been opened by design. The woman who came out from the shop gave a somewhat too startled exclamation at the sight of him.

"I've just been to the flat above," began Travers, wondering if she was taking him for a suspicious character. At once she was cutting in with all the goggle-eyed ardour of the fan.

"Are you a friend of Sir Jerome's?"

She was a smart, youngish woman, and Travers took her for the proprietress of the shop.

"Well, perhaps," he said. "I suppose you couldn't tell me why there's nobody in up there?"

"Oh, yes," she said. "Sir Jerome always goes out at about twelve and sometimes he doesn't get back till two o'clock. We always look out for him."

"But what about his man? He has a man, hasn't he?"

"Oh, yes," she said, "but he's away. He went away last Saturday about two o'clock. Gone on a holiday, I think. I know he had some luggage with him." She remembered something else. "Sir Jerome must be having his meals out somewhere this week, now the man isn't here."

"I wonder where I could find Sir Jerome?" asked Travers reflectively.

"He didn't go out alone this morning," she said. "A lady went with him. Two ladies, really, there were. The first one who called was a lady with red hair, then another lady called and they all went out together. My sister might remember when it was."

"A lady with red hair? I expect that would be his daughter Joy."

Her eyes were big with surprise. "If only I'd known!"

Travers smiled. "Known what?"

"Well"—she gave him a quick look—"if I'd known who she was, I mean. Anyone like that, you like to know who they are. You've seen her, have you? They say she's awfully good. A bit highbrow, they say."

Travers managed to get another word or two in.

"About that other lady who called. What was she like?"

"Well"—she thought hard—"she was a very pale complexion, I'd call it, but ever such a lovely face. She was dark—"

"Bernice—"

The startled Travers had let the word escape. Then he smiled to cover the slip.

"Miss Bernice Haire, I expect. The elder daughter, you know."

"The dancer? You don't say!"

Her eyes goggled, and then she suddenly was in the shop. The door was left open and through it Travers saw another woman, rather younger. She came forward, head on one side.

"This is my sister, Miss Rosamund Stopps," the first one said. "Rosey, this gentleman says the first one we saw this morning—you know, the one with red hair—was Joy Haire, and the other one was Bernice! Would you believe it!"

Travers smiled. "Surely you've seen them both here before?"

"They've been away on a tour," she said, "and we've only been here six months."

"Have you been to see Sir Jerome this week?" Rosamund cut in.

"I saw him at the Metropolis last night," Travers said.

"Wasn't it beautiful?" She looked positively ecstatic. "I think *The Decoration*'s one of his best, don't you?"

"He's very good in it," Travers told her tactfully.

"We knew he was going to do it, didn't we, Maud. We knew before it was even announced in the papers."

"Sir Jerome told you himself?"

"Well, no," she said. "We don't know him, not like that. I mean, he always speaks when we happen to meet outside"—and

Travers was judging that that was contrived very often—"but we'd never dream of taking a liberty like that."

"Last Saturday afternoon it was. We shouldn't have been here—"

Maud cut in. "You see, we happened to be working late, and then we heard a sort of loud voice upstairs and then we knew what it was. We both spotted it at once what he was rehearsing, didn't we, Rosey?"

"That's right, and we both said he was going to do *The Decoration*."

While talking, she had been making queer signs. Maud disappeared for a moment, and reappeared with a little book.

"Would you give us *your* autograph?"

Travers blushed. "Well, I'm afraid I shan't add very much distinction—"

"Oh, do give it to us!"

Travers wrote his name on the proffered virgin page.

"Nice for you to have such a famous neighbour," he said. "I don't think I'll wait any longer now. I may perhaps call back later."

He backed his way out through crepe de chine and rayon. The outer door closed and Maud said to Rosey, "Ludo—Ludo—can't read it."

"Ludovic Travers," Rosey managed slowly. "Never heard of him, have you? Nice voice he had, though. Wonder who he is."

"Didn't he look funny when he took his goggles off. I thought I was going to giggle."

Travers, unaware of that none too handsome appraisal, was thinking of that same moment when he had instinctively given his glasses a polish, which had been when it had seemed certain that both Joy and Bernice had called on their father. A chance meeting was all it could have been. Each naturally saw her father from time to time, and each that morning had chosen the same time.

He could hardly help a little chuckle at that. What frigid awkward moments the two must have spent up there with their father. But, wait a moment. *The three had left together.* Did that mean there had been some kind of reconciliation, forced upon the two by that chance meeting? If so, there might be great news soon for Barney. Or was the reconciliation a pretended one for Sir Jerome's benefit?

Then Travers smiled again. Why argue with one's self or rush to conclusions? On Sunday Joy would be sure to tell all about everything. Quite an amusing surprise for her too, to hear about the two fans in the lingerie shop, and how she had just escaped yet another autograph book.

As for Wharton, Travers knew there would be no news whatever for him, for the last thing Travers would even have hinted at would have been his private relationships with the sisters, or why that morning he had suggested Barney Josephs as the expert to consult in the case of the dead Furloe.

The saloon bar of the Spread Eagle was almost empty when Wharton walked in. Tom Moriarty, the proprietor, caught sight of him, motioned to the barmaid to carry on, and then came round to meet him, rolling down the white sleeves of his shirt and grabbing his coat on the way.

"Can I have a private word?" Wharton asked.

Tom took him into the office.

"After someone, Super?"

"Not this time," Wharton said. "Just want a little information. Did you see in the paper just now how an actor was found dying in the street? Between you and me, he was poisoned."

"You don't say!"

"Yes, and in his time he's been in here. A week ago today he spoke to Sir Jerome Haire and asked him for a job."

"Wait a minute." Tom raised a finger. "Was he an elderly man in a navy-blue suit? Respectable-looking and hatchet-faced?"

"You've got him."

"He's been in here only once, far as I know. Last Saturday morning, like you said. Let me see now. Sir Jerome came in with some big nob or other I didn't know, and they had a drink over there just inside the door, and soon as this nob went I saw this other man. Know his name, Super?"

"Furloe."

"Furloe? Furloe?" He shook his head. "Never heard of him. Still, as I was saying, as soon as I see him go up to Sir Jerome, I kept my eye on him. We're proud of having anyone like Sir Jerome come in here, Super, and we don't want them pestered, so when I sort of see Sir Jerome waving this bloke away, I was just going over to give him the push myself when he started doing a whispering act—"

He caught Wharton's quick look.

"You know, Super, sort of craned up and whispered something. Then I heard Sir Jerome say something and look surprised, and when I looked round again, there was the two of them going out, and this bloke still talking to Sir Jerome. And that's all I know, s'welp me."

"It's all I want to know," Wharton said. "But was he in here last night, by the way?"

"Not in here, he wasn't," Tom said. "Wait half a jiff and I'll let you know for certain."

The half-jiff was five minutes, but the report was definite.

"That's all right then," Wharton said. "I might have a word with Sir Jerome some time. In here regularly, is he?"

"He just drops in occasionally, like one or two of the old top-notchers do. It does the house good, Super. Gives it a bit of class. I knew some of 'em myself when I was in the profesh." He gave a wink. "Sir Jerome's a bit of all right. You'll get on well with him, Super. You haven't seen him this week, I suppose?"

"Saw him on Wednesday at the Paliceum," Wharton said.

Tom's face lighted. "Good, wasn't he! I'm best part of seventy and I've seen him a good few times, but I never see him in better form."

Then all at once the old pro was striking an attitude. Wharton stared agape till the words came and he knew what Tom was at.

He is *not* dead. They can't put me off with lies.

The attitude ceased. Tom's eyes swivelled for approval. Wharton nodded.

"Damn good, Tom. That was him to the life." He heaved a sigh. "When he's gone and you and me, there'll be few good 'uns left."

Tom chuckled. "We ain't gone yet, nor him neither. Sleeps bad, so he told me, but otherwise he never felt fitter."

"Well, thanks for the information." His hand went out. "Good-by, Tom. If ever you should want bail, send for me. Oh, before I go. You're a bit of a racing expert, so you can put me wise about something. Don't they say there're straight trainers and crooked ones?"

"Crooked?" Tom's shake of the head was heartfelt. "If the perishing stewards knew half what I've heard in here—"

"I shouldn't be surprised," Wharton said. "And, strictly in confidence, what sort is Charles Willshed?"

"Straight as a die," Tom said promptly. "Never heard a word against him. Besides, he usually trains for the right sort."

"Right," said Wharton. "Now if I can use your phone for a minute, I'll be obliged."

"Help yourself, Super," Tom said, and left him to it.

Travers arrived back at the Levantic in time to see Norris get out of a taxi with a man who looked as if he might be Corney Feathers. Corney was remonstrating, having evidently expected the talk to be elsewhere. Then Travers saw the bureau clerk make signs to Norris, and Travers interpreted them as a recognition that Corney was Smith.

But upstairs Corney and Osmund were parked in different rooms. Wharton was at the writing desk when Travers came in. He was not at all disappointed at the lack of news, and Travers saw for himself that what Wharton had gathered at the Spread Eagle had made a further statement from Sir Jerome not nearly so necessary.

"Norris saw that trainer," Wharton went on, "and we know now why Osmund got the push. What do you think his little game was? He approached Willshed with a scheme about stable secrets. Willshed was to have a share in the rake-off and Osmund also said he could do Willshed a lot of good with His Nibs. You know, claimed to have a lot of influence. Willshed blew the gaff and His Nibs was furious. That was last Tuesday, and Osmund had notice to go at the end of the week, which was yesterday for him. His Nibs told Willshed all about it yesterday morning. Oh, and by the way, Norris says Willshed's opinion of His Nibs wasn't openly given, but—well, you can guess." He listened for a moment, then nodded. "This will be Osmund. Sit over there as if you're only waiting."

Osmund came in with a deferential good-afternoon.

"Good of you to come," Wharton said, "and I've been thinking it was almost a pity to have troubled you. All I want to know is how many days old was the sheet of blotting-paper that was here last night."

"Well"—he frowned away for a moment or two—"I should say about three or four days. I didn't change the paper at regular times. It all depended on its condition."

Wharton nodded heavily, then suddenly smiled.

"It's just struck me, by the way, how strange you must have thought it—I won't say how lucky—that His Highness was bumped off *last night*."

Osmund peered at him sideways.

"Yes," said Wharton. "If he didn't go and die the very day your notice was up! Nobody to queer your pitch over getting a new job."

Osmund's eyes narrowed, but from the aptness of his reply it was plain that he had thought of all the questions and worked out all the answers.

"Notice, sir? That's not what I should call it."

"Oh? And what would you call it?"

"That His Highness and myself were parting amicably, by mutual agreement."

"Dear, dear, dear!" said Wharton, and shook a sorrowful head. "I wonder, Mr. Travers, what made that wicked Mr. Willshed tell all those lies?"

"He had to tell lies!" Wharton's heavy irony had touched him on the raw. "If you haven't heard the truth, I'll tell it to you. Willshed came to me with a certain proposition and I considered it my duty to inform His Highness. It was my word against Willshed's, and my word wasn't taken. Very well, then. His Highness and I agreed to part company."

"And why weren't we told?"

"But why should you be told?"

"I'll put it another way then," said Wharton patiently. "Why did you give us the impression, after you'd ceased to be in His Highness's employ, that you were still his secretary?"

"I don't admit that I gave that impression."

"Have it your own way," said Wharton mildly. Then he cocked an ear. "That sounds like Corney arriving. He'll tell us a few things. And then there's Lotta. How I hate to upset that poor girl after all she must have been through." His smile became positively roguish. "And so you were at the pictures last night, Mr. Osmund?"

Osmund made no bones now about throwing back the answers.

"I was, and it'll take a better man than you to prove I wasn't."

"Perhaps it will," said Wharton. "But you made an unauthorized entry here last night. Why didn't you ask permission to come up?"

Osmund smiled. "I know my rights. I'm answering no more questions."

"You prefer to make a statement?"

"About what?"

"Every detail from, say, eight o'clock last night till midnight." He leaned forward, and his tone changed. "And if I'm not satisfied with it, I'll have you in court at the inquest and grill hell out of you."

Osmund drew himself up with considerable show of dignity.

"I don't see why I shouldn't make such a statement."

Wharton pushed a bell and Norris came in.

"Take Mr. Osmund in there and take an official statement," Wharton told him. "And have Corney ready for me."

"Lotta was that Enfield girl?" Travers asked at once.

"That's right," Wharton said. "Lotta Laveen is the name she goes by. Norris says she's as dangerous a one as he's had. Used to be in the chorus and could do a duchess act if she wanted to."

He went to the lounge door and himself admitted Corney. Never had he been in a more affable vein.

"Sit down, Mr. Feathers, will you? Or would you rather it was Corney, as we're all friends. Don't mind Mr. Travers, by the way. He's merely an interested party." He beamed over the tops of his spectacles. "Or would you rather be known as Smith? Anything to oblige, as Lotta would say."

Corney kept his eyes on the carpet, and said nothing. He was not so big a man as Travers had imagined but his face was as described—thin and unhealthily sallow.

"Look at me," Wharton said.

Corney looked, and at once became voluble.

"If you want me to explain all about last night, Super, I can do so. You see, it was like this—"

"Just a moment," Wharton said. "I'd hate to deceive you, but this is not official—at the moment. Still, carry on."

Corney was far too old a hand to add apologies or excuses to his statement, and, as Wharton said afterwards, he knew there was no point in wandering from the truth. Through certain racing connections, he said, he had got wind of a certain two-year-old that could catch pigeons. The owner had been kept in the dark by the trainer, and was pushed for cash, so Corney worked it with the trainer to make a profitable deal with Amli. He had sounded Amli through Osmund—who was his cousin—and had been instructed to find out the terms. These of course had been worked out already by Corney and the trainer, but Corney took a few days before again reporting. Lotta had been in the swim to the extent of having asked Amli to buy her a horse of her own! Corney had rung up Amli the previous night at about eight-thirty, and Amli had told him to come at ten.

"Why so late?" asked Wharton.

Corney said he had been pretending to be ringing up from a certain training quarters quite a distance from town, and it would therefore be impossible to see Amli much sooner, though he would do so if he could.

"So you came at ten," Wharton said. "What happened then?"

"I own up," Corney said. "I did as he told me over the phone and came through to here. Then I saw him and bolted. You know why, Super."

"I can guess," Wharton said. "You knew you were a man with a record. Now what about the name of that trainer?"

Corney looked positively pained.

"You wouldn't ask me to give anyone away, would you, Super?"

"What do you mean by that?"

Corney had a look at the carpet.

"I'm not. That's all, Super. The deal's off and I've finished with it."

Wharton's lip drooped. "I see. Letting it be a lesson to you." Then he wagged a roguish finger. "I suppose this flyer of yours couldn't have been by Tea-shop out of Lotta? Foaled at Enfield?"

Corney looked up, moistened his lips, then looked down again, shaking his head.

"Like to make a full statement?"

Corney shook his head again.

"Like a grilling in the coroner's court instead?"

Corney looked up.

"Depends what sort of a statement you want."

"All movements from eight o'clock last night till two in the morning—including Enfield."

Corney's shake of the head was now a sorrowful one.

"You've got me in wrong about that, Super. Lotta was just a friend of mine, so I thought she ought to hear the news."

"Well? And what then?"

"Nothing," Corney said.

Wharton got to his feet. "I think you'll make the statement all right. If it helps at all, I don't mind telling you that Lotta's just making one—at the Yard. We didn't want this place all cluttered up."

In a minute Norris came in with Osmund's statement. Wharton read it and said Osmund might go, and would Norris get on with Corney instead. Then Wharton did quite a lot of phoning. It must have been half an hour before he came over to Travers.

"Nice little story Corney told us?"

"Yes," Travers said. "If it was true."

"It was true all right," Wharton said. "That racehorse business was a sideline. The real killing was to be when Corney found some pal of his to pose as Lotta's injured husband. Now do you see what scandal there'll be if the press get hold of the Enfield business?"

He shook his head.

"I don't like it. We're getting into a damn sight too deep water. If anyone does any blabbing outside, there'll be the devil to pay. The best thing I can do is make a report at once. And as for other things, neither Corney nor Lotta would be mixed up with killing Amli. You don't kill the goose that lays the golden eggs."

"I suppose that's right," Travers said. "I had the crazy idea a few moments ago that Furloe might have been mixed up with the gang. They might have accommodated him with a dressing room somewhere handy here—Osmund's flat, for instance. That's where he may have been poisoned."

Norris came in then with Corney's statement, and Wharton made him the audience.

"Mr. Travers has got a bee in his bonnet. What the highbrows'd call a Furloe complex. What is it you call him—the leaning man?"

Travers smiled but said nothing. Norris, more or less in the dark, said nothing either.

"What I will say," went on Wharton, "is that I don't trust Osmund. I believe he'd have double-crossed Corney and Lotta as soon as look at 'em. He's the man for my money. Lying to us like hell. Snooping round here last night and chucking that ruddy alibi of his in my face. Let me see that statement. About time I was at headquarters."

He read Corney's account through twice, then went to the lounge door.

"You may go, Corney. Make up your mind to be found nice and handy. Just one word, though. Come in here a moment."

He led the way to the far corner.

"Now, Corney, this is between ourselves. I'm a man of my word and you know it. Tell me this. When you were here last night, did you at any time by any chance see an Indian in a white turban prowling about anywhere?"

Corney shook his head.

"Did you touch anything in this room?"

"God's truth, no! I hadn't gloves on. All I did was wipe the prints off the door knobs."

"Ever hear of a man called Furloe?"

"Furloe?" He shook his head again.

"An old actor, he might have been. A man near seventy, hatchet-faced and usually wearing a shiny navy-blue."

"Never seen him in my natural."

"Right," said Wharton. "Now I'll surprise you. I *believe you.*"

Out went Corney. Five minutes later Wharton had gone too. Travers stayed for a brief yarn with Norris and then the two made their way to the lounge. As they neared the outer door, there was a tap at it.

"Come in!" bawled Norris.

The door opened and there stood an elderly clergyman.

"I went to St. Martin's," he said, "and was told to come here. I think I have some information about poor Furloe."

CHAPTER VIII
THE PARSON'S TALE

"WOULD YOU MIND coming through to the other room, sir?" Norris said. "Perhaps you'll make a statement for us." He whispered to Travers, "I'd better let the Super know."

Travers pushed across an easy chair for the old padre.

"Ah! thank you," he said. "I'm not so young as I was and I seem to have been on my feet quite a long time today."

"You've come far, sir?"

"From Bermondsey," he said. "Do you know it at all?"

He was a man of at least seventy years; tall, clean-shaven, scholarly, and with kindly grey eyes that wrinkled humorously at their corners.

"Now, sir," began Norris, "may we have full particulars? Names and so on."

"Spearing," he said. "Thomas Spearing. I'm vicar of St. Bede's, Bermondsey."

"I know the spot, sir," Norris said. "And you knew Furloe?"

"Very well indeed."

"That's capital then, sir. Tell us everything, will you? Begin at the beginning, if you know what I mean. We shan't interrupt if we can help it."

"Well, I'll try." He cleared his throat, settled in his chair, and began.

"I knew him—Walter Furloe, I mean—about six years ago. That was when I first knew him. It was through his married daughter, Mrs. Furloe—"

"You'll pardon me, sir, but wouldn't she be his daughter-in-law?"

"I'm afraid not," he said. "I'll try to explain." He smiled somewhat dolefully. "I'm rather a bad hand at this kind of thing."

"You're doing fine, sir," Norris assured him.

"Well, I should have said that Furloe *went* by his daughter's married name. His real name was Colson. Mrs. Furloe, the daughter, was a war widow with a pension. Not much of a pension but she hadn't any children and it was enough to get along with. A quiet sort of person, like her father, and very nice in her ways. I got friendly with her through church work and ultimately she told me all about her father."

"Walter Colson." He stopped at that and looked at both Norris and Travers. "The name conveys nothing to you?"

It conveyed nothing to either. The vicar smiled a quiet apology.

"Perhaps I oughtn't to have expected it. You gentlemen wouldn't be ardent theatre-goers like myself—or like myself of many years ago. I did remember the name as soon as she mentioned it. Well, before the war Colson was known as a man who was likely to go far in the profession. He played with most of the big men; with Alexander, I know, and Tree. I've heard him say, and I have no reason to doubt it, that he was able through lucky chances to give their first opportunity to some of our famous living actors. Still—"

"Pardon me," broke in Travers. "Take this question as confidential and not to go down in the statement. Was one of the actors he claimed to have helped Sir Jerome Haire?"

"Why, yes! How did you know?"

"In a purely private way that has nothing to do with the case," Travers told him. But he was glad at the lucky guess, for he knew now what Furloe had whispered to Sir Jerome in the Spread Eagle. "He must have been an older man than we thought, by the way?"

"He was over seventy," the vicar said. "But I'll go on explaining how I came to meet him. It was through the daughter. Colson had a tragic shock just before the end of the war. He and his wife were on holiday and the wife was drowned before his eyes. He tried to save her, and caught a very bad chill, and what with the illness and the shock and everything, his mind gave way. He spent the next fourteen years of his life in a mental home."

"Poor old chap," said Norris involuntarily. Travers, polishing his glasses, shook his head and said nothing.

"Yes," the vicar went on, "it was a very tragic affair. But he wasn't a raving lunatic or anything like it. Oh, no. He slowly began to recover. It was an exceedingly long process and he wasn't discharged till six years ago. His daughter naturally gave him a home and he took her name. Mind you, he was perfectly aware of his past condition, and he was very sensitive about it. I don't mean to convey that he was moody or anything like that, because he wasn't. He settled down at once, and the really curious thing was that he took no interest whatever in his old profession.

"Then the daughter died, and her pension with her. Something had to be done about poor Furloe, and at first I thought of applying to the Actors' Benevolent Fund, but when I suggested it, he absolutely refused. His tragedy had happened during the war when people's thoughts were on other things, and he had dropped so cleanly out of the profession that everyone by now would be thinking him dead, if they thought of him at all. Then I found a solution that was most satisfactory for us both."

He smiled beguilingly. "You see, I'm a bachelor. The old vicarage is still much what it was a hundred years ago. It has a deplorably untidy garden and an old-fashioned stable at the end, so what I did was to fit out a room above the stable and put in light and water, and there was a very nice home. The arrangement was that he should have his meals in the kitchen with cook and Alice."

He gave an apologetic, inquiring look.

"Please don't think I was snobbish. Walter Furloe was as good a man as myself, and in many ways a better. The idea was that as I'm the most erratic man in the world as to times, he would be able to have his meals absolutely regularly, instead of waiting till all hours for me. I must say he was most happy about it. He moved his few possessions to his new room and settled down at once. I paid him a nominal sum five shillings a week, to be exact—and he became responsible for little jobs about the house and for tidying up the garden. He was also very interested in our youths' and men's clubs. I should have said that the daughter died two years ago and he came to me at once."

He paused for a moment to collect his thoughts. Norris cut in.

"You were able to keep an eye on him, sir, up in that room of his?"

The vicar looked surprised. "But he didn't want an eye kept on him. I'm sorry if I gave that impression. You see, if I had a free hour of a night, he used to come in to me, or I'd go up to him, and we'd have a smoke and a yarn."

Then he frowned. "A year ago he began to change. I can't describe it except by saying that his old life suddenly began to appear in him. It was as if the great shock had put the theatre wholly out of his mind for good and all, and then it slowly began to come back. Every day he remembered more of his old life, and he began to get restless. I was very worried indeed."

He shook his head and his fingers were fumbling at his pocket.

"Fill your pipe, sir, by all means," Norris told him.

"Pipe?" He looked startled, then smiled. "I see. The bulge in my pocket. Well, I think I will smoke, if I may. Perhaps you'll try some."

"Not for me, sir; thank you all the same."

Travers with a smile of thanks accepted the offer, and as soon as the pipes were alight, the vicar's story acquired a new smoothness and fluency. It was not Furloe's mental state that worried him, he went on, but the means of finding some outlet for the new preoccupation. Things were also easier since Furloe himself realized that by no conceivable chance could he ever, at his time of life, get back to the stage.

"What I actually did," the vicar explained, "was to take him occasionally to shows in town, and I induced him to give little shows at our concerts. You wouldn't believe how well he went down, even with our kind of audiences. They used to clamour for him."

"He was still a good actor?" Travers asked quietly.

"He was. I've seen most of what are still household names— or perhaps only memories—and I say most emphatically that he could compare with the best. His very reticence gave him an extraordinary earnestness—I mean, the reticence of a man with a secret to keep." He gazed reflectively at the ceiling. "Perhaps his Sidney Carton was his best—"

"Pardon me again," Travers said, "but you don't mean an imitation of Martin Harvey?"

The vicar smiled with gentle reproof.

"It takes a good man to imitate, as you call it, and to hold the attention of rough lads and men. Still, his Svengali was first-rate, and his prosecuting counsel—you remember *Butterfly on the Wheel?*—was really masterly. I naturally had to answer all sorts of uncomfortable questions about him: why he wasn't a pro. and whether he had been.

"Then things began to get alarming. He bought himself a make-up set, and I saw it in his room, though I never referred to it. Then he acquired a definite mania for acting and everything connected with his old profession, and I began to see less and less of him. He used to go to shows by himself, and cook and Alice used to hear him prowling about in his room and talking aloud.

"Then I talked to him in my own way, and I discovered that he was just as sensitive about those years in the mental home. And yet he was now insisting that he might get back to the stage without anybody knowing about it. I had that talk with him about a fortnight ago. Then on Sunday he came to me of his own accord."

He sat up in the chair, and it seemed that the climax was at hand. His listeners had a new intentness.

"I should say that he was an actor to the finger-tips, but of the old kind. I mean, he pronounced his words well and he liked the sound of words and—I say it not unkindly—theatrical situations. He began his talk to me by these words. 'My benefactor!'"

A quick apologetic look and he was going on.

"He used to allude to me as that because he thought I *was* his benefactor, whereas, as you know, gentlemen, I was getting quite a lot out of our bargain. But, as I was saying, he came forward with his hand out, like this, and addressed me as his benefactor. I can't remember the exact words he then used but he spoke of a surprise I was soon going to have, and of a repayment. He gave me the distinct impression that he had after all succeeded in getting back into the profession. When I hinted at it and congratulated him, he merely gave his gentle smile. 'All in good time,' he said; 'all in good time.' And naturally I didn't question him."

He gave a sad shake of the head.

"I still don't think I was wrong. I know he'd have resented it—in a courteous way, of course, for he was always a gentleman. There was always a confidence, too, in his manner. Very reticent and self-possessed, and making you wonder what was in him and what his thoughts were, to make him so sure.

"Still that's merely by the way. We talked last Sunday, as I was saying, and I saw him no more. I'm always a busy man and this was a very busy week, and as it isn't gardening time I didn't see him pottering about. Then this morning Alice told me he hadn't been in to breakfast. When I questioned her she said he'd been away most of the week, except for breakfasts. He used to go out in his best suit—a navy-blue one—and that was all that was seen of him till the next day at breakfast."

He gave a sigh and a long, slow shake of the head.

"That's all, except that when I saw the newspaper bills I had a sudden intuition. Immediately after lunch I put everything by and came up to the hospital."

There was a long quiet in the room, then Norris gently cleared his throat.

"A remarkable story, sir, and what I might call a pathetic one. Now perhaps you'll answer a few direct questions. Was he at all addicted to drink, for instance?"

"Not in the least." The tone had a definite indignation. "He liked an occasional glass of ale, as I do myself. A most abstemious man. Most abstemious."

Travers cut in. "Would you call him wiry and tough? I mean, had he considerable physical strength?"

"At his age?" The vicar smiled. "Just the opposite. Gentle—that was Walter Furloe. A spiritual strength, of course, and alertness of mind."

"Honest?"

"As the day. The man was a natural gentleman. He was trusted with everything and he never betrayed the trust."

"Anything unusual about his room?" Norris asked.

"I saw it this morning, and there wasn't—to my knowledge. I should say that everything was unlocked, and there was nothing there that I didn't expect or had not seen before."

"We have to keep asking these questions, sir," Norris said. "And what about the make-up box?"

"It was still there."

"Had it been used?"

"It always looked as though it had been used."

"And did he ever speak of taking his own life?"

"Well, now you come to mention it, he did, just after his daughter died." He appeared suddenly to remember something. "Curious, you know, but he did mention something of the sort last Sunday, during our talk. Let me see—what were his words? That if he hadn't at last seen the end of the road there'd have been nothing left to go on living for. You understand what he meant, and what I gathered from it. He meant that if at last he hadn't got a job, he'd have given up everything."

"I see, sir." Norris nodded for a minute, then turned to Travers. "You any more questions, sir?"

"One more perhaps, one last thing. When he was even at the height of his craze for the stage again, was he ever definite? Did he mention any particular kind of play or parts he would like, or any theatre, or company?"

"There was never anything definite," he was told. "The word *stage*, if I may put it so, covered everything."

"Then if that's the lot, sir," said Norris, "we'll get you to read the statement over, though it's only for our private use. You'll be making a statement at the inquest, sir, in any case."

Norris lingered out the proceedings with the hope that Wharton might appear, but at last the vicar had to go.

"A fine old chap, that," Norris said. "There aren't many who'd have done what he did."

Then Wharton arrived.

"Just missed him, have I?" he said. "Let me see the statement."

He read it twice and made notes in his book, then remarked that things seemed to be fitting in.

Travers agreed. For one thing there was the explanation of what Furloe had whispered to Sir Jerome.

"And why he took him for a fraud," Norris said. "Everyone knew Colson was dead. And, of course, that unexplained gap made Sir Jerome naturally take him for an old lag."

"There's one most important thing that occurs to me," Travers said. "You may remember Sir Jerome's statement at the hospital last night, how in order to get rid of the man, he told him to come back in three weeks' time. He gave Furloe the impression that provided references could be found and the gap accounted for, then he'd find him work. Furloe didn't see that he was being got rid of. He took it only too seriously. The next day he had that talk with his benefactor."

"That's right," Wharton said. "Everything's perfectly explained and everything fits in—Sir Jerome's tale, the vicar's, and the bartender's. Wait a moment, though. I wonder if by any chance Furloe discovered the truth, that Sir Jerome was only getting rid of him? Some people would call that a suicide motive."

"He could have taken the poison at Bermondsey," Norris said. "If he took it in that room of his, nobody would have seen him go or come, because of the fog. After he'd taken it, and before it had begun to work, he might have come back to town. It'd have taken less than no time." He shook his head. "That'd rule out the possibility of him being Turban."

Wharton had been thinking of something else.

"Look here, Mr. Travers," he said, "you try to get hold of Sir Jerome. You'll do it better than us because you know him, so to speak, and I've got a conference at six o'clock. He and Furloe must have had quite a long talk, and Furloe must have let quite a lot of things drop, and you never know. You might get hold of some little thing that turns out to be just what we're looking for."

"As you wish," Travers said. "Anything happen at the Yard, by the way?"

Wharton sniffed. "Lotta says she met His Nibs somewhere, and she makes no bones about Enfield. Why should she? We may have her taped, but we can't pull her in for that." He shrugged his shoulders. "Corney was told about Amli by Osmund, and he knew Lotta's address and went to break the news. Osmund went with him for company. There we are then. We haven't got a thing on any one of them."

"What about Corney and the racehorse business?" asked Norris.

Wharton had his own code.

"Oh, no. I told him it was unofficial and that's the end of it. Besides, Corney could say it was a made-up yarn and then spin another."

Travers arrived home to find a message waiting.

"Sir Jerome Haire rang, sir," reported Palmer, who was evidently very impressed. "He understands that you called to see him, sir, and he says he'll be available at his flat till six o'clock." A little bow. "The message came soon after two o'clock, sir."

"Heavens!" said Travers, and made a bee-line for the bathroom. Now he saw how things had happened. One or both of the lingerie ladies had contrived to waylay Sir Jerome with the story about a caller.

A quick wash and Travers was away. The lingerie shop was closed but there was a switch that lighted stairs and landing. Sir Jerome opened the door at his knock, recognized him, and then let out a full-blooded "Ah!"

It was followed by: "Come in, Mr. Travers; come in. Not the most palatial of places but I—er—trust, hospitable. It suits me. Let me take your hat. My man happens to be away. Family trouble, poor fellow. Take this chair, won't you? Allow me to offer you some refreshment."

Travers mentioned sherry, if Sir Jerome was also having one, and then during the pouring, ran his eye round a room that was stuffy with photographs and souvenirs.

"Your very good health, sir!"

Geniality gave the voice a rare fruitiness. Even the dry question had a heartiness.

"And now what can I do for you?"

"If you wish to see my credentials, here they are," began Travers. "I'm really here on behalf of Superintendent Wharton of the C.I.D., to ask you to be so good as to help him by elaborating your account of your dealings with the man Furloe."

"Furloe?" He frowned.

"The real name appears to be Colson."

"Real, did you say?"

"Yes," Travers said. "Perhaps you saw in the papers that he was dead. Poisoned."

"Yes," he said, "I did see it, but it didn't give me the shock that you've given me by saying he really was Colson."

He had turned beetling brows on Travers who was feeling all at once like a small boy at tea with his house-master.

"I'll be frank with you, Sir Jerome," Travers said. "Please regard it as confidential but this is our information."

While Travers's recital went on he was all at once aware that the old actor was making the most of the situation. He was acting his listening, as it were, for he would thrust out that hooked beak of his whenever Travers paused, and he had anchored himself at the electric heater with arms well under his coat-tails. Occasionally a hand would emerge and make an appropriate gesture.

"Ah!" he said, when the explanation was ended. "He told me he was Colson, but how could I believe him? To the best of my knowledge, Colson was dead. I had never had much to do with him in any case, and then, perhaps, forty years ago. I thought the fellow was trying some confidence trick or other." Forward went the beak again. "You're sure of your facts?"

Travers smiled lamely. "Well, sir, our information was that he even claimed to have been of service to you years ago. He may have been boasting—"

"What's that? Of service to me!" Out came both hands and one was raised to heaven. "The man was a scoundrel, sir. A cadger. A common rogue!"

The blast subsided. Travers gently gave more details about the dead man, and guardedly mentioned the source of the information and its reliability. Then nothing was more comical than the expression that was all at once on his hearer's face.

"Then he was poor Colson?"

"Beyond any shadow of doubt, Sir Jerome."

"Oh, my God! And I misjudged him." He shook his head and then his hands went distractedly in the air as if feeling for words. "Not that he could ever have come back. The public wouldn't have stood for it. A man who'd been in an asylum." He shook his head again. "I shall feel the shame of this, Mr. Travers, till my dying day."

"But, why should you?" Travers began lamely.

"Can I do anything?" The question was eager. "Anything whatever. There's a widow?"

"Nobody at all," Travers told him. "Perhaps it was as well."

He had seen the quick glance at the clock, and he got to his feet.

"I won't detain you any longer now, Sir Jerome. By the way, you didn't see the man again after he came here?"

"Never. I'm sorry to say now that I avoided the Spread Eagle for a day or two in case I might be pestered again. Had I known—" He broke off with another shake of the head. "Any further help I can be to you, please call on me immediately. But wait a moment. An old friend is calling for me tomorrow and taking me in his car to the country. Not a place to stay in, this time of year. Still—"

He waved his hand vaguely and Travers gathered that there was to be more pleasure in the visit than had been admitted. A step towards the door, and he turned.

"I meant to have mentioned to you, Sir Jerome, that you once knew my sister very well. Helen, who was at school with your daughter Bernice."

"Helen? Helen Travers?" He shot a look at Travers as if for comparison, then smiled. It was his first smile since Travers had entered the room.

"Of course, of course. Why didn't you mention it before? You know my daughters then, my boy."

"Yes," Travers said. "But not so well as I could wish."

He flushed, dimly discerning he had dropped some kind of brick. Sir Jerome was actually chuckling.

"We're in the same boat, my boy. There was a time when daughters were daughters and fathers were fathers."

"And now?" asked Travers, and waited for the *bon mot*.

"And now? Well"—He waved a vague hand. "Now they—well, they go their own way. They've left the nest, as they say."

Perhaps he was aware of the anti-climax, for he took Travers's arm and began leading him to the door.

"I'm not so young as I was, my boy. I can't sleep as I used to. I take long walks at night—sometimes too long—but I don't get the sleep. That reminds me. Last night, when I saw poor Colson."

A click of the tongue and a slow shake of the head, then his hand went out. So firm was the grip that Travers was twiddling his fingers for a good minute after it.

Travers was not only gratified and flattered at the warmth of that handshake, he was also perfectly satisfied with the official results of that brief and chatty interview.

He saw for one thing why the old man had been harsh in his judgment of Furloe. The man had whispered in the Spread Eagle that he had once done Sir Jerome a favour, and there could be no surer way of putting his hearer's back up.

Prosperity and fame, thought Travers, are the peculiar and sole perquisites of their possessors, who necessarily resent reminders of helping hands, at however great a distance of time. Yet the bigness of the great actor had been seen in his confession of harshness and misjudgement, his quick humility and his offers of help.

But Travers could nevertheless smile at Sir Jerome's mannerisms and posings and his outworn cadences. A bit of an old windbag, there was no denying it, and a tremendous bore when away from the things of his profession.

So Travers was on good terms with himself when he entered his flat again. Then came the surprise and the enormous disappointment.

"Miss Joy Haire has just rung up, sir," Palmer reported. "She regrets she will be unable to keep the engagement for tomorrow, sir, but she's been called out of town."

Chapter IX
TRAVERS IN A HURRY

Travers spent an aimless kind of Sunday morning. Even when he forced himself to work at his book he could not settle down, for past murders seemed futile when all the time one was wondering about the new. But for the fact that Wharton had asked if he might drop in during the evening, Travers would have run down to Sussex after all.

He had been looking forward to that hour or two with Joy Haire, and not only because he saw arising out of it a possible solution of the mystery that was worrying Barney and had nagged so persistently at himself. There had been a novelty about taking out to tea a very charming and clever young lady. And Joy was Bernice's sister, and Bernice—though he was not prepared to admit more—was the most interesting woman he had ever met.

Just before lunch Barney unexpectedly rang up, and Travers had a sudden panic when he heard his voice.

"There's going to be good news, Barney," he said, and forced himself to believe that there had been something after all in that meeting of the sisters on the Saturday. "Besides I didn't promise anything till tonight or tomorrow."

Barney said he knew that but he had to have some comfort.

"If nothing happens, Mr. Travers, what shall I do?" Travers saw the palms rise quiveringly. "I'm finished. My name, my money—"

"You mustn't talk like that," Travers told him sternly. "Why, if there's no other way out you can always induce one sister to catch flu so that she's too ill to sign the contract."

"No more lies," Barney quavered. "I've got so that I can tell no more lies. And even if I could do it that way, Mr. Travers, it wouldn't help. The other parties think the contract is signed! Now do you get it?"

Travers got it, and knew there was the devil to pay. Business had been conducted direct by cable and phone, and Barney had so far committed himself as to allow New York to suppose that the signed contract was already on its way over. A bad business, and yet Travers could hardly blame him. Barney had let things drift after having been led astray by the sisters' first enthusiasms. Then he had hoped that they would prove possessed of at least the elements of common-sense. It was they who should shoulder the blame, not poor harassed Barney.

Then suddenly Travers felt a righteous indignation. What childishness the whole thing had been. All that pretence of indifference was nothing but silly temper and cheap affectation. And yet, were both sisters to blame?

Joy—yes. She was self-willed, headstrong, provocative, and recklessly indifferent to public opinion. Threaten her with the conventions and it was like waving a red flag before a bull. Joy it must be who had done what Bernice knew to be an unpardonable thing. For Bernice saw life rigidly, and her indifference was to the noisy and the vulgar. Poise and assurance were part of her; things born of long knowledge of herself and a belief in that self and life as she knew it should be lived. Obstinacy, some might call it. A better word was serenity.

But Travers found no peace of mind in trying to work out such psychological intricacies, and there was no wonder that during the afternoon he all at once had the idea of calling on Bernice. After all, she had agreed that he might ring. Better than ringing and finding her out, was to call with the chance of finding her in. The walk too would do him good.

He arrived at the hotel just before four. It was a different maid who answered his ring, and from the tan still on her face, he took her for the dresser who had accompanied Bernice on the tour. She would see if Miss Bernice was in, and she showed Travers into the anteroom.

She had entered the anteroom by one door and now she tapped at another, and opened it without waiting for a reply. Then several things happened. She halted just inside the door and gave a little startled exclamation. Travers looked round, caught a glimpse of a settee corner, and then who should move across his small glimpse of the room, but Joy Haire! And, most extraordinary, as she flashed across his view he could see she was dabbing at her eyes with a handkerchief.

"Close that door!"

It was Bernice's voice, and yet wholly unlike it. No serenity there but an angry, urgent order, with more in it than anxiety. So his fingers fumbled at his glasses and he moved towards the end of the room, and all the while he found himself listening for sounds.

Three minutes, and the maid reappeared.

"Miss Bernice will be here in a minute, sir."

The minute passed and five more after it, then at last Bernice appeared, but dressed for going out. Her face showed both pleasure and concern, but there was on it some other look that he had never seen.

"How charming of you to call! Unpardonable of me to keep you like this, but I was in the throes of dressing."

Travers bent over the gloved hand.

"Again I'm unfortunate."

"Yes," she said, and nevertheless waved a hand at the settee. "I have to go almost at once. But why didn't you give me a ring?"

"But that would have been worse," he said. "I shouldn't have been permitted to see you at all."

"But I might have arranged something—perhaps."

"Would you?"

She flushed slightly. "I mean—well, my going out mightn't have been so important."

All the while he knew a something unnatural, but there seemed nothing to do but prattle on.

"When shall I really find you in?"

"Well"—she frowned—"tomorrow I'm going into the country for some days. Shall I give you a ring as soon as I get back?"

"Will you?"

"Why, of course."

She rose then and he held out his hand with a look of humorous resignation.

"You still can't change your mind?"

She stared.

"Put these people off and come out to tea with me instead."

She laughed and with some curious relief.

"As soon as I come back—perhaps."

"I shall hold you to that."

"I shan't need to be held," she said, and then was closing the door after him.

Travers's face had neither ecstasy nor disappointment as he went past the elevator and down the stairs. As he went through the outer hall he glanced towards the elevator, but apparently Bernice had not yet come down.

Then as he left the hotel, and by its only door, it struck him suddenly that Joy would be leaving with Bernice, and he might be able to judge from their manner whether or not there had been a reconciliation. Joy would have to tidy her tear-stained face, and dress, and that was making the delay. But five minutes went by and nothing happened, so on a sudden impulse he crossed the road and stood at the corner with the hotel porch full in view. Five more minutes passed, and he turned up his coat collar against the east wind and settled dourly to wait.

Half an hour went by. Dusk was changing to night and lights were everywhere, and all at once he hailed a passing taxi. The fact that Joy's tears showed that there must have been a reconciliation with Bernice, was as nothing to his indignation at the trick that had been played on him.

What had happened? Joy had told Bernice that she should have been having tea with Ludovic Travers. But since the maid had announced no name, how did Bernice know that he was in the anteroom? Why then the urgency and almost fierceness in that snapped order to the maid?

Moreover all the windows faced south so his approach to the hotel could not have been seen. Why then was it so important that nobody should know that Joy was at the hotel? And, always, why had the possibility of Joy's being seen made Bernice speak like an angry fishwife?

Bernice, he was now sure, had never been going out at all. She had dressed to give that impression. In plain words, she had lied, and all as a theatrical covering up of the fact that Joy was in her room.

Then Travers shrugged his shoulders. Once more everything was childish and preposterous, and it would be as well to dismiss the whole thing from his mind rather than let temper get the better of him. And after all, something sensible did seem to have happened. There had certainly been some kind of reconciliation, so Barney's contract might yet be signed.

The thought cheered him and irritation faded, and in a minute or two the taxi driver was rejoicing at the size of his tip.

Wharton arrived soon after five and he brought Norris with him. His opening remark, while Palmer was taking the hats and coats, was that he didn't see why Sunday shouldn't afford a little relaxation.

Travers agreed amusedly, knowing what was bound to come. And he was right. No sooner were the pipes going, and the drinks ready on the side table, than Wharton was announcing that the only change to be looked for in the handling of the case was that the Enfield affair had been taken out of his hands.

"Suits me all right," he said. "Even the Archangel Gabriel couldn't prove a blackmail scheme. If His Nibs had certain requirements and Osmund and Corney supplied them—" He shrugged his shoulders for the rest.

"Osmund isn't included," Norris said. "We're still to keep an eye on him. Corney doesn't worry us. He couldn't have been in two places at once." He chuckled. "Damn funny to have seen Corney rigging himself up as Turban."

"Talking of Osmund," Wharton said, "I've got written down here all the various ways I think he may have been implicated in the killing of Amli—and possibly Furloe." He raised a hand at Travers's exclamation of surprise. "Wait till you've heard everything. First I'll take what even Osmund himself would be prepared to admit, *provided we could bust his alibi.*

"I think this would be his story once the alibi was busted: He and Corney had a preliminary talk at the Wardour Street flat, then Corney left for the appointment. At about ten past ten, Corney came back and he'd been running like hell. Osmund heard his tale and knew Amli's death meant there'd be the very devil to pay, so Osmund came to the hotel to see if he could get the Enfield papers. He was too late, so he made out he was there for some other urgent paper. In order to have an alibi for himself, he rang his brother and faked an alibi at the cinema.

"Now it wouldn't do him all that harm to own up to that much. But once, we knew the alibi was a fake, we could move on a bit. I think we could prove he was mixed up with the killing of Amli. We'll take that as a start."

"I really must ask the obvious question," said Travers. "A big scheme of blackmail in the offing, and yet Osmund killed the goose before the egg was laid?"

"Now don't you be in a hurry," Wharton told him genially. "We'll come to that later, but just think of this first. There were empty suites in that hotel, and there was Osmund knowing every detail of routine and being able to come in whenever he liked. The hotel people didn't know he'd been sacked. Why then shouldn't Osmund have entered the hotel at any time during the evening and been lurking in the offing? He might even have heard Amli tell Bond to go out, or he might have seen Bond go. He might have been present or at hand when Amli was killed, and then all he had to do was lie doggo again till the police arrived, and then pop out of his hiding hole bold as brass, as if he'd just arrived."

"Then between the death of Amli and the discovery of the body, he had at least ten minutes," Travers said. "Why didn't he help himself to the Enfield papers?"

"Panic, perhaps. Still, we can leave that objection till it arises."

"Did the clerk actually see Osmund arrive at any time that night?"

"He didn't," Wharton said. "He says it was his instinct to observe the unusual. Osmund wasn't unusual. He was a regular."

Travers admitted the interest of that. Wharton adjusted the antiquated spectacles and consulted his notebook.

"I want you to follow me carefully," he said. "As I see things, once Osmund's alibi is busted we can proceed along two well-defined lines. One is that Osmund himself was Turban, and the other that he wasn't, but was working with the man who was." Up went his hand. "No objections for the moment. You hear my case. And let's begin at number one.

"Osmund was Turban. Then his flat was his headquarters, and he dressed there. He rang Amli at 8:15 and made an appointment, making out—through his peculiar knowledge—that Turban was some Indian pal of Amli's, a pal who wore the beard and was a Sikh or something, as you said. He walked into the hotel, as we know. The interview took place, and what happened we know. Then he went back to his flat, changed, and reappeared at the hotel.

"Interesting sidelights are that when he phoned Amli he could have expressed a wish to be alone with him. He also might have known that Corney was having an interview at ten o'clock; that Corney intended to try and fix it for then, I should have said. Then there's all the special information that Osmund had acquired as Amli's secretary.

"And there's the motive. There we get a split into two parts, depending on whether Osmund intended to kill Amli. At the moment we might lump all the possible motives together. Hatred of Amli and revenge for being sacked? Had Amli threatened to expose him publicly? Was Osmund trying to free himself from Corney, who was a dangerous one to be attached to? Were there papers about which we don't know, in that wallet, which may prove to have been of tremendous importance? Was Osmund stuck on Lotta and therefore jealous of Amli?"

"You're raising some intricate—and, I'll admit, interesting—questions," Travers said. "Anything political, by the way?"

"Oh, no. I'm assured that there were no political troubles in the state. It's a thousand to one against Turban being a genuine Indian."

Travers nodded approval. All the same he had to point out that if Osmund was Turban, there was still to be settled the little matter of Furloe.

Wharton dug a finger in his ribs and chuckled to Norris.

"I knew we'd come to that. Very well then, we'll fit your friend the leaning man into place. Even you will admit that his eyebrows were darkened." Up went his hand. "No, don't tell me about theatre queues again. Norris and I have another idea. Furloe hinted to the parson that he had or was getting work. And when you come to think of it, what sort of people would employ an ex-lunatic?"

"I don't know," Travers said. "If he refused to account for a gap in his career or to supply references, then I can't say—unless he was to be employed on something shady."

"Out of your own mouth!" Wharton raised exulting hands. "Aren't there underground shows that might have employed him? Dirty little dens keep popping up all over the place. And what about the shady touring companies rigged up for abroad? South America, for instance. In order to ship their girls they fake a show of some kind. Furloe may have been one of the real turns. And suppose Furloe discovered just what sort of a show he was in, and threatened to blab, then wasn't that an excellent reason for getting rid of him?"

"Admirable," said Travers. "But where does the wallet come in?"

"Furloe may have picked it up. That will do for the present. If Osmund took the wallet it was for the papers. Besides, he daren't handle the money. Maroulis cashed Amli's checks and took the numbers of all fivers and bigger notes. Osmund knew that, and threw wallet and notes away."

Travers admitted that at least there was something to work on. But talking was thirsty work. Wharton sampled his favourite tipple, said that was better, then consulted the notes again.

"Now we come to the alternative," he said, "and it doesn't take any working out because we've gone over it before. But you always wondered where Furloe could have dressed, and changed back, and been poisoned." He peered over his spectacles. "Why not at Osmund's flat? Handy for everything, as you've admitted?"

"Furloe was Turban?"

"That's it. That's the second line to work on. And Osmund was the one who employed him and led him on. Both Osmund and Turban may have been in the room at the same time. What I mean is that Osmund came in when the struggle began, and if he took a hand it removes most of your objections about Furloe's physique. Everything now fits in, doesn't it?"

Travers was thinking hard, and said nothing.

"We think it does, sir," Norris said. "Furloe walked out of the hotel and Osmund slipped out too and joined him. Then he poisoned poor Furloe before Corney arrived, and turned him loose after giving him the wallet and notes."

"Quick going, surely?" Travers said. "Furloe had to change out of Turban's clothes. Still, we don't know if Corney went straight from the hotel to Osmund's flat. I take it you're checking up on that?"

"I'm seeing Corney at seven o'clock tonight," Wharton said.

"Before we go on," Travers said, "I'd like to mention something. According to the old padre's statement, Furloe had been heard walking about and rehearsing in his room during the week. He possessed a make-up box which always looked as if it was in use. Very well. When Furloe cleaned his face, what would have been easier than to have left a little mascara not cleaned off? *Was* it mascara?"

"It was," Wharton said. "Still, there we are. I've outlined the new plans of campaign and as I told you, they depend entirely on busting Osmund's alibi."

"Mr. Travers has bust a few in his time," Norris said.

"That kind of luck doesn't hold," Travers told him. "But you haven't told me the exact details of the alibi."

"It's this," Wharton said. "He went to the Rembrandt, in Gwynne Street, at eight-thirty, to see the big picture, and he was there till it ended. His brother can prove it."

"Seen the brother?"

"This very morning. He says some lights fused back-screen and he was going backwards and forwards attending to them himself. Osmund had an end seat and that's why the brother kept seeing him."

Travers smiled. "Fits too well. All the same, if it's faked, and the brother cares to risk perjury, we're helpless. The only possible method of attack is to break down the brother's alibi. If he wasn't where he says he was, then he couldn't have been aware of Osmund's whereabouts."

"Yes," Wharton said slowly. "That's not so bad. Tell you what, Norris; we'll put a good man or two on the job. We'll get in touch with everybody who was employed at that theatre on Friday night."

That was virtually the end of the discussion, though Travers made a note of Wharton's new lines of attack:

BREAK OSMUND'S ALIBI

Then work on the assumption that:

1. Osmund was Turban. This releases Furloe from all complicity.

2. Furloe was Turban and Osmund the instigator.

"Mind you," said Wharton when he rose to go, "I'm not implying anything against your friend Furloe, or contradicting the parson's evidence. If Furloe was induced to be Turban, then there's no knowing what yarn Osmund pitched him. Furloe might have thought he was doing an excellent thing." Then, with a speciousness of which Travers was only too aware, "What we should have done without you, I don't know."

"And no other job till you warn me?" smiled Travers.

"Not unless one occurs to yourself," Wharton said. "If it does, let us know. Later on I'll tell you what happened tonight with Corney."

After an early dinner Travers drew a chair well up to the fire, stretched his long legs to the warmth and settled down to a probing of Osmund's alibi.

What he had suggested to Wharton seemed the only way. Or, if any case whatever got so far as the court, then the line might be to discredit the character of the brother and prove him a bad witness. Prove a shady past, for instance, or association with Corney and Lotta in the Enfield affair. Then Travers remembered that the Enfield affair was being kept secret as the grave.

The phone rang. Travers thought that Barney was on the line, so he hunted for words while Palmer took off the receiver.

"Sir Jerome Haire, sir."

Travers hopped up at once.

"Yes, Sir Jerome? Travers speaking."

An ample clearing of a throat was heard at the other end, then came the deliberate voice.

"I'm just off in my friend's car to the country, my boy, but I wondered about poor Colson's funeral. Can't I help with the expenses, provided it's confidential?"

"Everything's being met by a friend," Travers said. "Most good of you, though, to think of it."

"Not at all. Not at all." Another clearing of the throat. "It's distressed me very much and I—er—hoped I might help. Oh, yes, and something else. That—er—statement by yourself that Colson had claimed to have—er—made me what I am, or some damn nonsense like that. . . . I hope that won't be mentioned at the inquest?"

"I'm certain it won't," Travers said. "By the way, the claim was only to have given you a helping hand."

"Well, I'd rather it wasn't mentioned. It might be construed as—er—something else. Very bad for people like me to have fables of that kind spread abroad. I've known a lifetime's reputation undermined by—er—talk of that kind."

"You can be absolutely certain that it won't be mentioned," Travers said.

"Thank you; thank you. Most grateful to you. If—er—you should hear anything of the sort, perhaps you'll take—er—appropriate action."

Travers was wondering what on earth that might be, and then became aware that Sir Jerome had hung up.

He put his own receiver back, stared for a moment into space, then did a curious thing. He darted off to the cloakroom and was back in a moment with hat and coat. Palmer, entering in time for the hurried exit, saw him making for the stairs at the double, and getting into the overcoat at the same time.

CHAPTER X
MORE MYSTERY

AT THE TIME when Sir Jerome phoned, Travers was still much exercised in mind and not a little irritated at the conduct of the Haire sisters. Bernice's duplicity had hurt him more than he cared to admit, and even Joy had treated him shabbily.

Then at the end of Sir Jerome's brief talk, an idea had flashed into Travers's mind. Sir Jerome was just off to the country. Bernice had said she was going to the country the next day, but as she had lied once, why not twice? Why should she not be going with her father at that very moment, and Joy with her? The general rendezvous would almost certainly be Sir Jerome's flat. And who was the friend whom Sir Jerome had mentioned?

In St. Martin's Travers hailed a passing taxi, and the driver must have been surprised to learn that his fare wished to be taken only the three hundred yards to Shaftesbury Avenue. It was a clear, frosty night, and outside Sir Jerome's flat stood a taxi. That was odd, for Sir Jerome had distinctly said the car of the friend was waiting.

"Turn here," Travers told his man. "When that taxi moves off, follow it."

A man—the valet-dresser by the look of him—came out with luggage. Sir Jerome was at his heels and inside two minutes the taxi moved off.

"Very well," said Travers to himself. "The rendezvous isn't here, so it will be at Bernice's hotel."

But the taxi headed the opposite way, down the Strand and over the river. A quarter of an hour later, when both taxis waited for the lights, Travers's man leaned back.

"How much further, guv'nor?"

"Keep going," Travers told him, and passed him a note on account.

The dingier suburbs were left behind, then the gaudier and gimcrack ones, and all at once the front taxi disappeared. It had turned down a private drive, and at the entrance was a board with a plain notice:

M E L C A N T O N   P A R K
Private Hotel

Travers's man asked for instructions.

"Too late to pay calls," Travers told him. "Take me back to where you picked me up."

On the journey back there was plenty of time for thought, and the more he thought, the more he was puzzled and intrigued. At first he was inclined to give Sir Jerome the benefit of every doubt. The friend had phoned that his car was out of order and so Sir Jerome had taken a taxi. Melcanton Park might, by certain comparisons, be described as country. Sir Jerome might be staying there with the friend or as the guest of that friend.

Yet there was something wrong. That taxi must have been waiting while Sir Jerome was phoning, and so there could never have been any such thing as a friend's car. And Sir Jerome had given the impression that he was going well out of town to stay at the friend's house. How could the manager of the hotel, or even the proprietor, be the friend?

Then why should Sir Jerome have seen fit to tell lies to a comparative stranger like Ludovic Travers, and about matters which never need have been mentioned at all? And why should all the Haires have suddenly become a family of liars, for that, in plain terms, was a summary of the happenings of the last twenty-four hours.

Travers went early to bed that night, but just as he was turning in, Wharton rang.

"Everything's working out fine," he said. "When Corney left the hotel he first rang up his pal, the trainer, and put him wise. Then he was on his way to Osmund's flat when he actually ran into Osmund in Piccadilly Circus. They had a quick talk and then Corney went to Osmund's flat, and waited, and Osmund went to the hotel."

"The times fit in?"

"Oh, yes. But here's something else. Corney says Osmund wasn't in on that racehorse game, so Osmund wanted to know what the hell Corney was doing at the hotel. Corney swore Amli himself sent for him, and while Osmund was with us, Corney was ringing Lotta at Enfield and telling her all about things and preparing the tale. Osmund and Corney had a row at Osmund's place and only patched things up at Enfield. Corney's sore at Osmund, and that's why he's talked—unofficially, of course."

"So far, so good then," said Travers.

Wharton chuckled. "Might be worse. But you wait till we've busted Osmund's alibi!"

Next morning Travers awoke with a resolution in mind. The whole Haire family, it seemed to him, had been setting out, for some obscure reasons of their own, to treat him shabbily. Very well then; why should he not do some obscure work himself? At the very least he was entitled to know what lay behind the obscurities of other people. Besides, Barney would be ringing up, and it might be as well to know the whereabouts of Bernice and Joy.

So Travers made no bones about ringing up a certain high-class private inquiry agency which he had found to be implicitly trustworthy and extremely efficient.

"I know I can rely on you for tactful handling," he said, "and I'd also like a report, if possible, before the morning. This is the job I want done:

"Sir Jerome Haire, and his valet with him, are at a private hotel known as Melcanton Park, near Sidcup. First, find out if Sir Jerome *is* there. Second, if he's there as an ordinary paying guest. Third, if he's with a friend, or by himself. Fourth, are his daughters—the Misses Bernice and Joy Haire—with him? Fifth, if they are not there, are they expected, and when? Last, find out how long Sir Jerome proposes to stay there himself."

That business over, Travers began to plan his morning, with Barney always at the back of his mind. By nine-thirty he would be in his office and ringing up to know what had happened at the tea-time interview with Joy; and what was worrying Travers was just what to say to him. Hint at a reconciliation, perhaps, though even that might not be true; and if it were true, it might not include a resumption of the old professional relationships. A cruel thing, too, to buoy up old Barney with hope.

Ten o'clock came. Nothing had happened and Travers lay doggo. As if by stealth he began working on his book, but with the phone bell on his mind, could not settle to work. Then he decided to tackle arrears of correspondence, and when he felt in his breast pocket for accumulated letters, there was the sheet of paper on which he had copied those fragments of words from the hotel blotting-paper.

There, ready for him, was a problem worth attention and attractive in its novelty. Once more he drew up to the fire.

ine . . an eakab ad.

He was glad he had copied that lettering down so carefully, and as a kind of map of the blotted line which it represented. Moreover, as he distinctly remembered, unless the remainder of the letter had never been blotted at all, those disjointed fragments represented the end of that letter, and there had most certainly been a full-stop after the final d.

Eakab seemed the most promising point of attack, but five minutes produced nothing. Then he tried the very end. What was required was a word ending in *ad.* He spent another quarter of an hour trying to complete a list of words ending in *ad*, bearing in mind that the spacing seemed to warrant a word of no more than five letters.

Then when he had his list, he could make no satisfactory application, so he shifted the attack again. He wondered if that e of the *ine* was really a smudged g, for *ing* was a much more likely word ending, and an ending, by the spacing, it certainly seemed. To make a list of all words ending in *ing* would take days at the least.

Five minutes later, Travers had abandoned the problem and was trying the *Times* crossword instead. But the morning was one of his bad ones, with his brain refusing to function, and after a few desultory minutes he laid the paper aside. Then he spent a minute or two at the window. A turn about the room and he came by the table.

He picked up the sheet of paper, intending to put it away in a drawer, and then his eye caught that lettering—*eakab*. The crossword brain, sluggish in itself, now joined forces with the still more sluggish cryptogram brain, and some new force came into action.

Of all the combinations of letters that one tried for the ending of an anagram, *ing, ion,* and *able* were the most likely, and as he saw the *eakab*, he instinctively made it end as *able*. He pronounced the result, and things happened. *Eakable—speakable—unspeakable*—that last was it! The obvious cliché presented itself— *unspeakable cad. An unspeakable cad*—that sounded right, but too much spacing between an and *unspeakable. And an unspeakable cad*—that fitted perfectly, and in the same moment the rest of the words stood clear.

Amli had been writing to some unknown and had ended the letter with:

(you are a) swine and an unspeakable cad.

The spacing fitted, even if the words were somewhat stilted. Travers nodded down at them, smiled, then rang the Yard and asked for Wharton. He happened to be in.

T. Oh, George, about that sheet of blotting-paper that was sent from the Levantic. Have the experts discovered anything interesting on it?

W. I expect it'd have been reported to me if they had. You-know-who have got it now. You know—all that foreign lingo there was on it.

T. Well, remember those fragments of words I copied down? I think I've licked some sense into them. Got a pencil handy? . . . Then take this down. First of all two words in a bracket, to be understood. *You are,* in a bracket. Now the actual words. *A swine and an unspeakable cad.*

W. (After a grunt or two) Just what's the meaning?

T. Well, wasn't Amli writing to someone, and calling him names? Doesn't that suggest reprisals? I mean, haven't we to look for a wholly new suspect?

W. (After more grunts) Well, it might be so. Wait a moment, though. (A chuckle) The letter was written to Osmund.

T. Come, come, George. How could it possibly have been? Amli sacked Osmund by word of mouth.

W. We're not certain. And if he had sacked Osmund by word of mouth, that isn't to say he didn't find out a few more things about him later. (Another chuckle) This letter of yours was the soldier's farewell!

T. (Somewhat amused) That's not so bad, George. Still, I'll leave the few remarks with you. Anything new at your end, by the way?

W. Nothing. Soon as there is, we'll let you know.

Travers, still smiling at Wharton's ingenuity, put the sheet of paper away. Then the outer door bell rang and he wondered who the caller could be. Ten to twelve, the clock said. Norris, perhaps—

"Mr. Josephs, sir."

Travers whipped round. Palmer was showing Barney in— and yet he was not, for Barney was showing himself in. He was rushing past Palmer like a human cyclone, his face one immense beam and his hand well out. Then his hand grasped that of the amazed Travers, and worked it violently up and down, and all the time he was talking.

"Mr. Travers, I want to thank you. I come here to thank you. How can I thank you? I don't know—"

The hand was relinquished and he shrugged his shoulders, but only to indicate that words failed him.

"You mean-"

"Signed! The contract is signed!"

Up went the palms and out shot the hand again. Travers shook it warmly.

"Barney, I'm delighted. When did it all happen? Tell me about it."

But old Barney was sinking into a chair and mopping his forehead. A full head of steam had been let off at one go, and now the reaction was coming.

"Let me get you a drink?" Travers said anxiously. "Beer? Sherry?"

"Sherry, beer, anything," Barney said, and then looked aghast. "What am I saying? Mr. Travers, I do not know if I am on my head or my heels."

Travers laughed, and poured out some sherry. Barney took a gulp, said that was better, then began getting his story out. Miss Bernice had rung him at his private address very early that morning and had asked to have the details of the contract read over to her. Barney, whom they had haunted for days, knew them by heart, and tremblingly obliged. Then she said she would be at his office at ten o'clock. She came, and Miss Joy with her, and after some discussion of the contract itself, it was signed.

"And what excuses were made for the delay?" Travers asked.

Barney shrugged his shoulders. As soon as the contract was signed, he had ventured on a humble reprimand. Miss Bernice had patted his shoulder and expressed regret, but the reasons were ones of health, she said, which were confidential. And she had wished to save Barney every anxiety.

"A pretty cool statement," commented Travers. "But how did the two seem to be getting along with each other?"

Barney said they seemed most friendly, but it was Joy whose health must have caused anxiety. Bernice had looked as cool and assured as ever, but Joy had been curiously quiet. Usually she would treat Barney to imitations of himself, and twit him about his exorbitant commission, and show high spirits generally.

"You believed that health excuse?"

"Mr. Travers," said Barney, and spread his palms, "the client is always right. But why should I worry? The contract is signed. I posted it myself. I tell you, Mr. Travers, I clutched it like this; like as if it was gold and diamonds."

"And when do they sail?"

"They sail—what is today? I cannot think." His fingers went distractedly through his hair. "Monday? Then they sail in ten days. Wednesday week, that is." He got to his feet. "Now I must get back."

"Don't forget your sherry," Travers reminded him.

Barney let out a breath and shook his head.

"What did I say? Still I don't know if I am on my head or my heels." He paused in the act of emptying the glass. "Mr. Travers, if there is ever anything I can do, let me know. Ring me. Come and see me. Write to me."

"Please, Barney," said Travers. "I assure you I've done nothing at all. I'm as delighted as you are but I can't let you think I contributed in the least."

Barney smiled knowingly, and shook his head again.

"I know, Mr. Travers. Some people would say they had done a lot. Everything, perhaps. You say you have done nothing. I know. I know."

"Ah, well," sighed Travers, "if you won't be convinced, then —" He remembered something. "There *is* a little something you can do for me. I'd like to see Miss Bernice on a private matter. Where is she at the moment? Do you know?"

Barney clapped a hand to his head.

"Let me think. . . . No, I have forgotten. Somewhere in the country for a few days. They were going at once—both of them." His face gaped with a look of comical dismay. "Wait, though. All the time I have it."

He showed Travers his personal address book, and as soon as Travers saw it, he was surprised, for the address was not Melcanton Park, but The Croft, Padgley Down, Sussex.

"How long are they going to be there?" Travers asked.

Barney rubbed his chin, then looked at the book again.

"Here it is. Next Monday. They did say there might be a good-by party, what they call a Columbus, or something."

There was more handshaking and then Travers saw Barney to the lift. There Barney began new thanks. Travers shepherded him inside, waved a cheery hand and went back to the room.

The room seemed curiously quiet when he drew his chair to the fire again, and he seemed always to be listening for something as he polished his glasses. Not a single mystery had been solved, as he saw things, but Bernice had been indulging in still more prevarication. How could health account for the relations that had existed for weeks between herself and Joy?

Then he was shaking his head. Bernice had suddenly become a wholly new, and strange, and very irritating person. Bernice, the rigid and moral, stooping to cheap and unnecessary lies. Bernice, the reposeful and assured, snapping out an order like an angry fishwife.

And Padgley Down, why the choice of that particular place? As far as he remembered he had never heard either Bernice or Helen even mention it. Quite an out-of-the-way little spot, and he could think of no friends of theirs who might live there.

Then he sighed. Some new mystery, apparently to be added to the others. But why should he not make a call at Padgley Down? Why not, indeed? It could be done without giving Barney away. On his journey to Helen's place on the Friday he might make a slight detour, and contrive somehow to run across either Bernice or Joy.

That same evening, during dinner, the report came in from the inquiry office, though only over the phone. The following were the answers to his questions.

1. The One-in-Question *is* staying at the hotel.

2. He is an ordinary paying guest.

3. No special friend of his is there, and the management have not been told to expect one.

4. His daughters are not there.

5. They are not expected.

6. The O-in-Q leaves on Sunday morning, according to present arrangements.

Within an hour the more detailed report had come, and it had two additions. Sir Jerome had informed the hotel management that his health had been none too good, and he had come for rest and complete quiet. He preferred to be known as Mr. Jerome, and the management had been asked to discourage questions and publicity.

In the course of that talk the fact had emerged that Sir Jerome was traveling up North on the Sunday evening to fulfil an engagement in Liverpool during the week following.

Now there was no new mystery in that report, unless it was that Sir Jerome, who was a courter of publicity, should all at once be avoiding it. Most decidedly he would be in need of quiet and rest after the strain of one week and as preparation for a new.

Yet one fact still remained, and one mystery was even all the more mysterious. Why, in heaven's name, had Sir Jerome seen fit to lie about those movements of his? And why had he chosen as the recipient of those lies a person so little known to him as Ludovic Travers?

The final event of that day was a letter which arrived by the very last post. It was from the Secretary of the Central Hospital.

DEAR TRAVERS,

A matter has arisen on which your views and advice would be welcomed.

There will be a meeting of the Finance Committee tomorrow (Tuesday) at 3 P.M. and we should be most grateful if you would attend.

Yours truly,

GEO. WILBURY.

Travers made a note on his engagement pad, asked Palmer also to remind him, and then thought no more about it.

CHAPTER XI

THE EMERALD RING

ONLY FOUR MEMBERS of the Finance Committee were present at the meeting. The agenda looked like pure routine and its various items were soon worked through, till at soon after four o'clock there remained only that usual endpiece—any other business.

Then Lord Abergayne looked at Wilbury. Wilbury cleared his throat, rose, remembered that the meeting had up to the moment been informal, and sat down again.

"A small package, gentlemen, reached here yesterday morning by registered post. It contained this letter"—he flourished it—"which bears no address. It says:

Sent to be sold on behalf of the Hospital's special appeal, by

A WELLWISHER.

The gift was this ring."

He passed the ring to the chairman who had obviously seen it before. A quick glance which had in it nevertheless a considerable admiration, and the ring was handed to Sir Arthur Barlet, the oil magnate. He looked, stared, grunted, then passed it on to Travers. Travers, whose eyes at the first glimpse of it had nearly bolted from his head, was now dead sure that the ring was the one he had seen on the finger of Joy Haire.

The chairman was speaking.

"I should say that the secretary and I had some talk before deciding to call this meeting. We have taken no opinion as to the value of the ring, but in my own view it is extremely valuable. What do you say, Barlet?"

"I'm no expert," Barlet said, "but I know it has that deep velvety green that really valuable emeralds have. What's it worth, Travers? A thousand?"

"Nearer two, I should say," Travers told him. "I don't know if you were at the de Marneau sale, but a rather smaller one made sixteen hundred."

"Well, gentlemen," said Abergayne, "we shall of course acknowledge the gift in the usual way in the personal columns. As for selling it, that, I think you will agree, is a matter in which we must move with the utmost circumspection. In fact, we oughtn't to sell till we're sure."

"You think it may be stolen property?" Barlet said.

"Well, there's the possibility. I do think the police should be consulted." He glanced at Travers. "We are fortunate in having a member who has contacts with the police authorities."

"Without moving a formal proposition, I suggest this," Travers said. "Let me take a description of the ring to Scotland Yard. Then if they decide to send an expert to see it further, we should grant facilities. Oh, and might I have the letter? Whose prints are on it, by the way?"

"Only the chairman's and my own," Wilbury said.

"That's most helpful then," said Travers. "I will take your prints now. Then the Yard will examine the letter and any prints that are not yours should be those of the sender. If the Yard have the prints, then their owner will be asked to explain. If the prints are unknown, then our minds should be considerably easier."

There was some hilarity as Travers, with gloved hands, took the prints. The whole proposal was moved and seconded and entered in the minutes.

"Now what about having the ring valued?" Abergayne asked. "And what expert should we get?"

"Why not my cousin, Henry?" Barlet asked. "It's his job, and I know he's consulted by the biggest people."

"The very man!" Abergayne said. "I propose Mr. Henry Barlet be asked. You'd better move it as a formal proposition, Mr. Travers."

"By the way," Barlet said, "he's got to be asked at once. I happen to know he's off to Paris tomorrow afternoon. Would some time in the morning suit everybody?"

Ten o'clock was decided on and Barlet agreed to warn the parties if Henry could not come. By the morning too, Travers might have a report.

Everybody was happy. The course of action was proposed and seconded and duly entered. Another five minutes and the four had gone their several ways.

Travers made for the Yard. Neither Wharton nor Norris was in but he found Collins.

"You don't want to know the age of the prints?" the sergeant asked.

"Only to see if you have them recorded," Travers told him.

"Then we'll have a squint at them here"—he blew the powder—"and then nip along to C.R.O."

Plenty of prints showed up. Wilbury had been right, for once his prints and Abergayne's were eliminated, one set only remained.

"Not unlike a woman's," Collins said. "Long and thin, and very clear. Now let's go and see what they've got, sir."

While the records were being examined, they went through lists of lost and stolen jewellery, and a description of the ring was prepared for the *Police Gazette*.

"We haven't got these, sir," Collins reported.

"Then would you mind just writing it down officially?" Travers said. "It'll be a kind of certificate to file with the letter."

Travers returned to his flat and, over a belated tea, began to work things out. Amazing that the ring should have been sent to his own particular hospital! And lucky too that he had examined the ring so closely before Joy was aware of it. And then she had distinctly given the impression that it was paste, a statement which even then he found hard to believe, marvellous though such reproductions could sometimes be.

Fortunate too for Joy that he had been there to handle things. Had it been Arthur Barlet who had recognized it, for instance, there might have been awkward questions—for Joy. Now nothing could arise, for there could be no danger in that paragraph in the *Police Gazette*. Joy was neither thief nor kleptomaniac.

"Shall I have a word myself with Joy, or shall I not?" said Travers. "But wait a moment. Maybe the prints aren't Joy's. If they are, there may be something fishy about that ring, and she'd only fob me off with fairy-tales. If they aren't, then she may have lost the ring. Better get a piece of paper and work the whole thing out."

The first thing that he assured himself was that he was not being merely curious. If the police and the hospital were making inquiries about the ring, and unknown to Joy, then he ought to undertake a kind of watching brief over her interests. Then, even before he began to put his ideas down on paper, he knew he was indulging in nothing less than pious humbug.

The truth was that yet another mystery was nagging away. A new puzzle was to be added to those others that during the last few days had accompanied every action and movement of the whole Haire family. To those mysteries he had no clue. Now, in the emerald ring, he had a clue substantial enough, and one that might be the solver of the whole mysterious series.

Now he settled down with pen and paper to clarify ideas and test them out. What was it he had said to Barney that morning in the Park? *"Cherchez l'homme!"* A good guess, surely. That quarrel between the sisters had arisen over a man. And during the homeward voyage. And precisely why?

a. Both had fallen in love with the same man, and Joy had been successful.

b. Joy had got herself secretly engaged to some man who was wholly unsuited to her.

The reasons seemed the only ones possible, and he proceeded to examine them closely. The first he rejected. For one thing he could not imagine Bernice as being in love at all, even—let it be candidly admitted—with himself. And she was not the kind—in spite of those irritating and bewildering actions of the Sunday—to take defeat ungracefully and, indeed, childishly.

But that second reason seemed foolproof. Joy's engagement to X was a secret one though she had confided it to Bernice. If it had not been secret, then it would have been announced. Bernice, while keeping the secret, had considered the match so unsuitable that she had put pressure on Joy by breaking off professional relationships.

Yes, thought Travers, it all works in admirably. There was, for instance, no point in going on with that American tour if Joy was determined to get married. And, of course, not a word could be breathed to Barney. Meanwhile Bernice was working hard and applying the pressure. Then Joy was the one to give way.

The man had been given up, reconciliation had followed and the contract was signed.

There, but for Ludovic Travers, the matter might have ended. Wharton had once said of him that the fact that there are two sides to every question, was for him merely an incentive to hunt for a third. Now Travers proceeded to find the leaks in that same cast-iron case, and probe for flaws and fallacies. Within five minutes he had the following questions to answer:

1. Why send the ring to a hospital? Surely it should have been returned to the man?

2. Why the anonymity and disguised writing?

3. Surely the ring was too valuable to be given as a mere engagement ring?

He was about to add a fourth question, as to why Joy had not worn the ring on her engagement finger, but he saw at once the needlessness of that. It would have been announcing an engagement. But she had taken the risk of wearing it on another finger, since it was something no woman could resist the temptation to wear.

As to the three questions, Travers lay back in the chair and with eyes closed did some hard thinking. His final answers were these:

Bernice had known the man was a wrong 'un. Joy would not listen to her, so, on her arrival in England, Bernice set to work to obtain evidence, and she had succeeded. She had even been able to prove that the man had no right to the ring he had given. Very well then; to avoid all scandal, the ring had been sent to the hospital. That ring had excited Bernice's suspicions from the start as being far too valuable for the man to own and give away.

Travers sat up in his chair and gave himself a smile. Those latest deductions were infallible. Still, for a final testing, how did they fit in with the amazing conduct of Bernice and Joy as far as concerned himself?

How did they fit? With a precision that was uncanny. Now Travers had a clear view of events. He knew what Joy had intended to confide to him on the Sunday, and why she had pre-tended the ring was paste. At that chance meeting at Sir Je-rome's flat there had been a partial reconciliation, and Joy had put off the engagement with himself. On the Sunday at Bernice's hotel the full reconciliation had taken place. But the risk of any scandal getting out was so terrifying to Bernice that she had snapped that order to the maid when the open door revealed the presence of Joy. As to the pretences of going out, well, if he had stayed on, Bernice must have asked him into that room, and it was most likely strewn with Joy's possessions. Or Joy might have had hysteria or a minor breakdown—Barney had described her as unwell and not herself on the Monday—and so Bernice had taken one way of getting rid of the man with whom Joy at that moment should have been having tea.

There was just one last thing which Travers felt he would like to know—the name of the man. He might, for instance, be a member of one's own circle and a rogue in mufti, so to speak. Joy might be impulsive and at times irresponsible, but it would be interesting to see the man who had carried her off her feet and for the possession of whom she had put up so good a fight.

Perhaps somebody at the *Record* office might know the name of the ship. After that he might some time run his eye over the passenger list and see if there was a name that was familiar to him. The clock said seven, which was early for the *Record*, but he managed to catch Matching of the gossip column. By way of bribe Travers mentioned the forthcoming departure of the Haire sisters.

"Thanks a lot," Matching said. "I'll take your tip and get hold of Barney Josephs."

"Remember my name's not to be mentioned," Travers said. "And now we're more or less on the subject, I suppose you can't tell me what boat the Haires came back on from Australia? I want to clear up a little argument."

"Hang on for a minute," he was told. "Or perhaps I'd better give you a ring later."

The information came just after dinner. Matching said the boat they had landed in England from was the *Deccan*, and they had sailed from Perth in the *Royal Emblem*.

"I don't quite get you," Travers said. "Isn't the *Deccan* one of the Provinces Line?"

"That's right," Matching said. "They came to Calcutta in the *Royal Emblem*, and left on the *Deccan* from Madras."

"Very stupid of me," Travers said. "I see it now. Good-by, and thanks very much."

So Bernice and Joy had done a short tour of Northern and Central India on their way home; which was something he should certainly have known for himself. Indeed, he remembered now something he had read somewhere or heard mentioned. But that engagement of Joy's must have been amazingly quick work! If Bernice and Joy had left India on good terms with each other, and they must have done if they had given their usual performances together, then everything had happened in that short period between Madras and London. Unless, of course, the man had been on the boat from Perth and had also landed in India.

But the main thing that arose out of that evening's deductions, and the certainty that those deductions were correct, was a certain shame in the mind of Travers for his mistrust and misjudgment of Bernice. Out of the humility came a quick surge of affection, and that night Ludovic Travers was nearer to being in love than he had ever been, even in those far-off susceptible days which maturity can view with tolerance and a kindly humour.

The morning's meeting at the Hospital was a very short affair. Travers presented his report and returned the letter, but made no mention of the fact that the previous evening he had very patiently made a copy of the prints.

Henry Barlet showed merely a courteous and expected surprise at the sight of the ring.

"Very fine indeed," he said, and took it to the window. There a strong glass was run over it, the callipers measured it and the scales weighed it.

"You realize," he told the meeting, "that a private sale would be more advantageous than a public one? There's always the luck element about a public sale, even with stones of this quality."

Travers was delighted. The last thing he wanted was for that ring to be on view before a sale, and plainly visible to some friend of Joy's. Indeed, he had not thought of that way in which talk might get about.

"You can find a private buyer?" he asked.

"I think so," Barlet said. "If I do, I shall hold out for eighteen hundred. I might need time, of course. And naturally I shouldn't charge commission."

The offer was accepted at once. The ring was handed over to Barlet and the necessary guarantees were given. It was a Paris buyer he had in mind, and unless in the meanwhile a warning were received from Scotland Yard, he hoped to have news before the week was out.

The morning was cold and bracing, and when Travers left the hotel he felt a sudden desire for a brisk walk. So he made the complete tour of St. James's and then headed for Piccadilly Circus, with Charing Cross Road and the book shops in mind.

He was opposite the Paliceum when he caught sight of Wharton coming from the entrance hall. A man was with him—the manager, by the look of him—and the two stood for a moment or two in earnest talk, and Wharton made a note in his book. A handshake and he was hurrying off. Travers cut across and headed him off.

"Well, well," said Wharton, and looked delighted at the encounter. "A bit early for you to be out, isn't it?" A tea-shop caught his eye. "You're not in a hurry? Right, then let's drop in here for a cup of coffee."

Travers knew from his manner that something was in the wind, for he had that air of quiet yet genial importance, as if his bosom harboured things of tremendous moment, but which to himself were merely new burdens on shoulders already sagging.

"You saw me leaving the Paliceum?" he said.

"I did. And I thought you might be making inquiries along the lines you indicated on Sunday night."

"Just what I was doing. I've paid three visits to the Paliceum inside twenty-four hours. Nothing that you would guess, though. By chance we happened to hear that an Indian was at the second house there last Friday night."

Up went his hand before Travers could put the question.

"I know what you're going to say. What sort of an Indian, and Indians are twopence a bundle, like radishes."

Travers smiled. "Very well, George. To save time, consider I've said it."

But Wharton was referring to his notebook.

"This Indian was the kind we're looking for. He wore a kind of frock-coat, white turban, gloves, and had a black beard. He was the same height as our friend Turban and the same build."

He peered over his spectacles to see if Travers was duly impressed.

"What's more, he walked just like Turban. The hotel clerk told me he walked as if he glided, and didn't swing his arms about."

"Very interesting," Travers said. "And the Levantic's about three minutes from here."

"Now we're getting to it!" The old General raised a suggestive finger. "Let's go back to Sunday night and our little chat. The Osmund-Furloe theory, if you like. Well, now, if you were coming from Osmund's end of Wardour Street and making for the Levantic, wouldn't you go past the Paliceum? Of course you would.

"Now listen to what happened last Friday night. The second house had begun about ten minutes when this Indian walked in and asked for a stall, and out of the two or three he was offered, he took a back one at the end of a row. The girl says he had only a slight accent. The program girl bears her out."

"They had a near view?"

"Well, naturally. I admit the girl in the box was behind her grille and the program girl saw him only in the dark. They admit he was an oldish man in spite of the black beard, but neither can give reasons. All the answers I got were: 'Well, he seemed so,' or: 'I thought he was.' Mind you, I'm not grumbling. They didn't say he was a much younger man than Furloe could have been."

Travers nodded. "And the crux of the matter is not when the Indian entered, but when he left."

"Exactly!" said Wharton. "And when do you think he did leave? At half-past nine! I can't get it nearer than that, but it suits me well enough. And he left by the side exit because the commissionaire saw him coming out of Winton Street and going in the direction of the Levantic. The commissionaire says he was a biggish man. In bulk, he meant, not height."

"But Furloe wasn't bulky," objected Travers.

"I knew you'd say that," Wharton told him with a vast complacence. "Can't an actor increase his bulk? What about Tree's Falstaff?"

Travers had to laugh. "George, first of all you put questions into my mouth and then you supply the answers. However, what's next?"

"Nothing but fitting things in," Wharton said.

"But first I'll be fair. I admit that London's swarming with Indians, and quite a lot are biggish men and have black beards. Even so, when I've finished I think you'll admit the odds are that it was our friend Turban. The trouble is, we can't get any further. He went into the fog and wasn't seen till he entered the hotel. In the same way, when he left the hotel he stepped into the fog and it's a million to one against us being able to pick him up. Already every taxi driver in London's been questioned about Turban as a possible fare. And about Furloe as he was when you saw him."

Travers was shaking his head. Wharton got his own arguments in first.

"Mind you, I know all your old objections to Furloe, but you hear all I've got to say. One of your objections I can remove at once. Furloe hadn't any scratches and the bruises on his wrists weren't much. Well, he was wearing gloves, wasn't he? We know that, or he'd have left prints. And what about this:

"Had Furloe been in a mental institution or had he not? You keep thinking about him as a normal person who'd once been abnormal. The leaning man!" He grunted. "Leaning man, my foot! And then there's the parson. A nice old gentleman, as I know, because I've spent several days down there, at odd times, I mean. He makes Furloe that same pathetic kind of character that appeals to you. But you're both wrong. You never had any contact with Furloe at all, and the parson hadn't seen him for days."

"Admitted. But what's it all lead to?"

"To this," said Wharton, and leaned forward. "Why should Furloe's actions have been normal during the last few days of his life? You and the parson have got it in your minds that he was a sane man who wanted to be an actor once more. I've got it in my mind that he was a man who'd become abnormal again. Mad, if you like, or just a puppet, but with someone else's brain behind him. Furloe, really mad this time, but under the control of that murderous devil Osmund."

"You're putting the argument rather strongly," Travers told him, "but I'll admit it's something that's never occurred to me."

"And another thing," went on Wharton triumphantly. "Furloe was ready to play his part as Turban, but there was still some time to wait. Where would an old actor like him decide to spend it? Why, at a show. He went past the Paliceum and thought he might as well wait there as anywhere else. And in the dark he'd be free from observation. Meanwhile Osmund was also in the dark—at the cinema, preparing an alibi."

He hailed the passing waitress and asked for the bill, then got to his feet. Travers had a final thought.

"But everything in the Osmund-Furloe theory depends on busting Osmund's alibi."

Wharton gave a prodigious wink.

"Don't you worry about that. I'm just off to see about that now. We've found a little crack in it already. If we don't prise it clean open, then my name's Higgins."

Chapter XII
TRAVERS IS FRIGHTENED

ON THURSDAY MORNING Travers woke with an uneasy mind. A problem was facing him, and it persisted as a kind of restlessness and dulled the interests of the day.

He had still the wish to make some kind of amends to Bernice, and above all to see her again after those two previous truncated visits. That rebound, after irritation and suspicion, was no temporary thing, and now the very distance from her was idealizing everything and casting about things a pleasurable vagueness. But for Wharton he would have gone down to Sussex that same day.

But Travers was refusing to face up to the truth. It was no loyalty to Wharton that was keeping him in town, for the chances were that Wharton would have no need of him. What he was really itching to know was the progress of Wharton's inquiries, and whether the crack in Osmund's alibi had as yet become a wide-open breach.

After lunch he took a walk round the area which had been connected with the affair at the Levantic. He stood for a minute or two looking at the window against which that poor devil Furloe had leaned.

Then he went past the Rembrandt, and its commissionaire dolled up like a Balkan guardsman. He had a good look at the Wardour Street shop above which was Osmund's flat, and then he turned back and made for the Levantic, passing the Paliceum on his way.

But there was never a sign of either Wharton or Norris, whom he had faintly hoped to meet, so he cut through to Whitehall and so to the Yard. Wharton was in his room.

"Got hold of something?" he asked at once.

"Wish I had," Travers told him. "The fact is I have to be away tomorrow, so I thought I'd hear the latest. I'm leaving Palmer at the flat, by the way."

"The latest," Wharton said, and pulled a wry face. "Well, the latest is this. If you'd asked me this morning how things were coming along, I'd have said Osmund was for the high jump. Now I don't know."

"You thought you'd busted the alibi?"

"Yes," he said. "And I still think we'll bust it. The trouble is it depends on the evidence of the commissionaire—or whatever you call those chaps who stand outside cinemas. He's a decent sort with a wife and two kids, and he's already had one spell out of a job."

"He daren't talk?"

"Not openly. What he's confided is this: Round about half-past nine on Friday night he saw a couple of suspicious characters just round the corner in Ravenal Street where some cars were parked, so he took a stroll that way. Only a dozen yards, or he wouldn't have seen anything through the fog. That's when he saw Osmund cross the road as if he'd just left the cinema, by the side exit in Ravenal Street. He knows Osmund on account of him being the manager's brother."

Travers nodded. "You don't want to run the risk of making the commissionaire lose his job."

"Yes, and as things stand, it'd be his single word against the manager's. But we've got another witness, if we can rope him in. The commissionaire described one of those suspicious characters and Norris thinks he's Tubby Tate—that's the moniker he goes by. Osmund bumped into Tubby, so Tubby must have had a good look at him. Norris is out after Tubby now."

"That's good enough, surely?" Travers said.

"Not so good as you'd think," Wharton told him. "Even if Tubby would talk, he's none too good a witness to have to depend on in court. His record's too well known. But what we might do is to get him and Osmund somehow face to face. That might set the ball rolling. How, I don't know. I was just trying to work things out when you came in."

"Anything from the Furloe side?"

"Nothing," Wharton said. "And there won't be. I've questioned the maids, I've been through the room with a fine comb, and I've turned the old parson inside out."

Just as Travers was going, Norris phoned to say he'd that minute heard that Tubby had been pinched that morning for a car job at Battersea, and would Wharton himself like to come over.

Wharton said he most certainly would, and fixed a rendezvous.

"If we can prove Osmund was out of that cinema at nine-thirty, then we're all right," he told Travers. "Everything will fit like a glove. When Furloe told Osmund round about half-past eight that he ought to go out and test the disguise, Osmund agreed. He said, 'Do as you like, provided you're at the Levantic at the time I've fixed up. I'll be there myself, and if there's any trouble—which there won't be—about you getting in, then I'll be there to make it all right.' You noticed, of course, that Furloe left the Paliceum at nine-thirty."

Later that night Wharton rang up.

"Tubby swears he was never within a mile of the Rembrandt on Friday night. Says he's got witnesses to prove it."

"That's awkward," Travers said.

"I'm not worrying," Wharton told him. "I know Tubby's witnesses. And he probably did a job himself near the Rembrandt on Friday and doesn't want it remembered. The very night for a car job." He gave a little chuckle. "Don't you worry about Tubby. He'll talk all right. They always do."

An early lunch on Friday, and Travers set off for Sussex. At three o'clock he reached the small village of Padgley Down, and there he had an astounding piece of luck, for just as he was about to pull the car up at a cottage to ask the whereabouts of The Croft, he saw Joy swinging along down the lane ahead of him.

He overtook her, then stopped the car and looked back.

"I thought I couldn't be mistaken. What on earth are you doing here?"

She was taken aback for no more than a moment.

"If it comes to that, what are you doing here?"

"Just off for my usual weekend at Helen's place," he said. "But what about a lift?"

"I'm only going to the post-office," she said, but got in all the same. "We're sending out invitations to Monday's party and we've run out of envelopes."

Travers let the car dawdle and chatted brightly away. The invitations, he learned in a roundabout way, were not for The Croft but for the Ballater Hotel on Monday.

"We sail on Wednesday," she told him casually. "Touring the States, you know, and Canada."

"Heavens!" said Travers. "How quickly you make up your minds!"

They were already at the post-office.

"Mind waiting?" she said.' And to his questioning look, "You must come to tea. Bernice would never forgive me if I didn't bring you."

A charming girl, Joy, he thought, and wondered once again how she could have been such a fool as to get herself entangled with an undesirable.

He felt for a match to light his cigarette and found an empty box. In the shop there was no sign of Joy, but as he was leaving it he saw her in the telephone booth with her back to him. He smiled at that. She would be ringing up the house to warn Bernice there was to be a third for tea.

Joy came out and called to him to wait another minute. She had to go to the baker's.

"Must feed you on something," she said, "I'm positive there isn't a thing in the house. We're both slimming."

The car moved off and she gave him the most delightful of smiles.

"I haven't seen you, Ludo, since that cocktail party. Wasn't it frightfully bad luck having to be out of town instead of going to some wonderful place for tea? Do tell me where you'd have taken me."

"Oh, no," Travers told her. "There may be a chance yet. But about the confidences. Too late for them, is it?"

She laughed. "But I never admitted there were any!"

Travers shook a sad head.

"You're taking a great risk. I'm the most inquisitive person, and sooner or later I'm bound to find out. I have the vaguest inkling at this moment."

There was a silence, and he knew he had startled her. Then she laughed.

"Well, what was I going to tell you?"

He hesitated for a moment, then smiled.

"Oh, no. Tell you what I'll do, though. In confidence between you and me, I'll throw out a hint or two before I go. Won't that be rather fun?"

"Here we are," she said quickly. "Just down this lane, and turn by that tree."

It was quite a large house, with an old barn that had been fitted out as a studio.

"It belongs to an artist friend of ours," she said, "and he's now abroad. The studio's marvellous for rehearsals. Leave the car here, Ludo, and I'll find Bernice."

He entered the hall at her heels, and she opened the drawing-room door. Then as he waited by the fire he heard her voice from just outside, at the foot of the stairs.

"Ber-NiCE! . . . Ber-NiCE! . . . I've brought someone to tea! . . . Ludo Travers. . . . He'll tell you."

There was a longish wait and then the two came in together. Bernice was lovely. The scarlet jumper and the black skirt suited her to perfection, and went delightfully with the flushed ivory of her cheeks and the velvety black of her hair.

"How fortunate of you to see Joy!" she said. "And you're staying to tea?"

"I insist on staying to tea," he said.

She laughed. "Let's go into the work-room. It's frightfully untidy but you won't mind that."

It was all quite littered, with what looked like dress materials strewn about, and the table piled with writing materials. Joy stooped and stirred the fire.

"Darling," said Bernice suddenly, "do keep an eye on the tea. Cook is out and Fanny burns everything."

"The scones," she explained as Joy went out.

"Rather a tragedy that tour of yours that Joy has just told me of," he said.

"A tragedy?"

"Yes. Apparently I shall have at least three months to wait for that private tea you promised me."

She smiled. "But you're about to have it!"

He shook his head. "Own up, Bernice. Was that in your mind when you promised?"

"No questions," she said. "I've hated questions ever since I was made to learn catechism."

"Ah, well," he said. "I expect you'd have had a very dreary time. I always insist on talking such a lot of nonsense."

"But I love nonsense!"

"Do you?" He shook his head. "But this might have been serious nonsense."

Their eyes met and it was hers that fell. Then Joy came breezily in and the moment of revelation and delicious intimacy had gone.

"Come along, darlings. Everything's getting cold."

So back to the drawing-room for tea. Travers felt enormously happy. He knew a sure understanding between himself and Bernice, and there was the cheerful prattling of Joy, the pleasant comfort of the room and the friendly informality of the meal.

"You're not looking so well as when I saw you last," Bernice told him.

"Age, with stealthy steps and slow," he said.

"You must discard all that on Monday," Joy said.

"So lucky your visit today. Now we shan't have to send your invitation. The Ballater Hotel, at five-thirty."

"Where's your father these days?" Travers suddenly asked.

"I believe he's staying in the country," she said. "On Monday he opens in Liverpool for a week's engagement."

"You're looking forward to your own tour?"

They began discussing it, and Travers at last tried a feeler.

"I'm afraid Joy will come back engaged to some charming young American."

She avoided his look and there seemed all at once a quick coldness in the room.

"Ah, well," Travers went blundering on. "I suppose you're determined to be wedded to your art and to live for your public."

"And why not?"

"Why not indeed?" he said. "All the same, if the truth were known, you've probably been engaged a dozen times already."

Again there seemed an awkward silence, then Bernice cut in, and obviously to help.

"Helen isn't too far from here, is she? I wonder if she could slip over?" She frowned. "Oh, bother! Tomorrow we have all sorts of people here."

"There'll be time when you return," Travers told her.

The talk went on but the gay indifference had gone. Something he had said had touched Joy closely, and it could have been only that reference to an engagement. It was only when he was ready to go that the old, unforced friendliness came back.

"You mustn't come out to the car," he said. "It's bitterly cold."

"I'll put on a wrap," Bernice told him.

Joy said good-by and it seemed for a moment that she was about to ask some question; then the seriousness passed and she was telling him to be early at the party. Bernice, shoulders hunched beneath the wrap, saw him off from the steps of the porch.

"Good-by," she said. "It was lovely of you to come."

"Really?"

She nodded. "Really."

He gave a queer shake of the head and moved the car on. The last glimpse he had of her was a darkness against the friendly warmth of the lighted porch.

Uncertain of his way in the now gathering dusk, he let the car dawdle through the narrow lanes and tried to put himself once more under the spell of the hour and its last few moments. But the mood was uncaptured, and soon the old Adam of curiosity began insidiously to work.

If Joy had phoned Bernice from the post-office, why had she pretended at the house that Bernice knew nothing? Joy had intended him to hear her call up the stairs, for she had called loudly enough to shake the very attic. And why had Bernice made herself part of the pretence? Was it necessary, and why, that Bernice should be aware that he was coming to tea and yet have to pretend to be unaware? But a more serious problem faced him when he regained the main road. What was to be done with those prints of Bernice and Joy that he had just secured? Surely there was something underhand in taking them, and doubly so in keeping them? Decency surely demanded that he should pull up the car, tear them up and throw them out of the window.

But somehow there never seemed to be a time when he could pull the car up, and he put the matter off till he should get to his room. But when the greetings were over and he really was at last in his bedroom, a moment of indecision ruined the fine intentions, and he was telling himself that to know exactly who Wellwisher was, was merely to serve the interests of both Joy and Bernice.

So he took out his copy of the Wellwisher print, dusted the card and envelope, and began to compare. Then the shock came. The prints were those of Bernice!

For a long minute he stood by the table, polishing his glasses and blinking away in the light. Then suddenly he smiled relievedly, knowing the sequence was clear. The talk at the tea-table and the very silences told him his deductions had been correct. The engagement theory had been the only possible one. Bernice had drawn Joy back to sense and safety, and it had been Bernice who had decided to send the ring to the hospital.

The weekend went its normal way: a round with the Major on Saturday morning, and then a lazy afternoon. Just after tea, Travers was called to the phone. The voice seemed vaguely familiar.

"Travers speaking."

"This is Henry Barlet. I've just returned from Paris, and Sir Arthur suggested I should get in touch with you at once. I rang your town number and your man gave me your whereabouts."

Travers had a sudden uneasiness.

"It's about that ring," Barlet was going on.

Now Travers was thoroughly alarmed.

"The emerald ring?"

"Yes. Something I happened to discover in Paris. Arthur thought we three had better talk things over between ourselves before letting the others know—if we do let them know. You know what Abergayne is like. He's a frightful stickler for red-tape, and he might panic."

Travers was more and more alarmed. So throaty and mumbling was his voice that he hardly knew it for his own.

"Something's happened and you and Sir Arthur would like to talk it over with me."

"That's it—if it's convenient. You're coming back to town to-day or tomorrow?"

"Tomorrow," said Travers promptly, and hoped he had not been too eager.

"Good! Be here at about tea-time. I'll arrange for Arthur to be here. My place is on your way. Holme-land House, Kingswood. Have you got it?"

Travers repeated, then cut in quickly.

"You there? . . . Oh, just one thing. I'd rather like to have some rough idea what the trouble is. I'd like to come a bit prepared, if you know what I mean."

"Well"—he seemed to be somewhat uneasy—"it's very confidential, even for the phone. But you remember a week or so ago there was a rather peculiar affair at the Levantic?"

Travers was moistening his lips.

"Amli, you mean?"

"You've got it. I won't say any more. The rest you can guess. At about four o'clock tomorrow then? . . . Good-by."

Travers found himself mechanically replacing the receiver, and all at once knew his forehead was damp and there was a chill in his bones. For a long indecisive moment he stood there, giving his glasses an aimless polish, and then he came to a quick decision.

But before he made his call, he listened, and cast a precautionary look round. Then he dialled exchange, and when he asked for Whitehall 1212, his voice was as low as he could make it. Then Helen looked in, but retreated at the sight of him still at the phone.

"Ludovic Travers speaking. Is either Superintendent Wharton or Inspector Norris in?"

"I'll inquire, sir."

"Just a minute," Travers cut in. "If neither is in, will you see I have this piece of information? On the Levantic case. On what boat and from what port did Amli sail from India? Got that? . . . I'll hold the line."

Within five minutes Norris was speaking.

"Hallo, sir. The one you want sailed from Madras on the *Deccan*. She's one of the Provinces Line. Any particular reason for wanting the information, sir?"

"I'm merely hunting about for ideas," Travers told him. "You never can tell at this game, as you well know." Then hastily, "Has a certain fat friend of yours done any talking yet?"

"Tubby?" Travers heard the little laugh. "Him and I are getting along fine. We're staging it so that he has a good look at Osmund. Nothing else, was there, sir? . . . Right you are then, sir. Good-by."

That was that. In less than twenty minutes Travers's whole outlook on life had changed. Before him was not the remainder of a pleasant weekend, but twenty hours of introspection and maddening, circling questions. Somehow he felt already that he would have given more than he cared to own to be in his car and heading for Barlet's place, where the truth was awaiting him.

On Sunday morning his golf was atrocious and the Major wondered what on earth had come over his game. But by the end of the round, Travers was certain of two things. That ring had been Amli's, and it was to him that Joy had surreptitiously become engaged.

As a kind of corollary to that, something stood out clear, and yet must never be faced. There was, he assured himself, no need to face it. The death of Amli had been merely a fortunate coincidence, and by no conceivable chance could Joy have been even remotely concerned.

CHAPTER XIII

TRAVERS TAKES OVER

IF THERE WAS one thing on which Ludovic Travers was resolved when he entered Barlet's house that Sunday afternoon, it was that he would fight like the devil on behalf of Joy Haire. If diplomacy still counted, then her name should never be publicly connected with that of the dead and unsavoury Amli.

But when Barlet had told his story, Travers knew that while there might be little danger of Joy's name ever being connected with the Levantic affair, there might be some rather awkward moments in store for himself if he still acted as the guardian of her interests. Yet it seemed the only possible thing to do.

Henry Barlet had been attending a European trade conference in Paris, and had displayed the emerald ring to a few friends, among them the Thonon brothers. Georges Thonon had at once recognized it beyond all doubt. Three years before, Bishan Singh's uncle, the then maharajah, had had certain jewels set or reset, and the emerald was one.

"There's no doubt whatever, then," said Travers. "But Thonon can't say who was the last owner of the emerald—the uncle or the nephew."

"How can he?" Barlet said. "It might have left the uncle's possession before his death, or the nephew may have inherited it and then lost possession. But couldn't the actual keeper of the jewels give information about that?"

"We needn't go that far," Travers said quickly. "But what was the special reason for calling me in this afternoon?"

"Well, this," he was told. "Amli was killed at the Levantic and, between ourselves, the idea has got about that a considerable number of things are being concealed by the police. All the same, if the ring was stolen, especially on the night Amli was killed, then the police would have a useful clue."

"Yes," said Travers dubiously, and at once began to cast a cloud of vagueness. "But there're ticklish matters which I daren't mention. Certain high authorities, strictly between ourselves, are very—well, I needn't say more. But I was present myself at the original inquiries."

He paused for that to have its effect.

"As to facts, the ring was *not* stolen from Amli that night. And we must bear in mind we're not concerned with what happened in India either to Amli or his uncle. If the ring was lost or stolen there, that was a matter for their servants or police. What we want to know is whether Amli had the ring when he arrived in this country six weeks or so ago. If so, did he lose it? I say no, or he'd have informed the police. For the same reason, he didn't have it stolen from him. But I do admit he might have given it away."

Sir Arthur raised his eyebrows. "A nice little gift?"

"He brought a collection of jewels over with him," Travers said. "He was small fry but very wealthy, and you know what such people are. Some of his kind could give away a bucketful of jewels and not miss them."

"But give to whom?"

Travers shook a solemn head. "In the very strictest confidence I may tell you that there was at least one pretty lady."

"I see," Sir Arthur said. "And if he had sold it, Henry, would the trade have known?"

"Not necessarily. But the point is, what does Travers suggest?"

"You have a buyer?"

"I have. And I can get eighteen hundred."

"Then sell," Travers said. "I'm not prepared to let red-tape and preposterous precaution stand in the way of the Hospital's getting a sum of money of which it's in urgent need. If you hear nothing further from me during the evening, then you'll know that Scotland Yard have no interest. After that I suggest you report officially to the Committee."

"And suppose anything should ever turn up?"

"I'm coming to that," Travers said. "Sell the ring, and inform the buyer that it once belonged to an Indian maharajah, and no one knows how it left his possession. Put a proviso in the receipt, if you like, but what I'm driving at is this. If that ring is ever claimed by the police or any other authorities, then I'll personally indemnify the buyer."

"I don't think that should ever happen," Henry said.

"If it does," Travers told him, "I stand by my word."

"A generous offer," Sir Arthur said, "and I'll take a half share if Travers likes. Sell the ring and be damned to it."

Travers smiled. "You fellows are hard-headed enough to know I shouldn't make such an offer if I thought there was the ghost of a chance of losing my money. Meanwhile, this meeting has never taken place, except for my private undertaking. Not a word to the Hospital, and certainly not to Scotland Yard."

As Travers drove towards town, he felt satisfied. He had told no actual lies and he had smudged but little truth, and he had so contrived matters that unless there was an astounding piece of bad luck, then no measurable human chance could ever connect Joy Haire with that ring.

But if anything did happen, then, and not till then, was it worth considering how to wriggle out of the extremely awkward situation in which he would find himself with the Yard. But Joy would be on the high seas by Wednesday night, and it would be three months before her return, by which time all danger should have passed.

But when he reached his flat he at once found Osmund's number and rang it. Osmund happened to be in. Travers recalled himself and asked for the favour of five minutes of his time on a personal matter, and gave a choice of meeting places. Osmund chose Travers's flat.

He looked just as shiny as ever, but his manner was uneasy and most deferential. When the small array of drinks and the proffered easy chair seemed to arouse suspicions, Travers once more assured him that the matter was a purely private one, and would come to the ears of no third party.

"And now, what will you have?" Travers said. "I recommend the sherry."

Osmund said he would have sherry, and he also took a cigarette.

"Here's how," said Travers amiably, and then drew his own chair to the opposite side of the fire.

"And now, Mr. Osmund, in the very strictest confidence, did you ever inspect that collection of jewels the late maharajah brought to the Levantic?"

"Never. I knew they were in the safe but I never saw them."

"You never saw him wearing a ring with a stone in it?"

Osmund shook his head again.

"He sometimes wore a showy sort of gold ring, but never one with a stone in it."

"You never heard him mention any ring? A diamond one, or emerald, or ruby?"

"Never."

"That's all right then," said Travers. "The ring I have in mind could never have been brought to this country. Another spot of sherry?"

"Thank you, sir, I will," Osmund said. "A very nice dry sherry, if I may say so."

"Glad you like it," Travers said, and was thinking that now he could with a clear conscience let the Barlets assume that Scotland Yard had no interest in the ring. Moreover, Osmund's negatives had seemed to prove that Amli had given Joy that ring on the boat. And there was something else which might be tested out while Osmund was available.

"Here's how again," Travers said. "And just one other little private matter while I'm about it. Did you ever in your life run across an old actor who called himself Furloe? His real name, I think, was Colson."

There was no start of surprise, no flicker of an eyelid, and no hesitation; nothing, in fact, to indicate that he had ever heard the name before. All he did was to look rather surprised at the question, and then shake his head.

"And you never heard the maharajah mention the name?"

"Never." Then he smiled. "The only actor I ever knew him to have anything to do with was Sir Jerome Haire, and I know very little about that."

Travers's heart missed a beat. His fingers went to his glasses, then shifted to the glass of sherry. A sip or two and he was himself again.

"Sir Jerome Haire?" He smiled. "Rather curious for those two to be friendly, wasn't it?"

Travers himself, the drinks, the comfort of the room and its informality, had all won Osmund over, and he began to talk at his ease.

"To tell you the truth, sir, I didn't know they were friendly. All I know is that about a week after I was at the Levantic, the phone rang one morning when His Highness happened to be at the desk and I heard him say Sir Jerome was to be asked to come up. I did see that when he heard Sir Jerome's name, he gave that nasty little smile of his. I was getting used to him by that time."

"And what happened?"

"I don't know, sir. But what made me think things at the time was that he said to me, 'Osmund, tell Bond to do so-and-so, and you might do so-and-so.' I forget what the jobs were, but I know he was getting us both out of the way. Oh, yes, I remember now. I had to go personally to a friend of his at Kensington. I had a word with Bond when I got back and he told me that he'd been notified that if ever Sir Jerome rang or called again, His Highness wasn't to be at home."

Travers gazed at the ceiling.

"I think I can put two arid two together. But did Sir Jerome ever call again?"

"Oh, yes, sir. He rang when I took the message, and when Bond took it. All he was told was that His Highness was out."

"Well, it's no business of mine," Travers said. "Still, you're a man of the world. What do people like Sir Jerome see people like His Highness for?" He waved a quick hand. "I know what you'll say. To get them to back some show or other." He nodded. "Perhaps you wouldn't be far out."

In the same moment he realized something. He was dead sure that Osmund had never known Furloe. Wharton's theory, it was, that, unknown to Wharton, had burst, and now there would be no point whatever in Osmund's refusal to admit the alibi had been somewhat cooked.

"I'm most grateful to you," Travers said, and got to his feet. "We've mentioned nothing important but all the same we agree that this meeting's never taken place."

He went with Osmund to the door, and then all at once halted with a wry smile.

"I wonder if in return for your kindness, you'd let an older man than yourself perhaps, do something for you. Just a word of advice. Suppose the police happen to be inquiring into the alibi of someone who shall be nameless, and I happen to know that if that someone tells the truth it will do him no harm; then oughtn't I to advise that someone to tell the truth?"

Then his hand went quickly out. "Good-by, and very many thanks. If I can do anything for you at any time, let me know."

Once more Travers was satisfied. When the first shock of the mention of Sir Jerome's name was over, he had known that that, too, fitted in. Bernice had confided in her father, who had naturally sought a private interview with Amli. Amli had told him in so many words to go to hell.

The Monday morning brought notice of the meeting of the Finance Committee to receive Henry Barlet's report. Travers attended that meeting, which authorized Barlet to sell, and then after lunch, when he was sitting over the fire with his paper, something caught his eye.

INCOMING LINERS EXPECTED TODAY
Deccan (Provinces) Due Tilbury

Once more his thoughts were circling round Joy and Amli and what had happened on that boat. Then all at once he made a desperate resolve to dismiss the whole thing from his mind. His final summing-up was this:

"I've been the one to blame. What I should have done was—and is now, for that matter—to go to Joy and point out the risks she was running, and ask for some confidential account of everything so as to be prepared. If I do so now, I can't avoid telling certain lies or making certain admissions. But Bernice will also have to be brought in, and, while I don't mind a certain amount of duplicity for her own good with Joy, I'm not prepared under any circumstances to lie to Bernice. Very well, then. I've straightened things out in my own way. The best thing to do is leave them alone and hope for the best."

And, as he knew, that same early evening he would be seeing both Joy and Bernice at that farewell party, and something might be let fall which would make both tombstone and epitaph for what had been an annoying and extremely delicate situation.

Now he had somehow got it into his head that that party was at six o'clock, so he allowed a quarter of an hour for manners and arrived three quarters of an hour late. The main room was packed, and yet there seemed nobody he knew.

"What's wrong with the theatre, my boy, is that—"

"I think Pavlova was very much over-rated."

"But don't you always eat your cherry first?"

"They say he never writes till he's half tight."

"Darling, you're joking. Not seen Ruth Draper!"

"Did you ever know a publisher yet who—"

"There's not the money in America there was—"

The snippets emerged from the giggles and gossip as he elbowed an apologetic way to the small open space at the far end where Bernice and Joy were apparently receiving. Each had a circle of her own, and Joy laughed back at him as he passed.

"Hallo, Ludo. You're dreadfully late."

He grimaced and made his way on. Bernice's smile seemed unnecessarily conventional, even considering the presence of the miscellanies with whom she had been apparently in the throes of some discussion.

"How do you do," she said. "So nice of you to come."

"I'm afraid I got the time wrong," he said, and then became aware that the group was straining at the leash to recommence the discussion. "Perhaps I shall see you later."

"But you must."

He smiled and backed. Over the heads of the chattering crowd he saw someone he knew holding a glass and looking forlorn. Travers elbowed a way with yet more apologies and caught Barney just entering a kind of annex. Barney had his glasses on and was gazing owlishly about him.

"Well, my old Bacchanalian?" Travers said heartily.

"Mr. Travers!" Barney emptied the glass, put it on the table and grabbed Travers's hand. Travers steered him to a corner where there were chairs and reasonable quiet.

"You're not drinking?" Barney said.

Travers smiled roguishly. "My digestion is not so good these days."

Barney missed the quip. He began recalling Travers's services and it was all Travers could do to edge the talk aside. Then drinks came by. Travers took a glass and Barney took another and was all at once in a confidential mood. Since he had last seen Mr. Travers he had had two more cables with regard to performances in private houses.

"Hostesses have to pay pretty heavily for that sort of thing, don't they?" Travers asked.

Barney leaned confidentially across.

"For one private show in India—four hundred pounds!"

"Good Lord!" said Travers. "Who was he? A prince?"

Barney leaned still further across and his voice was a husky whisper.

"A maharajah. The one who was killed in London last week."

His finger went to his lips and he gave a cautionary shake of the head. Travers did the leaning over.

"The Maharajah of Amli?"

"Sh!" went Barney, and raised frantic hands.

Travers refused to be silenced.

"Damnation, Barney, why all this mystery! Why shouldn't they have given a show at his palace? He was entertaining some Europeans, I suppose?"

Barney's hands rose quiveringly.

"But you mustn't! Mr. Travers, there is publicity and publicity." His voice was a whisper again.

"That's what Miss Bernice told me when he was killed. That private performance was never to be mentioned. Never!"

"And Joy? What did she say?"

Barney's mouth gaped with the most comical surprise.

"How did you know? Why, she said the same thing too. She rang the office." He gave a shrug of the shoulders. "That was the only thing they both agreed to do at the same time."

"I was merely having a guess," Travers told him.

"And they both heard Amli was dead, and both insisted that the private show should never be mentioned. Well, I see the point about publicity. And you needn't worry about me, Barney. I'll never mention a word to a soul."

Wilfred Braxwell, who was making such a hit in *Hornets' Nest*, came up then. Travers drew the two paternally together and made his way back to the main room. There he hung about till the crowd had thinned, and then got through to Bernice.

"Hasn't it been a crush?" she said. "Let's sit here, shall we?"

"Sorry," he said, "but I have to go."

"Go?" Her face fell.

"I must," he said. "But when can I see you alone?"

"Oh, dear!" She frowned delightfully. "You can guess what tomorrow will be. May I ring up if I can? And you will be at Waterloo. Ten o'clock, the boat train is."

"But suppose I have a lot of things to talk about?"

"Have you?" Her face lighted up, then from nearby came an apologetic cough.

"Well, cheerio, Bernice."

It was a man whom Travers did not know. Just behind him a couple of girls were coming. Travers's hand went quickly out.

"Good-by. Till Wednesday, or before."

He smiled, but when he came afterwards to visualize the scene, he seemed to remember that Bernice's eyes had been fixed intently on his own.

After dinner he drew his chair to the fire again, and at once his thoughts began circling. Soon he knew that he would never sleep. Some devil of insistence would hammer and hammer at his brain that the death of Amli had been only too apposite.

Let everything he had hitherto assumed be correct, and then why should Bernice and Joy each have so far forgotten their quarrel as to have told Barney separately to keep that performance a dead secret? Hatred of publicity had nothing to do with it. And why ring Barney as soon as Amli was known to be dead? If the engagement had been so secret, why be alarmed at Amli's death? How could that death bring the wrong kind of publicity to Joy when her name could never possibly be connected with his?

Then there was a dictum' of George Wharton's that would keep coming to Travers's mind: "You find the one who gets anything out of it, and I'll find the one who did it." And suppose that Wharton came suddenly into possession of all the facts, wouldn't there be the devil for Joy to pay—and possibly Bernice?

It was after ten o'clock and the thoughts had become maddening, and then he suddenly had an idea. Wharton was promptly rung at his private address.

"George, I've got an idea. I know it isn't worth a damn but I'd like to explore it, as I'm at rather a loose end and want a job. It's about Amli and the boat he came on."

"The *Deccan*?" Wharton grunted. "Norris said you'd inquired about that."

"It berthed this evening from India," Travers said. "My idea was that something may have happened on the voyage that may throw light on the rest of what happened."

Wharton grunted again. "You'll have to apply to You-know-who for that. They've taken all that over."

"But I want to work behind their backs, George. I'm making out that it's Osmund I'm inquiring about. Whether he and Amli knew each other before Amli arrived here."

There was a hesitation. Travers knew the decision rested on a knife edge. Then Wharton chuckled amusedly, like a man who gets something of his own back.

"Want to do them one in the eye, do you? Very well, then. You carry on. And you'd like me to advise the boat people that you're coming?"

"That's good of you, George. The Provinces Line, Tilbury." Then for fear Wharton should change his mind, "What's the news from your end?"

"Didn't I tell you?" Wharton said. "The most amazing thing. Osmund came to see me this morning and volunteered a statement. He says he left the cinema when Tubby saw him, but afterwards he decided to swear he hadn't, because he was afraid we might try to connect him with the murder."

"Doesn't that queer your pitch?"

"What!" Travers could see the glare. "If Osmund's not our man, then my name's Higgins. What do you think he volunteered a statement for, if he wasn't up to some new game?" A final grunt. "Well, goodnight. Just off up Wooden Hill. I'll get that call through for you first thing."

CHAPTER XIV

TRAVERS IS MAD

As long as he lived, Travers was to remember that day. There were times in it when his brain refused to function, and then, paradoxically enough, he was retaining his sense of proportion. At other times the ideas had never flowed so logically clear. But that had been when he was mad.

He woke early that Tuesday morning and all the night's uneasiness was at once in his mind. Soon there was an urgency with it, and a fear. Barney's disclosures might have been trivial and merely a reinforcing of what was already known, and yet, as he now realized, they showed the Levantic affair in a new and frightening light.

Neither of the sisters had shown the least interest in Amli and his doings *till after he was dead.* That was the vital fact. Neither had asked Barney to be desperately secret about that private performance in Amli's palace—that was the ominous thing. If he had had any hold over them, then they should have feared publicity when he was alive, not at his death.

Had two men been involved and not two women, Travers could have traced the progress of events. Amli alive had become a sudden menace and Amli had therefore been removed. As Wharton was sure, two people had been engaged in the removal. But could either Joy or Bernice have been one of them?

Bernice, who knew India well and doubtless could talk to Amli in Urdu, if not in his own native tongue, might have entered in Indian costume. Then who was Turban? Bernice could not have grappled with Amli or delivered that knockout blow.

What of Wharton's favourite—Osmund? But he could not have been Turban, for how could Bernice ever have come into contact with one of his kind? And if he had been Turban, he would probably at the moment be blackmailing Bernice and Joy both. Furloe then? How could Bernice have come into contact with Furloe, even if the other difficulties were overcome, or if one accepted Wharton's theory that Furloe had been mad again?

Those thoughts crowded in on Travers's mind as he drove towards Tilbury, and at last he had to force them to the background and keep his eyes on the road. It was shortly after ten o'clock when he reached the offices of the Shipping Company. Wharton's message had been received and the Captain was waiting.

"Shall we talk here or on board?" he asked.

"On board, I think," Travers told him, and started the ball rolling as they moved off. "You knew the Maharajah of Amli was dead?"

"Read it in India," the Captain said. "Naturally I spotted the name at once."

They talked in his own cabin. Travers said it was too early for a tot but he filled his pipe from the Captain's jar.

"And now, sir, what was it particularly that you wanted to know?"

Travers began by casting a veil of vagueness and secrecy of which even Wharton would have been proud. The bewildered Captain seemed relieved when he came down to facts and asked to be told about Amli's trip.

"I don't know that there's anything to say," he said. "He kept himself very much to himself. We carried few passengers that particular trip and he had one of the smaller statcrooms. He didn't make a show of any sort. Most times he'd have his meals in his room, and sometimes he'd be in the saloon. He brought no servants of his own aboard, and we found him a valet. A regular European you might have called him, but for his colour."

"Any acquaintances or friends? Or wasn't he the sort to make any?"

"Well, I don't see how his sort could strike up an acquaintance. The Misses Haire, they were on that trip and came aboard at Madras too. The elder one was friendly with him because I believe they'd met in his state where she and her sister had given a performance at some big do of his. You know what I mean by friendly. They'd bow to each other, and you'd even see them having an occasional chat."

"I see. Just polite friendliness. But he wasn't so friendly with the other sister. Joy, isn't her name?"

"That's right—Joy." He smiled. "She was out for a good time, with her own sort, of course." The smile became a chuckle. "What d'you think? We had a concert or two and at one of 'em, damned if she didn't do me to the life! If she'd been behind a screen you'd have sworn it was me—so they all said."

Travers smiled too. "I've heard she's very clever. But about Amli. Any private packages brought aboard?"

"Two," the Captain said. "I don't know what one was, but the other was valuables. Let me see now. The night before we berthed he fetched one package and signed, and I believe he told me it was jewels. It's all the same to us when it's signed for and sealed and in the safe. Later on he brought it back and it was resealed."

Travers shrugged his shoulders. "Well, that's all very interesting but it's rather wasting your time. To tell you the truth we hardly expected to find out very much. But I wonder if I might have a word with that steward who acted as his valet."

"Rench?" He hopped up. "I'll send him here at once. If you want me again I'll be in the office."

Rench, a hard-bitten individual of about forty, came smartly in.

"Yessir?"

Travers gave him a smile. "You're Rench?"

"'Sright, sir. Edward Rench."

"Make yourself at home. Have a cigarette."

"Don't mind if I do, sir."

He took the chair indicated and listened with strained attention to a few more of Travers' vaguenesses. There were also hints about the law and the consequences of all sorts of things.

"You acted as valet to the late Maharajah of Amli when he was a passenger last January?" Travers at last began.

"'Sright, sir."

"What was he like, in himself?"

Rench gave a quick look. "He wasn't so bad, sir."

The words had been far from hearty and Travers drew his own conclusions.

"Did he have any friends on board?"

"Friends, sir? He did—" Then he was shaking his head. "No, sir. He didn't have any what-you-might-call friends."

From his hip pocket Travers took a case. He removed some notes, put them in his waistcoat pocket and then replaced the case. Rench's eyes followed the proceedings.

"Listen to me," Travers said and leaned over towards him. "You said that he *did*. You said *did* in such a way that it meant he once had friends, and then something happened. Who was this friend or friends? He, or she, or both?"

"Sorry, sir, I was making a mistake. You know, sir. Mixing him up with someone else."

Travers kept smiling.

"You didn't understand me perhaps. Everything said in this room goes no further, whatever it is. Even the Captain will never be told. Now let's have the tale."

Rench shook his head.

"There ain't no tale, sir."

Travers rose reluctantly.

"Very well, then. I must arrange with the Captain for you to be brought to Scotland Yard at once."

"No, sir!" Rench was scared stiff. "I'll tell you, sir." He shuffled uneasily. "You won't get me in no row, sir?"

"You can rely on that," Travers told him. "Now tell the yarn in your own way."

Rench's story was this. The Maharajah had always been friendly with Miss Bernice Haire, and his ideas of friendship were the same as the Captain's. Then the night before docking—a cold, rainy night—he happened to see Bernice Haire and the Maharajah going towards his room. They were laughing like children and didn't seem to mind who saw them. The rain seemed quite a joke to them.

"I thought it was sort of peculiar, sir," Rench said, "him being what he was, if you get me, sir. I couldn't help wondering what he was up to, taking her in there alone. Then I remembered the vacant cabin next door, sir, only I couldn't go in because I was on a job of work.

"When I got back, sir, which would be in about ten minutes, I did nip inside, sir, and I don't mind telling you I listened, and they was still there, sir. You could have knocked me down with a feather, sir. I couldn't hear much because she wasn't shouting nor nothing, but from what I could make out she was telling him just where he got off. Calling him all the scum of the earth, sir. A—"

"Yes? A what?"

"Well, a *haramjadi*, sir."

Travers nodded at the questioning look.

"Yes, I know what it means. And what happened then?"

"Well, sir"—he grinned feebly—"I heard what sounded like a slap, sir. What I thought was he'd been getting fresh and—well, you know what I mean, sir. But when I heard that slap, sir, I nipped out like a streak of lightning, as you might say, and there she was, sir, going back along the deck cool as a cucumber, and just as if the rain hadn't been coming down fit to drown you."

"I know. Head held high. And what else happened?"

"Well, sir, I had to go in just afterwards about orders, and I didn't see him because he called through from the sleeping cabin. I was to take a chit to Miss Joy Haire at once and not let no one see me. Which I did, sir."

"Yes, go on. What happened?"

"Happened, sir?"

"Yes, happened. Weren't you interested?"

He smiled feebly again.

"I can't say as I was, sir. Now you come to mention it, I thought it was just an ordinary chit. You know, sir, just a letter about something."

"She didn't go to the cabin?"

"How should I know, sir. I didn't go to him any more because he distinctly told me he wouldn't want me any more."

"I see. And you've never mentioned a word of this to a soul?"

"God's my witness, sir. And how could I, sir, when I'd been where I hadn't ought."

Travers thought for a moment, then rose, and he was obviously disappointed.

"Well, Rench, I won't say that what you've been telling me wasn't interesting, because in a way it was. But the late Maharajah's private affairs are no concern of mine. I was after something much bigger and I thought you might have helped me."

He took the notes from his pocket and fingered them. Then all at once he was giving a queer look.

"It'd be pretty bad for you, Rench, now I come to think of it, if you ever told anyone what you've just told me?"

"As if I'd do such a thing, sir."

"Don't!" Travers told him curtly. "I've strong views about that sort of gossip, Rench. If anything ever gets to my ears—and we have a nasty habit of finding things out—I'll have you out of this job inside twenty-four hours."

He allowed that indignation to pass, then let out a breath.

"That's all, Rench, thank you. Take this for your trouble. And don't forget. It's confidential, like everything else that's happened in this room."

So urgent now was Travers's need for thought that when he left Tilbury he made for open country. A roadside restaurant caught his eye and he had a scratch meal there, then lingered on over the fire with his pipe. Out of the heterogeneous collection of facts that now comprised his own special evidence, a clear sequence emerged.

Joy had met Amli at that performance at the palace, if not before, and it was because of her that Amli had chosen the same boat for his voyage. The fact that Bernice was more with him than Joy was mere camouflage arranged by Amli and Joy.

Bernice had gone to Amli's room in a purely friendly way to inspect Amli's collection of jewels, but Amli had schemed all that in order to be able to break the news to her about Joy and himself. Bernice was horrified. Maybe she expressed certain strong objections which led to sneering recriminations from himself. In fact, he insulted her, whereupon she told him in his own language what would get clean under his skin. *Harem bastard* had been one name for him, and when he gave that sneering laugh of his, she slapped his face and calmly left the room.

Then Amli sent for Joy and told her some garbled tale. Joy was furious, and, when Bernice sent for her, made her own violent attack. The open breach then came, but Joy still had sense enough not to commit herself to a public engagement or to allow Amli to announce it. Most likely, indeed, after thinking over what Bernice had said, she broke the tacit engagement off, though pride and anger would keep her from letting Bernice know.

Bernice must have sought an interview with Amli soon after landing. But he had a revenge of his own already planned. He took out his wallet and showed her a series of letters—real or faked—and read compromising extracts. Then he asked her if she would like to slap his face again, and showed her politely to the door.

Thereupon Bernice saw her father. He had a talk with Joy, who refused to talk in return, so he interviewed Amli who in some gloating, sneering way proceeded to let him know that he had the whole Haire family where he wanted it.

Thereupon Bernice saw plainly that what she regarded as the honour of the family was being left to herself to defend. And as the elder sister she saw her duty clear. By some means or other she must get those letters from Amli, and take them herself to Joy, and prove beyond doubt what kind of blackguard Amli was and the tragedy Joy had so narrowly escaped.

But Bernice could not possibly act alone, so she looked about her for a confederate.

Turban was the man she employed. He must have been, for he was the man who was present at the killing of Amli. Then was Furloe Turban? Hard facts said that he could never have been, and his own intuitions had always told him the same thing. Yet miracles had happened. Indeed in this case, as Travers assured himself, they must have happened. But it had not been Furloe the leaning man who had been Turban. It was some other Furloe: the Furloe who, as Wharton had said, had been suddenly, struck by some new and worse kind of madness. And if all that were true, then how could Bernice have met Furloe, who was to be her tool and accomplice?

Travers sat with head in hands and strove desperately to think. Then an idea came, and an hour later he was in his flat. Palmer had a message for him.

"Miss Bernice Haire rang, sir. I said I expected you at any moment, sir, but she said there was no immediate hurry."

"As a matter of fact, I'm going out again at once," Travers said. "No matter who rings, say you can't tell when I shall be in."

He made his way to Shaftesbury Avenue and to the landing of Sir Jerome's flat. There he made much pretence of ringing and knocking, then came down and tapped at the side door of the lingerie shop. Maud, pop-eyed and gushing, opened it at once.

"No wonder you couldn't make anyone hear," she said. "Sir Jerome is away."

Travers clicked his tongue.

"How annoying, and there was a special matter I wanted to confirm. But, of course! you would do as well. It's really about the Saturday afternoon when you heard him rehearsing. Was he alone, do you know?"

"Oh, no," she said. "There was talking going on. We could hear it—you know, in the intervals."

"You didn't see Miss Bernice Haire go up the stairs that afternoon?"

"I couldn't say. She might have gone up, though. You see we were very busy or we shouldn't have stayed late at all."

So much for that, and before Travers had moved ten yards along the street he was feeling tolerably certain. Someone had been with Sir Jerome that afternoon, perhaps two people. Bernice had at least taken sufficient interest in her father to see him at the Paliceum, so perhaps she was one. Furloe had been there on the evidence of Sir Jerome himself. Or had he already been dismissed, and was Bernice the sole audience?

In any case he now knew how Bernice had come into contact with Furloe. Either she had been present that afternoon when Furloe told her father the tale, or else Sir Jerome had mentioned Furloe to her. At once she had thought of him as a likely man.

So she had got in touch with him at once, and had promised to use all her influence to get him work. That was the basis of those hints that Furloe had thrown out to his benefactor, Spearing. Then she had told him the story, or some story, and had won his sympathies.

So to the planning. She knew India well, and she obtained the disguise. She had also a key to her father's flat and knew he would be absent until at least a quarter past ten; and, of course, the dresser would be away too. She rang Amli and fixed the interview, and when Furloe left Sir Jerome's flat that night it was with a gun in his pocket and instructions to get the wallet.

But things happened. Furloe came back to the flat with a desperate tale. The letters he had, and he was given the notes as an immediate reward, but when Bernice heard the news of

Amli's death and how it would be taken for murder, then she panicked. Furloe panicked too. Then—

But then Travers realized just where his thoughts were leading him. The logical sequence stood clear. To go on was the easiest thing in the world, and yet he was afraid. Something, he told himself, must be wrong. Bernice could never have gone as far as that.

He looked up to find himself outside the flats, and in a minute or two he was in his bedroom. There he sat with head in hands and once more tried desperately to think.

Then a new idea came, and heartened him. The point was not what Ludovic Travers might or might not think of Bernice, or of what his theories might accuse her. The point was this. Suppose that Wharton obtained possession of the same facts, what would Wharton conclude *and, above all, what action would he take?*

The answer was plain. Wharton would set to work to prove things to the hilt, and for the purpose of securing a conviction. Very well then. Ludovic Travers must anticipate a possible Wharton, and inquire into every possible contingency for the purpose of proving not guilt but innocence. In other words, everything must be at once envisaged, and Bernice must no longer be thought of as Bernice, but as some impersonal thing.

He got to his feet at that. Now he could complete the story. Wharton would say that Bernice saw only one way out. That poisoning was a woman's work. Easy enough to drop something into a glass and forget about it. A man would have smashed Furloe over the skull and dumped his body. And so, as Wharton would know, when Furloe had quickly changed back and removed the disguise, she gave him the poison in a glass of whiskey. Doubtless she expected death at once, and she hurried him out of the flat and into the fog.

Next morning she warned Barney of the danger of mentioning that connection with Amli. She also called on her father to make sure no clue had been left behind, and she met Joy there. Later in the day she gave Joy various hints but the full story was not told till Sunday afternoon.

Now, thought Travers, if those were the conclusions Wharton would draw, how would he go to work to prove them? Only by seeing Sir Jerome, making a sideways attack on him and using a considerable deal of bluff, and getting enough further information with which to confront Bernice.

So Travers resolved that he himself would see Sir Jerome, and at once. But Liverpool was two hundred miles away, and there might be fog that would reduce the speed of the car to a crawl. The boat-train would be better than the car, and if he remembered correctly, it left Euston at about six o'clock and ran into Liverpool at ten. Sir Jerome was doing only two shows a night and there might be time to catch him at the hall where he was appearing, for his would almost certainly be the act to bring down the final curtain.

Travers rang the station at once. The Irish boat-train was at six, he was told, and there was a return train soon after midnight, a slow that ran into Euston at six-thirty in the morning. Travers decided to use both, and to travel with nothing but what he stood in.

It was not till after dinner on the train that he began to plan his brief campaign. First, how was the visit to be justified at all? Only by becoming a kind of Wharton, and bluntly mentioning the police. Then there might be a quick, vague reference to Bernice, and a hesitancy to act on what he had discovered. That would make the talk confidential and give himself an immediate ascendancy.

Then to the bluff, and the waiting for results. "Sir Jerome, I will tell you this much. I know what happened on the boat on the way home from Madras, and I know about a certain emerald ring."

But how introduce Furloe? That was a poser, unless the bluff became perfectly outrageous. "Sir Jerome, I know the part played in the death of Amli by Furloe, whom you once knew as Colson." That might produce some admission, for Sir Jerome must have suspected something all along. Otherwise, why had he so feared inquiry as to have bolted to the so-called country, and made up those lies about a friend and a car and a country house?

So Travers got out of the train that night with no lack of confidence. It was exactly ten o'clock as he went up to the taxi.

"Know what hall Sir Jerome Haire is appearing at this week?"

"Yes, sir."

"Right. Get me there quick. The stage door."

In five minutes he was speaking to the stage-door keeper. Sir Jerome's act was on at that very moment. Travers scribbled something on the back of a card. .

"Let him have this the moment he comes off. Find out if he can see me at once."

There was a wait of ten minutes before the doorkeeper knew the time had come. Out he went and he came back with a younger man.

"Okay, sir. Fred will show you the way."

Travers went through a room, past back-stage and along a corridor. His guide grimaced and pointed. Travers tapped at the indicated door.

"Come in!"

The voice was Sir Jerome's. A little nervous cough, and Travers turned the knob and entered.

CHAPTER XV

TRAVERS RUNS AWAY

SIR JEROME STOOD with the card in his hand, and he was snapping out an order to his man.

"Get outside and wait. Tell the taxi to wait too."

The man bowed, backed a yard or two as if his master were royalty, then left by the far door. Sir Jerome let his eyes rest steadily on Travers, and in his look were both suspicion and hostility. He had his back to the dressing-table, and was still in the costume and make-up of *The Decoration*.

"Well? You wish to see me?"

Travers felt uneasy. The reception was vastly different from what he had imagined.

"Yes, Sir Jerome. That's why I asked for five minutes of your time, even if it meant disturbing you."

The hooked beak went aggressively forward.

"Well, what is it you want?"

Travers flushed at the tone. It seemed to him also that he might at least have been offered a chair.

"I've come all the way from town to do you a service. I hope you'll believe that. In fact, I have good reasons for knowing that you believe it."

"Do *me* a service?"

"Yes, Sir Jerome. It's extremely awkward for me to state just how, but you were aware of the fact that I was connected with the police, and am still connected, in their inquiries into two deaths. One was the Maharajah of Amli."

"The Maharajah of Amli." He looked away for a moment, nodding to himself, then his eyes were fixed on Travers's face again. "I remember the affair, but how should it concern me?"

It might have been as a reinforcing of the indifference, but he looked again at Travers's card, then tore it in two and dropped it in the basket. Travers's prepared openings were lost in the presence of that queer hostility.

"I think you know the answer to that, Sir Jerome?"

He waited for some answer but there was nothing but that unwavering stare.

"What I would add is, that in the course of certain independent inquiries I have been making, information has come into my possession which might have very serious consequences. Very serious indeed. I preferred therefore to see you before reporting my discoveries to Scotland Yard."

The old man looked away again as if to think. He muttered something, then whipped round angrily on Travers.

"You're talking damn nonsense! Damn nonsense, I tell you."

"You know it's not nonsense," Travers told him earnestly. "I repeat. I'm trying to avoid serious consequences. If you're not prepared to hear what I say, then you must abide by those consequences."

He glared. "Damn you, sir, what d'you mean?"

"This. I know everything that happened on the *Deccan* during the voyage from Madras to Tilbury."

The stare was if anything even more intense. The words came slowly.

"You know what happened on the *Deccan*?"

"Yes. And to get nearer the point and convince you that I'm in deadly earnest, I know why you went to the Levantic."

The stare was distinctly menacing. Travers's fingers went to his glasses, then fell.

"You're not making it very easy, Sir Jerome. Perhaps we'd be on rather better terms if we talked about Furloe, the man you knew as Colson."

The old man turned away, shaking his head. His hand went to the front of the dressing-table as if to steady himself, and Travers, wondering what he was about, thought he must be posing for his benefit. That wave of the hand in the empty air, and that sinking heavily into a chair.

"Get out, sir. Get out!"

He had leapt from the chair like a madman. Travers drew back before the waving of arms and the mad glare in his eyes.

"Do you hear? Get out!"

"Sir Jerome—please—"

"GET OUT!"

Travers still backed before the onslaught.

"As you wish, Sir Jerome. All I hope is that you won't regret—"

But the hand had grasped his shoulder and whirled him round. In a moment the door was closing on him, and then it slammed. Travers stood for an indecisive moment in the corridor, dismally shaking his head.

The night was raw with a bitter east wind, and he turned up his collar and hunched his shoulders as he walked back towards the station. Somehow he was feeling desperately ashamed, and for the life of him he could not have said why. For a score of complex reasons, perhaps: that he hated brawling, that he had been badly treated, that the old man should have behaved so unreasonably and indeed almost like a lunatic, and that he himself had been made to look very much of a fool.

But that last was wrong, and he drew himself up as he walked. There had been no loss of dignity on his part. Maybe too, what had angered the old man was that a comparative stranger should walk into that dressing-room and begin talking so calmly about the most intimate private affairs of his daughters and himself.

Then all at once Travers stopped dead. A supplementary theory, startling in its implications, had flashed into his mind, and now was crystal clear.

No wonder the old man had suddenly begun raving like a lunatic. Every deduction had been true, *but with this addition*: not only did Sir Jerome know the truth; he had himself been implicated. Bernice could never have poisoned Furloe. Furloe himself might somehow have taken the poison by mistake, but a far more likely happening was that Sir Jerome had reached his flat that night to find that Bernice and Furloe were there. Their dilemma had been such that they were bound to admit him to the secret. Sir Jerome had then sent Bernice home, and had solved the problem himself by poisoning Furloe so that he should never speak.

Yes, it was conscience that had made him know that the police, in the person of Travers, were after him. There had really been no need for bluff, for a guilty conscience had worked in its place. Even the make-up had not concealed the fact that he looked desperate and worried, and no wonder, with the anxiety of days gnawing at his brain.

There too, as Travers had known, was the explanation of those trumpery lies that had been told about the country and a friend's car. Sir Jerome had been suspicious from the start about Travers's visits, and he had bolted to that private hotel to be out of the way of questioning.

And so much being certain, what was the next move? Not the move that Wharton would make, for the last thing Travers was minded to do was to confront Bernice or Joy. Perhaps the best thing to do would be to plan ahead during that crawling journey of the train.

But there all Travers's calculations went badly wrong. He secured a first-class compartment to himself and was assured by the guard that he would not be disturbed. The compartment was deliciously warm, the cushions were soft, and Travers was worn out in body and mind. Before he had gone ten miles he was sound asleep, and it was not till the train neared Euston that he really woke again.

It was well after seven o'clock when he got back to the flat. Palmer reported that nothing had happened except a call from Wharton. Travers's conscience smote him and after a bath and a change of clothes, he rang Wharton at his private address.

"Sorry, George, I couldn't let you know what happened yesterday. As a matter of fact there was nothing to report."

Wharton grunted. "When Palmer said you were away, I thought you might have got hold of something."

"That was only a personal matter," Travers said, and was hating himself for the lies that had to be told. "Oh, and, George, I'm going away for a time. Just the usual Spring holiday. . . . To-morrow, perhaps, unless there's anything you particularly want. . . . I see. Cheerio, then. I may see you later."

So on the spur of the moment Travers had decided to run away from the case. What he was most afraid of was that Wharton might question him at a time when he was no longer prepared to tell lies. Let Wharton have ten minutes with Rench and there'd be more than the devil to pay.

The old tag about deception and the weaving of tangled webs was still true. Living on a volcano was as nothing compared with the situation in which he was likely to find himself. And there was something else of which he was afraid. At a quarter to ten there would be people on the platform at Waterloo, and two days ago he had looked forward to being there himself. Now he was running away from even that. No more lies and pretence. Far better let Bernice think he was a philanderer and had changed his mind.

So Travers read his paper, cleared up arrears of correspondence, and began drafting a preface to his new book. Then he caught himself with eyes once more on the clock, and all at once he fetched his hat and coat and made his way to the garage.

Never had he felt so miserable, even to the marrow of his bones, and all the time it was as if some heaviness was pressing on his brain. So he turned the car northwards and made for a golf course where he sometimes played. There he borrowed clubs from the pro and managed to find an opponent.

After a late lunch he felt somewhat easier in his mind. He could now regard impersonally the hands of the clock and know that an Atlantic voyage had already begun. Bernice must have wondered, and perhaps she had been hurt. Or had she guessed that he knew about Amli? Cold silence might have told her that, and in any case it had been the better way out.

It was four o'clock when he came back to the flat again. Palmer said there had been no letters or phone calls. Travers nodded to himself, then made up his mind.

"Tomorrow we'll leave for somewhere south. We might try Italy for a change. Pack what we're likely to need for a month or so."

After tea he busied himself with his packing, and wrote a letter or two, and then Palmer came in with the evening papers.

"Good heavens, sir!"

Then there were quick apologies.

"I'm sure I beg your pardon, sir. I'm sorry, sir, but I happened to glance at this front page."

Travers took the paper. His eyes narrowed, and then his fingers went to his glasses. A shake of the head and he was turning away.

DEATH OF SIR JEROME HAIRE
Famous Actor Dies in His Sleep
THE DRESSER'S STORY

The headlines flared across the page, with pictures of the great man and the hotel where he had died. Travers ran his eye along the larger print.

. . . unwell for days . . . suffered from insomnia . . . found beside his bed . . . account given by his dresser . . . with him for many years . . .

For a moment he looked away from that blur of words, then turned to the second column and the dresser's story.

William Prossman, for twenty years valet and dresser to the dead man, had told a pathetic story. His master had been unwell for some days, and even a short holiday in the country prior to the Liverpool engagement had not done the good that had been anticipated.

On the previous night, after leaving the stage, Sir Jerome had received a caller in his dressing-room, but a few minutes later he rang for Prossman again. His manner was most perturbed but he was at pains to impress on Prossman that the interview had had nothing to do with it, but that he was suddenly very-feverish and tired.

On reaching the hotel Sir Jerome at once went to his room. Prossman was dismissed and told he would not be required again that night. The usual decanter of whiskey and the siphon were at the bedside.

Next morning Prossman looked in at ten o'clock, which was his usual hour. Since Sir Jerome rarely fell asleep till well into the morning, he slept late, and recently he had become rather afraid of the effects of the sleeping tablets he took. Prossman at once saw that his master was a sick man; moreover the bed had not been slept in, and it looked as if Sir Jerome had tried to doze in the easy chair where he then sat. He admitted he had not slept.

"He was very irritable when I spoke to him," Prossman's account went on, "and positively refused to let me send for a doctor. When I remonstrated with him he said he would take some tablets and try to get to sleep, and he was on no account to be disturbed before four o'clock. I assisted him to the bed and left him as directed. I noticed that a fair quantity of the whiskey had been drunk and that the box of sleeping tablets was by his bed.

"I listened outside the door soon after lunch but could hear no sound. At four o'clock I went to rouse him as directed, and found the door locked, which was a thing I had never known before. I obtained the desk key and returned with the manager, and we found Sir Jerome dead in his bed."

According to the paper, medical evidence showed that he had died within an hour of his dresser's leaving him, and it was hinted that, in his craving for sleep, he had taken a considerable overdose of the tablets.

"What adds pathos to the tragedy," the general account went on, "is that while Sir Jerome, unknown to everybody, was lying dead, his daughters—Bernice, the world-famous dancer, and Joy, the equally well-known diseuse—had left Southampton for their tour of the States and Canada. We understand that a message has reached them, but at the time of going to press we have no further information, though it is extremely unlikely that there will be much modifications of plans made so far ahead. Our sympathies go out . . ."

Travers let the paper fall, and for a long minute lay back in his chair with eyes closed. Then suddenly he jumped to his feet as if in answer to some quick alarm. Another second and he was at the phone calling Barney Josephs.

Barney was at the office. There had been little doubt of that on that particular night.

"Yes?" he said, and there was an incredible snappishness in his tone.

"Travers speaking, Barney."

"It's you, Mr. Travers." The tone changed at once. "You have heard the news."

"Terrible," said Travers. "Perfectly terrible. And will it make any difference to the tour?"

"How can it? How can they come back? I was just now on the phone to the boat and Miss Bernice assured me herself that it must make no difference."

"She was upset?"

"Why shouldn't she be?" Barney asked plaintively. "She's a brave woman, Mr. Travers."

"Yes," said Travers lamely. "But did Sir Jerome leave any message at his bedside."

"How should he?" asked Barney. "He didn't know he was going to die, did he?"

Before the receiver was replaced, Travers knew he should have known that for himself. Sir Jerome had told Bernice nothing and had given no warning about what Travers knew. He had had to give the impression of natural death, for only suicides leave messages. And he had timed his death so that it should not be discovered till after his daughters sailed.

For Travers had now made a slight adjustment of the pieces, and could see the completed whole. He himself had been the instrument of justice. Sir Jerome had been afraid from the very beginning. For days he had waited and feared, and the sight of Travers's card at that strange hour had been enough to disturb his last mental balance. He had not tried to sidetrack with blandishments in order to discover what his caller knew, for his fearful mind told him that that caller could have come for one thing alone. The first words he had heard had been overwhelming confirmation.

Travers sat on in the quiet room, and then, in that mood of resignation, found himself thinking of Bernice, and above all as she had been that afternoon at The Croft. Suddenly a weight seemed to go from his mind, and a pressure was lifted, and he stared as if aghast at some strange abnormality that had taken the place of his humdrum and everyday self.

Mad, temporarily mad—that's what he must have been. How else, in God's name, could he have harboured such thoughts of Bernice, and even allowed himself under the sham guise of Wharton to think of her as having murdered Furloe!

The planning that Furloe should get the letters—yes, that much she had done. And she had awaited his return in her father's flat. But the rest—no! It cut across every knowledge and every memory. She had been sent home that night from the flat, and then her father had dealt with Furloe himself. It was madness ever to have thought otherwise, and now her father's suicide proved it.

Then all at once his bowed head was in his hands, and when at last he rose from the chair, his mind was made up. Theorizing and argument belonged to the past. Everything was now too late, and the meticulous details of the truth were of no interest. Sir Jerome was beyond the law and the law could never prove, even if by some amazing chance it might happen one day to suspect.

He alone knew the main truth. As for the rest, it was also best forgotten. Sir Jerome, Furloe, Amli—those main actors in the tragedy had gone. Bernice was on the way to America, and he himself was going somewhere abroad. Death for some, as it were, and a new way of life for others. That was the way of it, and somehow he could tell himself that he was glad.

So, with what seemed to him the virtual solving of those two connected mysteries—the events on the *Deccan* and at the Levantic—Travers left England the following day, and stayed abroad for five weeks.

But he was wrong in that confident assumption that he had as good as solved two problems. It was a kind of madness that had led to the first main theories, and it was tiredness and wretchedness of mind that now led him to abandon them with their gaps and rough edges.

Neither problem had been solved. Rarely, in fact, had he been so near and yet so utterly wide of the mark. But he was to have no inkling of that till the very end of his holiday, when he was feeling rested again and his sense of proportion had been recovered. The sub-conscious mind, too, must have completed its own inquiries and begun a new investigation.

Chapter XVI
TRAVERS KNOWS

TRAVERS REACHED PARIS late at night, and the next morning called at the post-office for his mail. Among other letters there was one from Wharton, the gist of which was that the case was fizzling out, the H-and-M were probably glad of it, and that he himself had not abandoned the hope of pinning something on Osmund.

Travers felt a tremendous relief at that. On his return home he need not fear the kind of questioning that Wharton was likely to go in for. And the first thing he had better do was to ask George to lunch or dinner and so hear all the news.

It was that one word *dinner* that set his thoughts stirring. Within five minutes he was seeing the serious flaw in the reasoning that had produced those confident deductions. At once he changed the day's plans, and pushed the car on to Boulogne for the early afternoon boat.

The evenings were now clear and drawing out, and he drove fast from Folkestone to town. He was just in time to catch the lingerie sisters before the closing of the shop.

"I thought I'd drop in," he said, "as I hadn't seen you since Sir Jerome's death."

"Wasn't it sad?" Maud said. "Rosey and I fairly sat down and cried when we heard it; didn't we, Rosey? But you've been away, haven't you? Your face looks ever so tanned."

Travers pinned the conversation down.

"We all have to have holidays. That's what I thought about Sir Jerome. If he'd given himself a lot more rest, he'd have been alive today."

"That's just what we said ourselves."

"And probably not even getting his meals properly," Travers said. "Take that week when he was doing four shows a night, and his dresser was away. I suppose he went without dinner? He couldn't very well go out in costume."

"Oh, but he used to look after himself," Rosamund said. "We found that out. You see, he used to make up and dress here, and after the first two shows the taxi used to bring him back here, and he used to go up and have something by himself. It wouldn't have paid him to have dressed twice. Then the taxi used to come for him again soon after nine o'clock."

"That's right," Maud said. "There was a lot of that in the papers during the inquest."

Travers was satisfied. If Sir Jerome was in his flat that Friday night from eight o'clock till nine, how could Bernice and Furloe have made it their headquarters? Furloe could not have made up there as Turban, for Turban had been seen in the Paliceum at half-past eight and he had not left it till an hour later. Therefore it even looked as if Bernice and Furloe had not been accomplices after all.

But when he cast about for some variations on the theme—always using the same material—he always came to a dead end. Nothing emerged to throw any light on the Levantic affair, and Wharton—sedulously pumped without knowing it—could let fall never a word which could be made to lead to a clue.

So Travers shifted his interest to what had happened on the *Deccan*. If one branch of the theories had its flaw, why not the other? If Bernice, for instance, had not employed Furloe, might it not be because there was nothing on which to employ him? That—might one assume?—there had never been any compromising letters?

With that as a beginning, and building surely on the simple, steadfast and unalterable traits in the character of each sister, he achieved something that was altogether new. A week before Bernice arrived back in England, he knew his old theories about the happenings on the *Deccan* had been woefully wrong. On the eve of her return he knew his new theories must be incontrovertibly right. It seemed to him too, that Bernice herself might be brought to some admission, if not confession.

The May morning was a sunny one and he took special pains over his clothes. When he appeared in the grey—it was the brown that had been laid out—Palmer thought it probable that he was going somewhere in the country. But not till the afternoon, for Superintendent Wharton was coming to lunch. Travers reminded him of the fact.

"Anything particular that Superintendent Wharton likes for lunch?"

"I'm not really sure that I know, sir."

Travers laughed. "Well, find something good. One o'clock, if he should ring up to make sure. I shall be out most of the morning, by the way." After breakfast he completed the preface to his book, and began wondering about a title. But his eye was always on the clock, and at last he phoned.

"The Velasquez Hotel? Miss Bernice Haire, please. . . . It doesn't matter about the name. Say, a friend."

He waited gravely for at least two minutes, then his face lighted.

"Morning, Bernice. This is Travers."

"Oh, yes." The voice was prim. "How are you, Ludo?"

"Much better," he said. "I've been away on rather a long holiday, you know. You're just back?"

"Yes. The day before yesterday."

"A wonderful time you had, so Josephs was always telling me. He's a very old friend of mine, you know."

She was plainly puzzled, which was what he had intended from the start.

"By the way, could you spare me just ten minutes on an urgent matter? . . . Anywhere you like. At your hotel, or in the Park?"

There was a hesitation. "I think I might manage it. Shall we say here?"

"Splendid!" he said. "I'll be with you in twenty minutes."

She was in a small drawing-room overlooking the river.

"Lovely to see you again," he said. "And you're looking so fit—and so cool."

She smiled. "Shall we sit here? It's rather jolly watching the river."

"How's Joy?" he said.

"Very well indeed. She's staying with some friends in Sussex at the moment. At Padgley Down. But you know it! You came to tea one day at The Croft."

Travers gave a quick shake of the head at that chill epitaph. But as they talked he knew she was waiting for something. Two questions would soon have to be asked, and at last one came.

"Did you say you'd been unwell, and away on a long holiday?"

"Hardly that," he told her. "I'd been none too fit, so I did go away. It was the day after you sailed."

A hesitation, and the second question came.

"You never told me that you knew Mr. Josephs? I had no idea he was a friend of yours."

"Lord, yes," he said. "Josephs has told me a good many things in his time."

Then all at once he was getting to his feet.

"Bernice, I hate prevarication with you, just as I think you once hated it with me—"

"What do you mean?"

He shook his head. "What's the use of our fencing like this? May I talk to you very frankly, just as if it was three months ago?"

"But it isn't!"

He smiled gravely down at her.

"Let me tell you something; something impertinent perhaps, but that I believe to be true. I should have been at Waterloo Station one morning, but I wasn't. You're now wondering if it was an illness that kept me away, and you feel less angry with me because I've told you that I always inquired after you from Josephs."

A quick shake of the head and she looked up.

"And even if that should be true?"

"Then you would be wrong," he said. "I was not unwell. I deliberately avoided you because of something I had been forced to believe. I admit I was wrong to believe it—even mad, perhaps. It was only a few days ago that I knew what must have happened."

She had been frowning up at him.

"What on earth are you talking about?"

He was still smiling gravely down.

"I'm coming to that. But tell me something, and forgive the frankness. Three months ago, if I had asked you to marry me . . . would you?"

"Yes," she said slowly. "I think perhaps I would."

"And now?"

She looked away, shaking her head.

"That makes it easier then." His fingers began unhooking his glasses. "It's wonderful for us two to be able to talk so openly and—well, as if we trusted each other after all. I mean—well, I shall have to say it and get it over. Forgive me again if I hurt your feelings. Will you tell me yourself, in your own way, just what happened that last night on the *Deccan*?"

She stared frightenedly, then suddenly was getting to her feet.

"What do you mean?"

"Something that nobody now knows about but you and Joy and myself."

She moistened her lips.

"How did you know?"

"I was concerned with the police in the investigations into Amli's death. Then there was the emerald ring, which you yourself sent to what I call my hospital. But what I found out I've never mentioned to a soul. And it's partly why I was not at Waterloo Station."

She moved across the room to a chair, and sat there as if she was unaware that she was seated at all. Every now and again she shook her head, and her fingers fidgeted restlessly.

"There's nothing to be worried about," he told her gently. "Nothing at all. Everything's over. Now will you tell me what happened? . . . Or would it be easier if I tried to tell you?"

She had given a quick nod, and he was looking out at the river while he talked. More than once his fingers nervously polished his glasses.

"You were courteous and friendly on that boat, because you had met Amli with his guests at his palace, and he was English, so you thought, in everything but colour. You were thrilled at inspecting his jewels. Perhaps you might have hesitated on any other night, but that was the night before reaching home and you were excited and different.

"You particularly admired an emerald ring, and no wonder. Then, very coolly and cynically, he told you at what price you could have that ring. When it dawned on you what he meant, and what had been his scheme throughout, you told him just what he was. You took pains to get well beneath his skin. That was why he planned an extraordinary revenge.

"No sooner had you left him than he sent a private message to Joy which induced her to come to him. She was shown the jewels, and he virtually forced her to take that emerald ring. You can't blame her for taking it. It was the perfect ring, and she took it—but, of course, only on the condition that she would never say where she had got it.

"But you happened to see Joy admiring that ring. You demanded that she should say where she got it. She indignantly refused, and she probably told lies. Those lies told you the truth. You knew where she had got it, and what she had paid. You as good as told her so. She refused to deny it, but said she would never speak to you again in her life. Which, perhaps, is what Amli hoped would happen."

He shook his head as he hooked the glasses on again.

"That's all—and I'm sorry. You weren't to blame, any more than I was to blame for having precious little faith in you."

He knew somehow that she was crying, but when he turned, her eyes were dry, though her face seemed drawn and tired.

"I think you'd better go now, Ludo."

He took her hands.

"I was right?"

"Yes . . . you were right."

Then she was looking urgently up.

"Who did kill him? Tell me who killed him!"

He smiled. "That will never be known. Even if it ever is known, it will never be made public. But they think it was some intruder. Probably some Indian."

She seemed to smile at that, though the fright was still there.

"I was terrified. All the time I thought tales would get out about him and Joy."

"I knew," he said. "But it's all over now. But there's one thing I'd like you to tell me. How did you and Joy find out the truth—about each other?"

"That was through poor daddy," she said. "I confided in him and he had to find out the real truth. But he wouldn't see him—that dreadful man, I mean—and then daddy finally cornered him somewhere in the country and forced the truth out of him. Wasn't that wonderful of him?"

But Travers was moistening his lips and staring away at nothing.

"Don't you think so?"

Travers came to himself. "Oh, yes. Yes. It *was* wonderful. Very wonderful indeed. And when did you hear about the confession?"

"On the very day he was killed. I mean, when we read it in the papers."

Once more he nodded gravely down.

"Well, it's all over now and we're never going to mention it again. You and I cut sorry figures. I lost faith in you as you did in Joy. Not that she was without blame."

"You must be going now," she told him. "I have a dreadfully important engagement."

"Honestly?"

"Honestly."

They went out to the corridor together. He held out his hand.

"Only one thing to do now."

"To do?"

"Yes. Choose a lovely afternoon and get back that tea-party we lost."

"But that was with Joy," she told him, and flushed.

"Oh, no," he said. "Am I to ring, or you?"

She smiled. "Perhaps I will—some afternoon when it's fine."

At first he made for the Embankment, then changed his mind and turned back towards the Park instead. No need now for any thought. Bernice had unknowingly revealed the truth. The main outlines were crystal clear, and at any moment he could give each detail of what had happened that night at the Levantic.

But he lingered out his walk till just before Wharton arrived. The old General was in great form. Life was easy, the weather was good, his digestion was perfect and he certainly appreciated that special half-bottle which Travers insisted was for himself.

After the meal they sat and yarned till nothing was left of Wharton's long cigar but the shortest of stubs. Then he regretfully rose.

"Well, this won't buy the baby new socks. I suppose I've got to leave the palaces of the wealthy and get back to my attic again." His roving eye caught the manuscript on the desk, and his lip drooped. "Still writing that damn rubbish of yours?"

"Still plodding on," Travers told him amiably.

Wharton grunted. "Still telling just how you'd have fired the shots and slit the throats."

"Hardly that, George."

"Ah, well," he said, and wiped his vast moustache with wide sweeps of his voluminous handkerchief. Then he suddenly chuckled. "I've got an idea. You're telling us how murders ought to have been done. Why not go one better. You tell us all about Amli and Furloe."

Travers smiled dryly. "You're showing considerable faith. But why drag all that out of Limbo?"

"Drag it out of Limbo?" He grunted and glared. "That's what you're doing with those other cases, aren't you? Resurrecting things, aren't you?"

"Yes, but in those cases I know all the answers."

He snorted. "Don't tell me. You're picking out all the nice, pretty cases, but soon as I suggest one myself, then you start to hedge and back out."

"Even if I tried to follow your suggestion, you forget that people are still alive. My other murderers are all dead. And there's still a law of libel."

"Ah, well," said Wharton graciously, and moved off towards the dining-room again. "One of these days I might have a little shot at it myself."

Travers stared. "You have an idea?"

Wharton smiled complacently. "No more than I always had. Besides, I often think to myself I might do something in the author line." He nodded. "Mind you, I admit we were never able to pin anything on him, but if that oily Osmund wasn't in everything up to the neck, then my name's Higgins."

Travers smiled relievedly. The elevator was heard ascending, and suddenly he thought of something.

"Tell me, George. Who exactly is, or was, Higgins?"

"Higgins?" He glared, then shook a reminiscent head. "My old dad used to use that expression when I was a nipper. One day I asked him the same question and what answer do you think I got?"

"Don't know," said Travers, as Wharton entered the lift. "What answer did you get?"

"A clip over the ear!" Wharton told him. His hand lifted in farewell and Travers could still hear him chuckling as the lift took him out of sight.

But Travers was not smiling when he came back to the study. That account of the Levantic killings would never be written, fascinating as Wharton's idea had been. But it would have been interesting to see Wharton's face if he had read the things that might have been written. Take the clues, for instance, that had been under his nose, as they had been under his own.

Take Furloe. Only a distorted vision could see him as the man who wrestled with Amli and struck that knockout blow. Furloe, the man with the frail physique and the gentle disposition. But Jerome Haire, in spite of his age, had wrists and fingers of steel, though of that perhaps, Wharton had not been aware.

Then there had been the words on the blotting-paper, and in Amli's writing; the words Jerome Haire had forced at the pistol point; the full confession, the last words of which were: *I am a swine and an unspeakable cad.* Only Jerome Haire could have dictated words as stilted as those.

Then there were the things which Wharton had not known, and which would come as staggering surprises. There was that bow drawn at a venture in the Liverpool dressing-room. Not the reference to Furloe—that had been comparatively unimportant—but the words: *I know why you went to the Levantic.* That first interview had been meant, but the guilty conscience had taken it for the interview of the murder night.

Then there were the revelations of the lingerie sisters. Furloe had been with Sir Jerome that Saturday afternoon. Sir Jerome had certainly recognized him as Colson, and Colson had as certainly once given Sir Jerome his chance. But that afternoon Furloe told the other what he could do, and he mentioned *The Decoration.* That was what the sisters heard—Furloe giving Sir Jerome an example of his work. The other voice was the critical or congratulatory voice of Sir Jerome himself. Probably it had never previously occurred to the great man how easy it was for even an ordinary mimic to assume his voice and to copy his pronounced mannerisms.

Haire, as Travers saw it, had been frightened at the prospect of four shows a night, even for only one week, and so he had toyed with the idea of using his old friend Colson as a kind of ghost. Probably there was a try-out at either the Paliceum or the Metropolis early in the week, and Furloe came through with flying colours.

That was it. The valet was sent away on Saturday as soon as the idea entered his master's mind. Sir Jerome's flat was the only dressing-room required for that week, for he would remain in costume all the night. After the first performance or two there would be no need for any conference at either of the halls, and inquiries would probably elicit the fact that Sir Jerome had deliberately discouraged talk.

On that Friday night, then, after the long interval for dinner, the taxi took not Sir Jerome but Furloe to the Paliceum, and then on to the Metropolis, and it was Furloe whom Travers had actually seen. No wonder he had thought the performance somewhat different from that one just after the war! Meanwhile Jerome Haire, in Indian costume, had watched Furloe's performance at the Paliceum, and had then gone straight to the Levantic. He had previously rung up under some kind of false pretences and arranged for a private interview. That first phone call coincided, by the way, with his free hour.

As soon as he entered the room he covered Amli with his gun and extorted the confession which on the Saturday he was to tell Bernice he had obtained somewhere in the country. Amli blotted it and then whipped open the drawer and got to his own gun. The other wrenched it from his fingers, and the rest was as Wharton had reconstructed it. Then Haire took the confession, and when he looked at Amli to see if he were really dead, he saw the wallet half out of his pocket, and had the sudden idea of taking it so as to give the impression of theft.

At about twenty past ten the taxi brought Furloe to the door of the flat. While he was getting out of the Russian uniform and removing grease-paint, Sir Jerome was thinking. If Furloe ever blabbed about that week's work, he would be the laughing-stock of the world. His reputation would be gone and for the rest of his life he would be his daughters' pensioner. And Furloe dead would mean a perfect alibi for himself in the matter of the killing of Amli.

He must have known that the poison in some form or other was in the house. Perhaps it had been bought for removing stains from some costume, and was still in its blue bottle. But he insisted that Furloe should have a stiff whiskey, and then he probably expected the poison to act at once. It acted quickly on the empty stomach but not in the expected way. Instead of a dead Furloe who could be got out to the fog and through the alley to Soho Square or further, there was a red-faced, obstreperous man, clutching at his throat, making passes in the air and gasping for breath. Sir Jerome had tried to calm him and it was then that Furloe's wrists had been bruised.

Finally Sir Jerome had panicked. Furloe had a minor collapse, perhaps, and at once he was half-dragged down the stairs and out through the alley. Then the other followed him at a convenient distance when at last he got to his feet again. But Furloe was in no condition to talk, even if a passer-by had questioned him. He fell again, and Sir Jerome, always at his heels, suddenly remembered that that damning wallet was still in his possession, and at once he thrust it into Furloe's pocket.

Furloe once more got to his feet again, and by those unfrequented alleys reached St. Martin's and the shop window against which he had leaned. For a last time Sir Jerome drew near. He decided to mention that he knew the man, and he suggested that he was drunk. He also made much talk about evening constitutionals, and he craftily discredited Furloe without going too far from what the police might discover to be the truth.

A hellish business. Everything had been hellish from the start. That scheme of Amli's on the boat, then the death of three men that came from it, and how it had gone near to ruining the lives of three more—four, indeed, if one included Barney.

But it was all over, whatever legacy remained. About what had happened to himself he had no complaints, for he saw much of it as his own fault. And he did not blame Bernice. Few would have acted differently, especially when Joy's obstinacy fostered the lies.

As for himself and Bernice, time would be sure to close rifts and make possible something of what had been before the hellish business began. Friendship at least was sure; the morning had told him that.

Then while that mood of not unpleasant melancholy was on him, there was a tap at the door. His thoughts had been too near for the phone bell to be heard.

"Miss Bernice Haire rang, sir."

Travers was up in a flash and making for the phone, Palmer at his heels.

"No, no, sir. She rang off, sir."

Travers turned on him, and not for years had Palmer seen him so annoyed.

"Rang off? Why didn't you call me at once?"

Palmer gave that incipient bow of his, though with a shade more humility.

"I told her to hold the line but she insisted you were not to be disturbed."

Travers shook his head. "I'm sorry. And there was no message at all?"

"No, sir. Only to say it was a fine afternoon."

He stared, then remembered.

A moment, and the smile had gone, for he had remembered something else: something he had discovered and which she must never know. How could he see her, and talk and be questioned? What he knew was something that, unknown to her, must colour both their lives.

A fine afternoon—the words came of themselves. But she was wrong. That afternoon at The Croft, three months and more ago; that was what would always come back to his mind, in spite of its east wind and its frost. But life had changed since then. There were the things that brought a quick shame when he remembered them; the things over which he had slurred too easily that morning—the thoughts he had let seize on his mind that mad day at Tilbury. . . .

And yet, after all . . .

Palmer, watching anxiously from the far door, saw him hesitate and turn back, and he wondered why he should be smiling so queerly to himself as he slowly polished his glasses. Then Palmer thought he knew. A monitory cough and he was giving his little incipient bow.

"What hat will you require, sir? The grey?"

"What's that?" Travers hooked the glasses back. "Hat, did you say?"

Perhaps he remembered that quick annoyance, for as he smiled, his hand went to the other's shoulder.

"Yes. I think perhaps I *shall* want a hat. It'd better be the grey."

THE END